CW00428635

Robert Ronsson lives in the Severn Valley with his wife Valerie. He retired early from a career in financial services to start writing full-time. Robert is a film enthusiast and he and Valerie help run their town's community cinema.

Once upon a time
in Chinatown

ONCE UPON A TIME IN CHINATOWN

ROBERT RONSSON

Patrician Press

Manningtree

First published as a paperback edition by Patrician Press 2020

Copyright © Robert Ronsson 2020

The right of Robert Ronsson to be identified as the author of this work has been asserted in accordance with the Copyright, Designs and Patents Act of 1988.

All rights reserved. No part of this document may be reproduced or transmitted in any form or by any means, electronic, mechanical, photocopying, recording, or otherwise, without prior written permission of Patrician Press.

British Library Cataloguing in Publication Data. A catalogue record for this book is available from the British Library.

ISBN paperback edition 978-1-9997030-5-9

Published by Patrician Press 2020

To Valerie with undying love and thanks for your support...

"History will be kind to me for I intend to write it."
Winston Churchill

"Forget it, Jake. It's Chinatown."
Final line of dialogue in the screenplay of *Chinatown* (1974)
Director: Roman Polanski Writer: Robert Towne

OPIUM DEN (1933) Interior. Sunset.
He holds the smoke in his lungs for a long time
before letting it spiral out and up towards the ceiling.
The smoke is harsh and kind and cleansing.
It wipes out memories, strife, mistakes... and Time.
Screenplay for the final scene of *Once Upon a Time in America*
(1984)
Director: Sergio Leone Writers: Leonardo Benvenuti, Piero
De Bernardi, Enrico Medioli, Franco Arcali, Franco Ferrini
and Sergio Leone. Based on the novel by Harry Grey.

KUALA LUMPUR TO LONDON

10th May 1996

I am composing a waking dream. Cocooned in the thin British Airways blanket, near-horizontal on a business class seat, I crave sleep so that I won't be a total zombie when we arrive in Heathrow. Hypnos, though, is a teasing gatekeeper. He opens the door and signals me to enter but, as I pass the threshold, he steps across my path.

Is it guilt keeps me awake? Or is it fear of being found out? I have not led a blameless life but I have nothing to be guilty about, no reason to be fearful. Despite this, like Dorothy's Texas tornado, my imagination spins out of control and I'm falling, falling into the grasp of my nemesis. She is the archetypal, TV-hard, dogged detective who can construct a murder case out of coincidence. She is the witch of my insomnolence.

Since I can remember, my infallible method for finding the oblivion of sleep has been to fantasise about the future: wild, irrational tomorrows when all my hopes are fulfilled. When it works, as it invariably has until this night, I fall asleep before the blissful finale.

When I was a boy, my fantasy was that my father would

come home alive from the war, a victim of amnesia, but otherwise whole. Later, when I knew how limited our lives were by lack of money, it would be Mum scooping the football pools and we'd never want for anything again. In adolescence, the latest object of my crushing desire would find me irresistible and we would enjoy a life together filled with companionable days and passionate nights. In my thirties, Mum's illness would be arrested, we could share a proper conversation and I would be able to resume a normal life. Like I said, wild imaginings.

Now, after seeing the house and meeting Nancy, it's impossible to fantasise a wild, irrational future when I'm still trying to figure out what to make of the last six years. The events are recorded on time's ticker tape. It can be interrogated, spooled from palm to palm under an inquisitive eye; reviewed but never edited.

Immutable it may be, but the past is open to interpretation. Yesterday can be changed in its recollection and retelling, particularly if you have something to hide.

PART ONE - 1990

PART ONE 1990

1

There's no doubt about it, Mum was having a good day the day she died. As on every day, I coaxed her out of bed and dressed her. A good day meant she didn't scream at me when I changed her pad. She accepted me as her son and understood I was trying to help her. She even said, 'Goodbye, son,' when I kissed the wispy, silver hair that hung over her forehead before leaving for work that Friday morning, the last day of August 1990.

Mum and I share the surname Cross. It's a non-name – anonymous. A cross is the mark you make when you can't write. She was given it when she was taken in by Dr Barnardo's a few years after the first world war. She was a new-born and the shamed mother who left her on the doorstep didn't leave a label. It was a starry night so Barnardo's named her Stella. Stella Cross never married; Cross is the name I bear and no family to share it with.

That work day didn't finish until the early hours of the next morning. The heat wave earlier that month had dissipated but the night was still humid and day-warm. Perhaps this powered my growing sense of apprehension as I approached the house. My footsteps echoed and, as I passed underneath the Aquinas Street lamps, my shadow pirouetted around me as if it were my partner in a Viennese waltz. My key scratched in the lock.

Her bedroom door was open. I could see it from the foot

of the stairs. Either I'd forgotten to shut it properly or she'd wanted to use the toilet and had remembered how to work the door handle. It had been a good day for her, remember. I took the stairs three at a time, clambered over the stair gate and hurried into her room. Her chair was empty. She could still have been on the toilet. No matter how long she'd been sitting there, she'd be mouthing the word 'finished' waiting for me to clean her.

She wasn't sitting on the toilet. She was in the bath in her nightdress. Her head was under the clear, cold water. Her white hair drifted in tendrils.

It was one of the paramedics who called the police. I stood in Mum's bedroom with the blue strobe lights from the street flashing across the ceiling. The police constable was young – no older than the girls at work. He led me downstairs and we sat at the kitchen table. He had a notebook in his hand and explained how it was important to have an immediate record of what happened. He asked me to describe my day. 'Why did you come home so late?'

'It was always going to be a long day,' I said. 'I work for Scotia Mutual in the City and earlier this year the directors announced its demutualisation. Today was the deadline for the carpetbaggers to buy in—'

'Carpetbaggers?'

'The people who buy bonus bonds knowing they'll get a windfall pay out when the company's privatised. We processed an avalanche of applications before the midnight deadline. They were still bringing them in at ten.'

'You spent all day at the office?'

'No. I came home at lunchtime and I also popped back about five to check how Mum was. I went back to the office around seven.'

'Was your Mum all right when you came home earlier?'

I wiped a hand over my tired eyes. Tears welled up. 'At

lunchtime, I changed her pad, gave her a sandwich and settled her in front of the TV. She was fine. I was back again sometime after five – it only takes me twenty minutes to get here. She was asleep in her chair with the television on. Her cushions were dry.' I sobbed. 'She was having a *good* day.'

He waited for me to compose myself, his pencil hovering.

'She leant on me as I walked her from the toilet to her room. She still smelt fresh from the day before. She goes to the day centre every Monday and Thursday for a bath and stuff. I don't do this – care for her – every day.'

He nodded. 'We can do this later – this afternoon. If—'

'No. Like you said, it's better to have it right.' I took a deep breath. 'I left her sitting in front of the television. "I have to go back to work this evening, Mum. I won't be able to sit with you," I said. She didn't make a scene; she was having a *really* good day.'

'And you went back to the office. How long does it take?'

'Like I said, twenty minutes. Walk to the station, Waterloo and City line, short walk to Cheapside. Twenty minutes, door to door.'

'Once you were there?'

'The business was stacked up and I pitched in logging the forms and cheques. It's not normally work that I do but it was every man on deck. We had handled a record for a day's business by the time we finished at 11.37 – I made a note of it – and we opened a bottle of Champagne the boss had left for us. I gave the girls their taxi fares from petty cash. After they were safely on their way, I set the alarm, locked up and got a taxi myself.

'Did your mother often try to bathe herself?' he asked.

'Never. She had difficulty working the handle on her bedroom door. She had difficulty with the geography of the house. Basically, she only felt safe in her room.'

'She's never run a bath before?'

I shook my head, 'Not for the last five years... at least five years. She couldn't work the hot tap. It's too stiff. I didn't get it loosened. It seemed safer to leave it that way.'

'But she could turn the cold tap.'

'It's much looser. I can only think she must have filled the bath with cold water. When she got in, even if she felt the cold, she was probably too frail to get out.' I choked back a sob. 'Perhaps she slipped – the cold water would have made her weak – would hypothermia...?'

'I'm sorry. This must be difficult.' His stubby pencil paused. 'And you're sure she couldn't have worked the hot tap.'

'Go up and try it yourself, Constable. It's hard, even for me. No, *she* couldn't have done it. I wouldn't want her scalding herself.'

He looked up sharply as if he was trying to discover something behind my eyes. 'But you said she was unlikely to make it to the bathroom alone, so you could have had the hot tap fixed without it being a danger to her.'

'You haven't cared for an adult relative, have you? You've got to allow them some dignity. I leave my mother alone in there when she's able to tell me she wants the toilet. I wouldn't forgive myself...' I covered my face with my hands. 'In any event, I use the bathroom downstairs. She hasn't had a bath – other than at the day centre – since... I don't know when. I can't remember when that tap was last used.'

The sun was rising by the time I was alone again. I slumped in Mum's armchair – the one she should have been in when I came home. A sense of elation seeped across the dry-grit of my exhaustion. I was free at last.

At the inquest, the pathologist reported there was no evidence of scalding and, in any event, it was unlikely Mum could have turned the hot tap. Because of the water, the usual calculations to determine time of death weren't reliable but nevertheless, she tentatively estimated that Mum died between 9pm and midnight. There were no marks on Mum's body to indicate she had been mistreated or there had been a final struggle. The young policeman confirmed that the girls at the office and the taxi driver had verified my whereabouts.

The coroner concluded that Mum had run the cold bath herself and her condition would have prevented her knowing that she had to get out of the water. His verdict was death by misadventure.

My verdict? She had been having a good day but not good enough.

As Mum's body passed through the curtain into the fire, I turned to check the chapel for the last time. I was still alone. Mum and I had lived in a bubble of inter-dependency. The future was a narrow ridge-top path with chasms of despair on both sides. Time pushed me in one direction; there was no retracing my steps even as the ground ahead crumbled beneath my feet.

The house's silence fell around me like a shroud. The floorboards no longer creaked as she shuffled from bed to chair and back again. There were no more gasps or growls, no cries of 'Finished!'. The blue light from her television had stopped projecting the spectres of soap actors across the landing.

I sat in the kitchen grasping a mug of coffee and took stock. My churning gut, my bubbling thoughts, underscored the conclusion that I was a sad, lonely, middle-aged man connected to nobody outside my work. But I must have had a family. Everybody has a family... somewhere.

Families have secrets. Or, more accurately, there are shadows at the edges of understanding that nobody dares ask about. For instance, Mum must have told me, when I was young, that my dad died in the war. Did she also tell me he was one of the first to land on the D-day beaches on the 6th June 1944?

Whether she did or not, it was always my belief that he had died a hero on a Normandy beach – seven months and four days before I was born. I'd also absorbed from the fabric of the house and from the gaps between Mum's sentences, that she and Dad were going to get married when the war ended. He died and I was excess baggage.

Mum had a cleaning job in the City that meant I woke myself up and dressed myself for school from an early age. Her evening shift work at the cosmetic factory made me a latchkey kid, returning to an empty house. At my grammar school I was one of the few boys wearing a jumble sale uniform and leaky shoes.

We couldn't afford television so I read books from the library and found another, better world solving crimes with the *Secret Seven* or the *Famous Five*, sharing adventures with the *Swallows and Amazons*. This was how the muscle of my imagination was nurtured and I exercised it by re-enacting my father's warrior death times beyond measure or by conjuring up his miracle return.

I didn't see my birth certificate until I was fourteen. 'The school's doing a trip to France at Easter, Mum. Everybody's going.'

'You're not. We can't afford it.'

'They say that kids who get free school dinners don't have to pay the full amount.'

She was wearing, as she always did at home, her 'housecoat'. It was a blue-checked, nylon cover-up with a thin cotton belt around the waist. If an unexpected visitor rang the front-door bell she would, in a slickly choreographed routine, whisk off her housecoat before she reached the kitchen door, swoop to open the cupboard under the stairs as she passed and toss the housecoat in.

We were chatting in the kitchen. Me sitting at the squeezed-in table, Mum fussing by the gas-stove, apparently mulling over whether the poor-family subsidy made a difference. 'I won't take any charity,' she finally said.

'It's Normandy.' This was as near as I could go to the taboo subject of my father.

She was facing away from me and hunched over as if my words had loaded something heavy on her back. 'You haven't got a passport.'

'They say I can use an identity card because it's a school trip. I can get one at the post office.'

'Why are you so keen?'

A terror gripped my throat. If I said the wrong thing now... 'It'll be good for my French. And I'm thinking O' level History: 1066, the Bayeux Tapestry and all that. It's educational.'

She turned and smiled. 'Well I can't stand in the way of your education, can I?'

I jumped down from the stool. My knees nearly gave way with relief. 'I can go?'

'How much is it?'

I told her, watching her face to see whether it was beyond our reach.

She didn't flinch. 'If you're that keen, you won't mind it being instead of a birthday present, will you? And you'll have to save something out of your *Colonial Stores* money.'

She was referring to my job as an after-school, grocer's delivery boy. I had the bike with the big basket on the front and a *Colonial Stores* apron to wear while I was delivering. It was a proper job. 'Really? I can go? Thanks, Mum.'

She hugged me and I was tall enough to be able to rest my chin on her shoulder. I didn't want her to see my face. 'I have to have a birth certificate to get an identity card. I do have a birth certificate, don't I?'

She gripped my wrists and held me at arm's length. 'Course you do, you silly ha'porth.'

A few days later she showed it to me. She pointed to the blank space. 'They wouldn't let me put your dad's name on it.'

'Why not?'

She shrugged. 'They said the father had to be there in person because I didn't have a marriage certificate—'

'But that's because you were waiting until after the war—'

'—and when I explained that he'd been killed—'

'— and he *couldn't* be there in person—'

'—they said it had to stay blank.'

'It's not a problem though, is it, Mum? It won't stop me getting an ID card.'

She shook her head and smiled but her eyes were sad. 'No. It's not a problem, son.'

She applied at the post office for my *British Visitor's Passport*, which was basically a fold-out card with my name and picture in it, and I went on the school trip, a free-lunch oik on the coach to Dover with the other boys ragging me as they compared their fancy holdalls to my scruffy suitcase.

In France, I stood on the promenade overlooking one of the beaches imagining a place at the high-tide mark where my dad was killed. No doubt he was leading a platoon like in the war comics. 'Come on, lads. We're outnumbered but we'll make the Jerries sorry they ever stood in our way.' The rat-a-tat-tat of fire from a hidden machine gun zig-zagged across the imagined page. 'We're caught in cross-fire! Aaargh!' He stumbled forward and down.

I picked my way across pebbles to the place where I imagined he fell. The stones thinned out and waves lapped up to dark sand. A line of pollution foam marked the water margin and bubbled like the tissue in an open chest wound. It wasn't a picture in a comic book anymore.

I was alone in the house in Aquinas Street. Earlier that September Sunday morning, I had walked to the middle of Hungerford Bridge with the plastic urn the undertakers had delivered. The river carried the zest-fresh scent of the sea and the sun, spying on me from between fluffy clouds, was still low over the skeletons of the new buildings at Canary Wharf. The wafting breeze came from behind and I upturned the container so that Mum's ashes cascaded, in a grey, gritty shower, onto the turbulent water below. The heavier stuff went straight to the fishes, but the powder settled as a surface scum and, softly singing Mum's favourite song *Waterloo Sunset*, I followed its progress towards Waterloo Bridge. I was hardly more than mouthing the final words, *As long as I gaze on Waterloo sunset, I am in paradise*, as the lace-thin membrane dispersed. I turned for home. A mass of dark cloud churned over Vauxhall Bridge to the south threatening the end of summer.

Mum's house – mine when probate was complete – was a two-bedroomed terrace. When it was new, it had probably been built for the sort of people who didn't know how to use a bathroom and hung torn newspaper on a string in the backyard privy. The original upstairs box-room became the bathroom where Mum died.

Downstairs was open-plan, one-room with a front door directly on the pavement. I'd had the partition walls removed in the early 80's. The furniture was low, minimal, dominated by my television and the bookcase containing my video collection. I had cleared the things away after a late breakfast during which I'd read the colour supplement from the *Mail on Sunday* while eating eggs on toast. The coffee was strong and black.

I loaded the dirty crockery into the dishwasher – the fitted kitchen was another part of my modernisation – before returning to the living room and, with a sigh, climbed the stairs. There was no stair gate to climb over. Up here, the house was stuck in 1977 – a time even before Margaret Thatcher was Prime Minister. Mum couldn't have dealt with change. The wallpaper was floral and curled at the corners. The skirting and dado rail were painted to create the illusion of woodgrain. The single light fitting had a slurried-pink, glass shade.

The dust-must of heavy, brown furniture clogged my tubes and my mood flatlined in the gloom. I had charity-shopped her clothes, so the wardrobe and all the drawers of the chest save one were empty. The house-clearance dealer was coming to take her furniture away the next day and I'd arranged to take time off to be there. I couldn't put it off again.

I pulled out the drawer containing her personal papers and placed it on the stained mattress. The walls closed in and my eyes filled with tears. Rushing out, gasping for breath, with both hands holding the drawer, I leaned into the wall as I stumbled down the stairs. Safely at the bottom, once under the kitchen's bright lights, I placed the drawer on the worktop. With my hands flat on the surface and my head bowed, I waited for my breathing to slow.

There were three cardboard boxes – a shoe box that reached to the top and two that were shallower, wedged in to fill the base. Four smaller jewellery cases slid about on top. There were no loose papers or envelopes.

I lifted out the jewellery cases, placed them on the work surface; which should I open first? In my imagination, Mum held my thin, childhood wrist and shifted my finger from one to the other. 'Eeny-meeny-miney-moe. Catch a tigger by the toe...' I plumped for the long narrow one. It was blue, its lid embossed in gold with the name of a jeweller I didn't recognise. The resistance of the spring lid was enough to have prevented Mum from looking inside even if she had wanted to.

A single strand of pearls lay on a blue velvet cushion. The jeweller's name was repeated on the inside of the lid with a Bond Street address. I poked the beads with my forefinger and picked them up by the clasp. I knew there was a way of verifying genuine pearls and gently bit across the surface of a larger one. It was rough and grainy. Did this mean it was real or synthetic? Rebuking myself for knowing only half the test, I decided to have the necklace properly valued.

I imagined my father in his army uniform – a smudge where his face should have been – standing behind my mother. She held her dark curls in a bunch to one side while he fiddled the two halves of the clasp together with his soldier's fingers. It was an intimacy that was easy to picture but my father's lack of identity made the scene fade, like in a movie when a scene dissolves into a drift of virgin snow.

The second box was a garish red and, when I opened it, the lining was made of frayed white satin with no cushioning. I recognised the tracery of gold-coloured metal wound around a large red stone. It was the brooch Mum wore when we went to the pictures together. I had given it to her for her birthday when I was about ten. I'd saved up my pocket money and bought it at Woolworths. I had to swallow hard as I closed the box.

Number three was more promising. It was navy-blue again, from the same jewellers as the necklace but this time the box was smaller, deeper. It revealed a pair of drop pearls on clasps similar but not identical to that on the necklace. A later purchase perhaps? No, I decided. *This* was the earlier present. My dad's relationship with Mum would have been getting serious with the earrings. But the necklace cemented it.

The fourth box was the clincher. If only Mum had shown it to me when I was a teenager. It was maroon leather with the words 'Asprey' and 'London' gold-embossed on the lid. Two rings nestled together in the opulent velvet as they might have looked on Mum's finger. The plain gold wedding band snuggled up against a solitaire engagement ring with the stone offset to give the pair a singularity that explained why Mum had never worn either. The diamond ring would have looked odd, unfinished, without its partner. She never became a bride. If anything made me legitimate, surely it was these twin rings.

The story of Mum's relationship with Dad told in three items of jewellery. And the final piece – Asprey's – never worn. I decided to take the rings and the pearls to a jeweller.

It was probably the jewellery collection that prompted me to track down my father. I needed to know something about the man who had contributed half to make me and was so committed to my mother that he had married her in every possible way bar the ceremony. If only he hadn't died on that Normandy beach.

I set the jewellery cases to one side. Perhaps I wouldn't sell the three expensive pieces. They were my proof of him until I reached a better understanding of who he was. I tossed the Woolworth's trinket into the waste bin and lifted out the shoebox with the words *Arding and Hobbs* on the lid. I vaguely remembered a department store that was a short train ride from Waterloo on the Surrey line. Was it in Wimbledon? I had always thought the first name was 'Harding' and Mum adopted a Cockney accent and dropped the aitch whenever she talked about going there but, on the box, the name really was, *Arding*. A collection of black and white photographs lay inside. We never had a photo-album. This was Mum's equivalent.

The earliest picture of me was a full-length studio portrait of mum holding a baby. I was struck by how dark her skin was alongside the white of my christening shawl. Obviously, I was aware from an early age that she was different to other mums, with her brown skin and recognisably African features. When she talked about her foundling origins, she guessed that her mother was probably white and felt she had no option but to abandon her mixed-race child. I could have gone through school as a darker, frizzier-haired version of the others, but for Mum's appearance when she attended parent-teacher events.

It was after the first of these that I was teased in the playground. The other kids tugged my hair, waggled their forefingers against their lips and called me a wog. The bullies were only satisfied when I burst into tears or lashed out at the nearest of them. The name-calling only stopped at the grammar when a teacher, trying to be helpful, admonished my classmates, 'You shouldn't call Cross a Wog, you know, chaps. The letters 'W', 'O' and 'G' stand for "Worthy Oriental Gentleman". Young Cross here is of African descent. Your name for him only emphasises your ignorance.' It didn't take long for them to come up with an alternative: Sambo.

The new nickname stuck and the boys would have said that they used it affectionately but, when one of them shouted, 'Oi, Sambo!' across a crowded bus, it didn't feel that way.

Flicking through the other photographs, I found the earliest I remember being taken. It was of me standing in the back yard swamped inside my first infant school uniform. Mum must have stood in front of the kitchen door, wearing her housecoat, hunched over a Kodak Box Brownie, shielding the viewing screen from the sun with the curled palm of her left hand. A hand bare of rings.

One Christmas, in my early teenage years, Mum gave me a sleek modern Brownie 127 with its eye-level view-finder. The holiday snaps of Mum – some with Aunty Millie – in Shanklin on the Isle of Wight or on the beach at Brighton, were taken by me using that camera. Aunty Millie – this was the first time I'd thought of her for ages – was Mum's best friend from the cosmetics factory and in the snaps she appeared as vivacious and attractive as I remember. I blushed, recalling that, when I was thirteen or fourteen, I had a crush on her even though she must have been at least twice my age. She died the week England won the World Cup. Cancer. She was thirty-something and I was twenty-one.

Mostly though, the snaps recorded my achievements: the primary school nativity; the grammar school drama productions; receiving the sixth form essay prize. There was one of me in my first suit – brown with flared trousers – that I wore the day I started at Scotia Mutual aged 17. I did the sums. I'd worked in the same building for the same company for something like 28 years. The pictorial record continued to skitter across the high points in my life, never dipping down into the murk of its lows.

What to do with these pictures? As I tossed them back into the shoe box, I thought that I might compile the album that should have been. The one I could have placed on Mum's lap and coaxed her, 'Here, Mum. Look at this. Perhaps you'll remember. Can you remember Millie?'

The flat boxes next. They were both tray-shaped and one layer deep. The first had a reproduction of *The Haywain* on the lid, the other *The Blue Boy*; my mother's life in chocolate-box clichés.

The Haywain contained correspondence from a solicitor that alluded to Mum's purchase of this house in 1948 when I was three. The original purchase price was smaller than my monthly salary today. Its ownership now made me worth over half a million pounds.

I made a mental note to look for the deeds to the house. I was going to need them for title to be transferred. Perhaps the solicitor in the letterhead would know their whereabouts – provided the firm still existed forty-plus years on.

A paragraph in one of the letters shone out as if it were marked by a celestial highlighter. It told Mum that, *the third-party funds making up the bulk of the completion monies have been transferred into our client account and we are ready to proceed on your confirmation that you wish us to finalise the purchase.* Who was this 'third-party'? Was my father's family involved in financing the house? If so, why weren't they involved in my later life?

The last box, *The Blue Boy*, was mine. Obviously. It must have been the one she looked in when we needed my birth certificate for the school trip. There it was on top. The gaps where my father's name and signature should have been might as well have carried the word 'bastard'. School reports tracked my undistinguished academic life from 'happy and bright' primary to 'must try harder' and 'could do better' at the local grammar.

From beneath the thin layers of school certificates and cub and scout achievements, the yellowing edge of a white card peeked out. With the tentative fingers of an archaeologist lifting an artefact, I nudged aside the papers of later years and revealed the shiny finish of a certificate that Mum had never shown me. Its heading was a picture of Christ with children gathered around the hem of his robe. The caption was: *Suffer little children to come unto me.* Further down, beneath the heading *Baptismal Certificate,* the gold, gothic text read: *This certifies that* (my name was handwritten in black ink) *was this* 11th March 1945 *BAPTISED by me in the name of the Father, and of the Son, and of the Holy Ghost, and is thus acknowledged as a member of the Church, to be brought up in the nurture and admonition of the Lord. Place and date of birth:* Clapham, London. January 10th, 1945. *Minister:* The Revd. John Maley (or Haley? The signature wasn't clear.) *Mother:* Estelle Cross. *Father:* Anthony Kellie-Smith (Deceased).

For the first time since Mum died, my breathing stalled and then surged up in a choking cry of misery and elation. Dad had a name.

3

On the Friday after I learned Dad's identity, the sales guys and I went out to lunch to celebrate the previous month's record production. They had given the girls a bottle of bubbly each before we left for the blue-smoke fug of the *Golden Fleece*. We'd reserved a table and before long I was digging into sausages and mash and knocking back a pint of Young's bitter.

As was usual with these events I sat apart with Peter Dell. We'd joined Scotia as trainees at roughly the same time and he'd negotiated the route into sales while I'd stayed on the clerical side. Right from those early days, I felt most comfortable in his company. His kindly eyes and gentle manner were so unlike the rugger-bugger aggression of the others, which reminded me of the torments I had suffered at school.

The other salesmen were posturing and jabbing, like cocks in a fighting pit, as they debated the cases for and against Britain joining the European Exchange Rate Mechanism. In the calm of our table, between mouthfuls of gammon, egg and chips, Peter was emphasising how important one of his brokers called Alvie Sessions was to Scotia Mutual and how his end of year bonus depended on my department's ability to speed the final three months' business through the administration process.

I took a deep swig of ale. 'Do you mind if we talk about something other than business?' I asked.

He nodded and his posture shifted as if to encourage confidence. I could see why Peter was so successful. He not only listened; he gave every effort to the act of listening.

'You come from a military background, don't you?'

'Why d'you say that, old chap?'

'You've mentioned your Dad's medals in the past – from World War Two.'

He put down his knife and fork and frowned. 'Yes, my father was in the Life Guards – his father and his uncle too.'

I nodded. 'I thought I'd remembered.'

'Father was in the second show, Gramps bought it in the first.' He took a swallow of beer to wash down the food. 'They both got gongs.' He adjusted his tie. While the others went for the paisley-patterned, wide sort, Peter's were always narrow, striped – regimental.

'Is your dad alive?'

'Oh, yes. Father has a place in Cobham.'

'He got through the war, then.' Now I had the opening. 'My father was killed.'

'Really?' He wiped a piece of bread around his plate.

'Yes. D-day. On the beaches.'

'That was a tough show, old chap.' His brow furrowed. 'You must have been a baby.'

'Conceived. But not born.' It was a phrase I had dreamt up in my teens but perhaps this was the first time I'd said it aloud.

'You never saw him? Rough business. And now your mother...' He looked at me with a new appreciation. 'But you'll have his campaign medals to remember him by.'

'No nothing. Mum didn't keep anything. Perhaps his parents did.'

'He'll be on the Honour Roll though. The army doesn't forget its fallen comrades.'

'Honour Roll?'

'In the Public Records Office.'

Armed with my knowledge of the existence of the Honour Roll and my dad's name from my Baptismal Certificate, the following Tuesday lunchtime I stood outside the Gothic frontage of the Public Records Office with the London traffic bustling behind me. The building was a strange mix of styles. At the lower levels, the mullioned windows and complicated corners and buttresses brought the Houses of Parliament to mind. But, when I looked up, squinting against the sun, the cupolas and towers looked as if they'd been imported from a Rajah's palace in colonial India. It reminded me of pictures I'd seen of Victorian railways stations in far-flung corners of the Empire.

I followed the signs for the search office and entered an anteroom. A polished teak counter top extended across from the left-hand wall to a doorway on the right. Scuffed linoleum covered the floor. The base of the counter and the walls and window frames were painted in governmental green. The door through to the room beyond the counter was marked 'No entry without authorisation.'

The indifference that seeped from the walls settled around me. The anteroom would not have been out of place in 1984 and I shared Winston Smith's despair. On the other side of the counter there sat two desks, the type my schoolteachers had used twenty-five years before, and two similar desks carrying microfiche machines. None of the four chairs was occupied.

Beyond were the banks of shelves. These extended to the end of the room some fifty feet away. The shelves were stained dark brown and high as a man. The frayed ends of manila files and envelopes were visible where they had been half-pushed back into place. The distinctive smell of filed paper wafted across on the dust motes.

The man and woman who tended the records walked up and down with clickety-clackety steps swerving past haphazard heaps of files that lay in their paths like the droppings of some elephantine beast. The minders cradled bundles of papers and occasionally stopped, and stretched or stooped to insert them into place.

A woman entered from behind a partition to the left. She wore a pinched-waist jacket and the bulk of her body above and below the straining buttons made me think of Rosa Klebb in the James Bond film *From Russia With Love*. She tapped her crimson nails on the counter-top. Her fingers were stained with nicotine. 'Can I help you?'

'I'd like to trace someone in the World War II Army Roll of Honour.' I chunked out the words to be sure I put them in the right order.

'Of course.' She reached across to a stack of pigeon holes and her talons closed in on a pile of forms. She slipped one out and passed it across the desk. 'Fill this in.' She signalled behind me. 'Pens are over there.'

I turned to face a narrow shelf equipped with quill-shaped, ball-point pens. I took the form and filled in the details I knew – my father's surname *Kellie-Smith*, first name *Anthony*, date of death *6th June 1944*. There were other spaces for his date of birth, regiment and rank that I had to leave blank. But there wouldn't be more than one with that surname that died that day, would there? I handed the form back to Rosa.

'Mmm. Is this all? No date of birth?' She peered at me over the top of spectacles. There was a waft of antiseptic perfume as she turned to a card index. She spoke over her shoulder. 'Are you sure of this surname – Kellie-hyphen-Smith?'

'I think so.'

Her head dropped forward and she sighed. 'Could it be plain Smith?'

'I don't think so.' My lack of knowledge was shameful.

'I'll order up *Hulton to Kepner*. Have a look at that first. You don't want to look at the *Smiths* unless you have to.' She filled in the lower section of the card and signed it with a flourish. She handed it back. 'Take it through to the reading room and sit at a desk. We're not busy. It shouldn't take long.' Muscles worked in her cheeks and stretched her lips across her front teeth. It took a moment before I realised she was smiling.

I turned and hesitated. Was I to go through the door? I looked back and Rosa shooed me towards it with the back of her hand.

The young man click-clacked over as soon as I sat down. He gave my card a cursory look and said, 'I'll bring it down.' He returned to the safety of the stacks, walking the long corridor with an athlete's roll of the hips.

I put down my briefcase and wished I'd brought something to read. Too nervous to tuck into the lunchtime sandwich in my bag, I sat and waited.

After a few long minutes, the young man returned with a leather-bound foolscap book about three inches thick. A lot of death. He put it down in front of me. '*Hulton to Kepner*,' he said. 'Alphabetical. You'll find Kellie towards the end.' He stood with his hand on his waist. It looked awkward; his thumb pointed forward. 'Is there anything else I can help you with?' he asked, flashing his teeth.

But I didn't find my father. There was no name between *Kellhuy, Andries* and *Kellifer, Percival*. No Kellies at all. Perhaps he was in the register but misspelt as Kelly. I flicked on and found a list that stretched to three pages. None of the Kellys was coupled with Smith. I sat back and considered what this meant.

Firstly, the names were of all the British army's WWII

dead. It wasn't important that I may have been mistaken about his date of death.

What did Rosa at reception say? 'Could he be plain Smith?' I looked around. The young man was sat at another desk between the shelves about halfway down the room. I picked up the heavy volume and scraped back my chair.

He looked up and hurried over. 'Stay there,' he said, smiling.

'I've drawn a blank,' I said.

'Oh.' He took the book in both hands and tossed back his fringe waiting for me to say more.

'I wonder whether I should have looked at Smith. The name I'm looking for is Kellie-Smith, you see. Double-barrelled.'

'That would be *Slaney to Szarkow*, he said. 'All the Smiths are there. Pages of them.'

'Could I see it?'

'Of course,' he said, as he turned away, hugging *Hulton to Kepner* to his chest. 'You need to ask Miss Turvey for the correct card.' He nodded towards the door I had come through earlier.

I repeated the card process with Miss Turvey, who was less hostile second time around. She didn't even remind me that she had predicted I would need the *Smith* book. When I returned to the reading room, the young man was waiting by the door. He took the new card and nodded towards the table where I'd been sitting. The required volume was already on the desk.

'Very kind,' I said. 'Thank you.'

'Any time,' he said as he strode away towards his station.

I had to check more carefully. There were 33 lines of *Smith, Anthony* Only one was Anthony K Smith – the others with the same initial had full middle names – *Karl to Konane* –

none of which was 'Kellie'. The *Anthony K* died in France in May 1940. It wasn't him. There were no other possibilities.

I scraped back my chair so my minder knew to come back.

'Not there?' he said.

I shook my head.

'Sorry I couldn't help you.' He cocked his head to one side as if he expected me to respond – as if we should make a conversation out of my disappointment. I mumbled something about only having an hour for lunch and left him with the book.

As I hurried back to Scotia Mutual, a seed of hope germinated. If Dad wasn't in the Roll of Honour, he either hadn't been in the army or he didn't die in the war. Could he still be alive? My heartbeat sped and a surge of electricity tingled at my fingertips. I urged myself to calm down.

My christening certificate was the only proof of Dad's existence but equally, the same certificate was the only proof of his death. I now knew that the man named as my father hadn't died in Normandy. If he still lived, had Mum perhaps told me a story to hide the fact that he'd run off?

Suppose the third-party money that helped her buy the house had come from my father or his family as some sort of pay-off. If the war brought together two people from completely different social spheres, had my father run away from the idea of an inter-racial marriage as the clock struck midnight? The jewellery shops he used were way out of my mother's experience. She was a black cockney, brought up in a succession of children's homes with no airs or graces. How would she have been received by the presumably middle class Kellie-Smiths?

In one train of thought, my father had died a hero. The jewellery made him as real as the diamond on Mum's engagement ring. At the other extreme he was a snob who couldn't go through with the marriage and his death was my mother's cover story. I already felt guilty about the manner of her death. I hated myself for being thankful that she was no longer a burden to me. Now, I was in danger of resenting her for inventing the hero-father I thought I had. There was only one way out of this. I wouldn't give up the search.

4

Some days after my disappointment at the Records Office, I stood in the doorway of Mum's bedroom after the clearance men had removed the furniture. I'd been in a deconsecrated church once. It was emptied of pews and at the far end there stood a cuboid of empty space where the altar should have been. Then as now, I had only seen the things that weren't there.

Mum's deterioration had started 13 years before. Now, in the last decade of the 20th century, who else did I live this life for but myself? But when I thought about my future, all I could predict was retirement with a generous Scotia Mutual pension. What of the intervening twenty years?

Why not move out of this house? If it was sold I could easily buy a good-sized flat further out. In Chelsea, perhaps, close to the football ground. I could re-kindle my affiliation to the football team.

The glum room stared back. Would I be able to entertain women here – in Mum's room? I'd had women friends before 1977 but I was a slow starter – not unusual for a young man who had gone to single-sex schools and whose only female close acquaintance was his mother. It was only after I joined Scotia and had a bit of money in my pocket that I started going out with a girl I'd met through work. We clung to each other for too long and it finished when I had an affair with an older woman who was married. She gave me the confidence to play the field which mostly involved me asking girls for dates only after they had shown an interest in me. Nothing developed into anything meaningful because, if the girl started talking about the future, I broke it off. I could never imagine how sharing my life would be better than being alone.

After Mum moved upstairs, I exploited my sole use of the ground floor with a few dalliances. I had affairs with two married colleagues in the post-pill seventies – free and easy Gloria and giggly Maz – but, after the firework fizz of the initial naughtiness, both spluttered out. Perhaps with a flat, I could cut a rakish dash. I smiled grimly – me, rakish. My life had become constricted by responsibility. Caring for Mum had confined me, compressed me into a tight bud of thwarted ambition and it was too late to break through its skin and blossom – not at my age.

Before Mum, I used to take my girlfriends up the West End to see films at the *Empire Leicester Square* only a day or two after their premieres. There were still traces of the sticky-tape where the red carpet had been. The films were epics like *Dr Zhivago* and *Lawrence of Arabia*. Later there was *The Godfather* trilogy, others: *Jaws* and *Taxi Driver*. I peered into the mirror-shaped, non-faded area of wallpaper. 'You talkin' to me?' I said out loud. 'You talkin' to me!'

Even though Mum hadn't lived in the house before my dad died I imagined him standing where I was, looking at his reflection in the recently removed mirror. A pale version of my face looked back at me out of the rectangle. Perhaps I would never know if he was dead or alive.

Action! I needed something to snap me out of this. I looked down at the nylon carpet. Stupid! I should have asked the clearance men to take it even if it was so obviously fit only for the dump. The stains between the oblong of deeper colour, where the bed had been, and the doorway, where I stood, said it all. I bent over and picked at the edge by the faux-grained skirting. My hand jerked back with pain. One of the teeth of the carpet gripper had pricked my finger. I examined the minute hole and sucked off a bead of blood. It reminded me of the brooch I'd given Mum. With a pang of regret, I remembered tossing it out.

Further along, almost at the corner with the outside wall, the carpet edge looked frayed. Loose strings of plastic thread stuck out. I knelt and shuffled on my knees across, picking up thick rolls of dust on my Levi's. When I reached the other side, I flicked the dust away and sneezed – once, twice. I tugged a tissue from my pocket and blew my nose.

The ragged edge of carpet parted company with the gripper easily. It had been pulled away before. Using it as a starting point, I soon had the carpet free all along the wall. With more effort, I'd folded a quarter of it back into the middle of the room. Scabrous patches of desiccated underlay clung to the floorboards. I picked idly at one of the newspapers lying haphazardly. The headline was: *Moorgate – 43 Feared Dead*. The date was March 1st, 1975.

Back where the carpet had been loose, there was a knot-hole in the centre of a section of plank about four-to-five inches square, its edges askew. I pushed my finger through the hole and prised the square of plank upwards. A small cotton-wrapped bundle nestled in the gap between the joists.

I picked up the package. The dust-flecked wadge of... something... fitted easily in my palm and had a little heft to it. What could it be? Had Mum secreted another jewel? Some money? I estimated that it weighed about the same as my wallet. Was it a roll of £20 notes put by for a rainy day before she was ill?

Still on my knees, I picked at the edges of the handkerchief. It revealed a pocket-diary sized book with a faux-leather cover. The embossed silver writing told me it was *The Book of Common Prayer*. I opened it. The crisp paper was tissue-thin with heavy black print that showed through both sides. The edges were silver-blocked. A dark line about half-way in betrayed that either one of the pages was folded over or someone had inserted a bookmark. I allowed the book to fall open at the page. A blank card was marking the start of a section entitled: *The Form of Solemnization of Matrimony*.

The bookmark had the stiffness of a photograph and my hand trembled as I turned it over – a man alone in a military uniform. He was posed in front of a neutral, swirling backdrop, the sort used by professional photographers. The name of the studio *JA Alonzo* was printed across the bottom right-hand corner. This and the picture's size made me think it was a proof sample for a bigger, professional portrait.

The man had his cap tucked under his arm and his forehead and hairline bore an eerie similarity with the man I had confronted in the imaginary mirror moments before. His eyebrows met in the middle as mine did. Unlike me, his hair was straight, his nose narrow and his lips thin but there was something in the self-consciousness of his smile and his pose that made me think of my first photograph in school uniform. The wings emblem on the front of his cap and above the left breast pocket of his jacket made it clear that Dad was RAF not Army. Why did Mum lie?

I looked down into the gap between the joists to see if there was anything else there – another clue. I scrabbled to the sides blindly and reached along as far as I could but the space was empty. Nothing else. But why hide this? I could only theorise that she always regarded my father as her secret. She never spoke to me directly about him. Even when I asked she would only answer obliquely. The onset of dementia must have made her fearful that she might inadvertently let the secret go – let him go – so she had hidden him away, to keep him for her alone.

With the handkerchief – his perhaps – the book and the photo in one hand, I stood up and flicked at my dusty knees with the other. I was cold and shivery. The search for Dad was on again. Somebody who knew these things would be able to tell me his rank. Perhaps the original photograph could be traced through the studio's records? Maybe Mum hadn't lied about him being in the army. Just as she hadn't lied about him dying on a beach in Normandy. Her only sin was omission. As I grew up, I had accreted layers of my own made-up stories to build a shell that protected me from my ignorance. My one certainty was that my father had died. But if I'd been wrong about so much else...

My mind was a jumble of unknowns that pointed to futures I dared not anticipate. I turned away from that desolate room and closed the door on the past.

The photograph was on my desk as I waited for Mr Thurslow to arrive. When Scotia Mutual wanted to dispute a claim that we thought might be dodgy, we employed an investigation firm in Leadenhall Street to look into the circumstances. The man we dealt with at City Investigations was invariably Mr Thurslow and I'd asked him to come in so we could talk about 'a personal matter'.

When he entered my office, he was even more solemn than usual. 'How are you today, Mr Cross?' he said as he deposited his bowler hat on the surface of my desk. It squatted there as if it was hiding something.

'Tea or coffee, Mr Thurslow?'

'Coffee. Excellent!' He stroked his thumbs along the sharp creases of his striped undertaker's trousers.

I lifted the telephone handset. 'Coffee for two, please,' I said.

Thurslow stayed silent. He was waiting for me to

unburden myself. He was probably expecting me to ask him to follow my cheating wife.

'This is rather a delicate matter,' I said, relishing the idea that I was keeping him on the wrong foot.

There was a knock on the door and the new girl came in balancing a tray with two cups of coffee on saucers, a milk jug and a sugar bowl. She placed it alongside the bowler hat and I slid a coaster across to Thurslow. Julie – or was it Tracy? – shifted one of the coffees to Thurslow's coaster. I reached across for mine.

Thurslow waited for the girl to leave. 'You were going to tell me about a delicate matter.'

'Yes.' I leant back in the swivel chair. 'It's a family matter.'

'You can rely on my discretion.'

'It goes without saying.' I shifted forward. 'The thing is, my mother wasn't married.'

Thurslow's face stayed blank. 'I see...'

'I've only recently discovered who my father was. I had always thought he was killed during the war – on the beach in Normandy – on D-Day but I tried the Public Records Office and he's not on on the army Roll of Honour. Having drawn a blank I thought I'd hand the job over to a professional.'

Thurslow's grey eyes were as impenetrable as smog. He must have learned neither to react nor to lead. He waited like a buzzard, hunched atop a telegraph pole its eyes fixed on a point below – a vision conjured by his greying eyebrows and hooked nose.

'His name was Anthony Kellie-Smith...'

I paused while Thurslow reached into his jacket pocket for a notebook. It was inside a black leather cover that he flipped open. It reminded me of the police officer on the night Mum died. A small silver biro appeared between his finger tips and hovered over the page. 'Kellie Smith,' he said, 'hyphenated?'

'Yes, I think so. And the Kellie part is spelled with 'i-e' at the end, not 'y'.

He crossed out the name and rewrote it.

'As I said, I'd always thought he was in the army but I've discovered this photograph...' I passed it across.

Thurslow put down his pen and picked up the picture. 'RAF.'

'Yes.'

'And you're sure this is him?' He tapped a knuckle against the picture.

'Not one-hundred percent. But I think there's a likeness... don't you?

He looked from the image to me and back again. 'I see,' he said. 'Can I keep this?'

I gave it a long moment's thought. I couldn't bear to lose it. 'Yes, but look after it. It's the only copy I have.'

He nodded and slipped the picture into the notebook cover. 'And you'd like me to find out what exactly?'

I shrugged. 'You're the expert. What is possible? Firstly, I need to know if he's still alive. I don't think he can be but...'

Thurslow looked towards the window as if he was reading from the glass. 'We can work out his rank from the photograph. That's easy. From there we can search RAF records and get his date of birth. From there we go to his birth certificate – marriage, family details. That's when we'll know.' As he spoke his white feathery moustache oscillated on his top lip.

'Know what?'

'If he's dead there will be a death certificate. If he isn't we'll try to locate him. If the photographic studio is still operating we may get a lead to the family. Portraits like this were customarily commissioned by parents or spouses. If we can find out what happened to the original it may take us to his family, if any survive.'

Although I desperately needed to know the answers, I could see a big bill ratcheting up. 'Will it cost much?'

'Nothing to you, old boy. Happy to do it as a favour. We'll lose it in the billings to Scotia. It's legwork – public records, a few phone calls. We'll put a junior on it. Good training.' He saw me start at the word 'junior' and held up a hand. 'Don't worry he won't know who our client is. Anyway, he's bound by our confidentiality guarantees.'

'Of course.'

'We'll find out what happened to your father and maybe uncover some relatives. That's gratis...' He picked up his hat fingered the brim. '... but if you want us to trace them... or him...'

I shook my head. 'That's not necessary.' I turned to the window. 'I only need to know if there's anybody out there.'

Thurslow stood up. 'I'll call you when we have something, Mr Cross.'

I swivelled back, stood up and walked around my desk to offer my hand. 'Thank you, Mr Thurslow.' I was aware that our relationship had crossed a line. As I closed the door, I had to screw up my face to hold back the tears.

5

A week later, Thurslow's bowler was back on my desk. He had placed it there without even lifting an eyebrow in my direction. I was ticked by his presumption and the blank look in his grey eyes. He was giving nothing away. But he had asked for the appointment; it should mean progress.

'Well, Mr Thurslow?' I didn't offer coffee. If there was to be bad news, I wanted him to give it quickly and leave.

He leant down to his side, unzipped a black leather document case and took out three foolscap sheets. He had something after all.

'This has been an interesting assignment, Mr Cross.' He touched a finger to the wings of his moustache. 'I can give you the bare bones.' He referred to the typewritten sheet. 'First, I can confirm that, sadly, your father *is* dead.'

I sighed. Thurslow had casually extinguished a fragile flame of hope but it was a relief to know that I hadn't been misled for forty-odd years.

He looked up, waiting.

'Go on.'

He returned to his notes. 'His name *was* Anthony. His last name has been written differently: always 'Kellie' – 'i–e' – always Smith. But sometimes the words are hyphenated and sometimes they're not. He was born in 1915. We haven't seen his birth certificate because it appears he was born in Malaya – now Malaysia. This information appears in his service record. He never married – at least not in the UK and was a single man – again according to the RAF – when he was killed—'

'He *did* die in action.'

'Not exactly. On 30th June, 1944 there was a massive VI rocket attack – you know – 'Doodlebug'. It exploded not far from here in *The Strand*. Your father was among the fatalities.'

'*30th* June.' I tried to remember why I thought he had died in Normandy. Had my young brain conflated June 1944 with D–Day and had it all been in my imagination?

'Your father was a Wing Commander in the RAF. Quite a senior position. He was awarded the Distinguished Flying Cross in September 1940 – perhaps he was one of *The Few*.'

A hero after all. The valour I had invested in my incarnation of him was not baseless. Only now I pictured him in the cockpit of a Spitfire, a Hun bomber in his sights and the thumb of his gauntleted hand pressing the red firing button. Tracer from the wing-mounted cannon darts across the sky over London. 'Eat lead, Jerry! I'll make you regret taking to the skies over our green and pleasant—'

Thurslow interrupted my reverie. 'But by 1944 he was flying a desk – I believe that's what they called it.' He smiled. 'We can assume he either worked at or was visiting the Air Ministry offices in *The Strand*. It looks as if he had been meeting a relative when the bomb fell and both were killed. The relative's name was *Kenneth* Kellie-Smith. He is on the list of casualties alongside your father. Interestingly *his* name is hyphenated on the death certificate.'

'How were they related?' The skin behind my ears prickled into life. Of course, *he* had a family. I flapped my hand to encourage Thurslow to hurry along.

He looked down at the notes. 'I have the bare bones here. We'll submit a full report. It seems he was your father's uncle. We went back from his death certificate to his birth certificate. He was born on the same day as your father's father in the north of Scotland. They were twins.'

'You've seen my father's father's – my grandfather's – birth certificate?'

'Our young man has.'

'And his name?'

'Sorry. I can't share our employee's—'

'My grandfather's name!'

Thurslow looked down again. 'Of course. William. The interesting thing for you, though, is that your father had a sister–' He turned to the second sheet.

'An aunt – *my* aunt.' My mind was in turmoil. I had relatives – alive.

'Exactly. Helen Kellie-Smith. She was the person who registered your father's death but her surname then – she had married – was Escobar. We tracked her back from there. Your aunt.'

'Where is she?' I had a family. Beneath the desk, I took a handkerchief from my pocket and wiped the sweat from my palms.

Thurslow made a show of straightening the paper in his hand and studied it theatrically. 'From her marriage certificate, we discovered that the man she married was a Portuguese national – Jose Escobar. The wedding was in 1927. There was nothing after that in London – no death certificates, she hadn't registered any births.'

'A dead-end then,' I said, my voice cracking with disappointment.

'Not exactly. Our clerk really earned his spurs on this one. Because the man your aunt married was Portuguese, he wondered whether the absence of records in the UK meant that she had emigrated with him after the war. He started looking at passenger records for sailings from Southampton to Lisbon after June 1945. On the off–chance.'

I shook my head. 'There must have been thousands.'

'Not that many. I imagine the sailings didn't start straight after the war. Each ship's passenger list is in alphabetical order. He was looking for Escobar and 'E' as an initial isn't that common. It was good training.'

'Did he find anything?'

'Yes. Your aunt Helen and her husband sailed to Lisbon. They sailed out and didn't return inside three months – not by steamer.'

'She could still be alive?'

He shook his head. 'Sadly, not.'

'I thought you said you didn't find any more.'

'Not in England. We've been in contact with Lisbon. We know people there – a firm, reputable, like us. They tracked her down. She's buried in the British Cemetery next to her father William – your father's father.'

'My grandfather. You know where he's buried!'

'Yes. In Lisbon.'

'Hold on!' I put up a hand and slipped my chair back. 'You said it would cost me if you started tracing people. I didn't give you—'

'Normally we would have to bill you. But what could we do? As I say, our junior had the bit between his teeth. Once he set that particular hare running...' He shrugged. 'We know the firm in Lisbon. We put work their way. It was only a small favour. Happy to do it for you – for Scotia.'

I pulled my chair back up to the desk. 'Go on.'

He tapped a forefinger to the paper. 'Your aunt – Helen – and her husband – Jose – stayed in Lisbon and had a child.'

'What!'

'Yes, a cousin, *your* cousin.'

'And is *he* still alive?'

'Yes.'

A surge of elation rushed through me. I had a cousin. All

the years I had thought of myself as some sort of remnant, a loose end. Thurslow had, with this one word, shifted me from winter into a spring burgeoning with new possibilities. Nevertheless, I couldn't hide my irritation. 'Why the hell didn't you tell me this at the start!'

'I'm sorry – I thought...'

'Get on with it!'

'His name is – Luis Kellie Escobar. His date of birth, 23rd April 1950.

'Shakespeare's birthday.'

'Pardon?'

'Nothing. Carry on.' I imagined my family tree. Up to my father, across to his sister, down to her son – my cousin. Alive. In Lisbon. I could visit him. Perhaps he had never been to London. I pictured us striding across Westminster Bridge, me pointing out the Houses of Parliament and Big Ben, talking about our imminent boat trip from Westminster Pier to Tower Bridge. My handwriting was shaky as I scrawled *Luis Kellie Escobar 23 April 1950* on my blotter.

'We'll put together a comprehensive report.'

'Thank you.'

'We know where he is – your cousin.'

'You've contacted him?'

'No. We wouldn't do that without... The firm we used – our counterparts in Lisbon – they know of your cousin.'

'They do? How?'

'Apparently, he used to be a policeman. Ironically, he runs an investigation business himself. One man – you know – divorces, missing relatives, that sort of thing.'

'Really?' I shrugged. 'Why ironically? He has to do something, doesn't he?' Touché! That was for holding back the key information.

'You're right. I suppose it is just coincidence – you know – we use an agency and they find a man who's in the same line of work. Anyway, his details are in the report. Should you wish to contact him.'

'Thank you. When will I have it?'

'About a week?'

'And if I want to contact him before then – Luis...' I looked down at what I'd written '... Escobar?'

He bent over the desktop and with his silver ball-point pen wrote two lines directly onto my blotter. I read the words upside down as he wrote them: *Escobar Investigation Agency* and a long telephone number starting 00351. He clipped the ball-point into the inside pocket of his jacket and looked me in the eye. 'Now, if there's nothing else.' He swept up his hat with a flourish.

I escorted him to the door. 'I'll await your report, Mr Thurslow,' I said.

After he had gone, I stood for a moment, thinking. I had a living relative – a cousin. Okay, he happened to be Portuguese and his name was Escobar but... but well, we were both Kellie-Smiths and... I couldn't get to grips with exactly what this meant. I only knew that I was no longer alone.

I was relieved that Thurslow had been able to confirm that my dad had died in June 1944. Dad being one of *the Few* meant he remained the hero I imagined. He had died because of enemy action and his reputation shone as brightly as ever. A father to be proud of and a cousin to share some sort of future with. A good day's work and it was only midday.

I wiped my eyes, took a few deep breaths and picked up the telephone. I could hear the buzz in the outer office as Tracy responded.

'Yes, Mr Cross?'

'Come in, now, Tracy. You'll need your pad and please bring a new blotter.'

I wasn't on form. Normally I could rip through dictation without thinking. Most of the letters followed a formula:

requests for first premium cheques; telling brokers that their clients had been rated; confirming commencement of cover; that sort of thing. I should have been able to dash them off without thinking.

If Tracy hadn't been new to the job I could have told her the paragraph headings and let her get on with it. But she was inexperienced and I was distracted by my family tree. A father, a grandfather, a grand-uncle (if there was such a thing), an aunt and a cousin. All now took their places joined by marriage to my mother. There was nothing on her side and no hope of ever finding where she came from. But my family tree had sprung up from nowhere and I was on one of its branches.

Tracy was infected by my distraction and it was a difficult session. I stumbled over the flow of phrases, sentences, paragraphs and she interrupted to ask me to spell technical terms and to clarify standard words. It was no wonder that by lunchtime I needed a beer.

Perhaps because of the two pints of *London Pride* inside me, I was less inhibited than I should have been when I called the Lisbon number.

6

The plane descended west to east across the northern fringes of Lisbon. I had a window seat with a view of the city below. I'd studied the *Fodor* guide before I left so was able to identify the Avenida de Liberdade spearing southwards from a park's triumphal colonnade. As it entered the city proper it narrowed between the encroaching hills, proceeded pinch-waisted through an arch before it exploded into the paved Praça do Comércio on the waterfront. This abutted the Tagus River extending east and west like a ribbon arranged on each side of a knot. I focused on the point where the Avenida plunged into the grid of the old city. That's where *his* office was. Luis Escobar's. My cousin.

Over a week had passed since the afternoon I had called him: 'Hello, Mr Escobar? Você fala inglês?' I had no idea what I would say if he answered with, 'Desculpe, não'.

I held my breath and let it go when he not only said 'yes' but added in perfect English, 'How may I help you?'

'You are Mr Luis Escobar of the Escobar Investigation Agency?'

'Yes. How may I help you?'

My throat felt so tight I had difficulty forming the words. 'I'm calling long-distance from London, England so I will get straight to the point.'

'Please do, Mr...'

'My name is Cross but it won't mean anything to you.

My father's last name was Kellie-Smith. The same as your mother, Helen.'

I heard him shift the phone and flick a cigarette lighter. After a long intake of breath, he said, 'How do you know this?' There was coating of smoke on his voice as he exhaled. 'Who are you?'

'It's a long story, to be honest. Basically, I'd like to come and see you to tell you the whole thing but the gist of it is that you and I are related. Actually, I'm your cousin.'

Another deep inhalation. 'How can it be?'

'Your mother Helen had a brother. His name was Anthony. He was my father.'

'Yes. But he died in the war.'

'He was still my father.'

'Are you sure of this?'

'Sure enough to want to come and visit you in Lisbon.'

'Okay.' He didn't sound convinced.

I said that I would make the arrangements and call him again to fix a meeting. I replaced the handset with a flourish. I may not have had a father as I grew up but I was going to fill the void of his absence with family — a blood relative somewhere over in Europe.

As the taxi from the airport sped down the same Avenida that I had observed from the sky, I tried to recollect when before in my life I had ever been so overcome with the anticipation of what might happen next. My brain whirled with the possibilities and my mouth was dry.

I took deep breaths and distracted myself by watching the passing buildings set back on either side behind the thickly laden trees. I had given the driver written details of our destination and, after crossing the carriageway by a cinema, we passed a terrace of shopfronts before pulling up outside the *Garden Hotel*.

The room was pleasant enough with a Juliette balcony

overlooking a shabby square lined with parked cars. After a quick change of clothes, I was ready to wander downtown for the meeting with my cousin. The interlude had done nothing to calm my nerves and, to keep my excitement in check, I purposely maintained a leisurely pace and carefully observed my surroundings.

The autumn sun was noticeably higher at this latitude and the sky cloudless but there was a cool breeze from the north that riffled the back of my shirt as I entered the Praça da Figueira. Heading towards Baixa, the oldest part of the city, I crossed the black and white chessboard paving, passed an equestrian statue and entered Rua Augusta, the constricted continuation of the Avenida that led down to the river.

I was determined not to be early and, with my heart thudding, dawdled past the tables set in the centre of the street. Tourists and locals, some drinking coffee, others wine, shared pastries or slices of tart. At two minutes before 3.30pm, I turned left off Augusta into Rua Sao Julião and fifty yards along, stood outside 110. The heavy wood-panelled door was crusted with flaking, green paint. There were four tarnished brass plates, three for lawyers and the fourth for the *Agência de Investigação Escobar, 20 andar*. I ducked inside and had to wait a few seconds for my eyes to adjust to the gloom. I was in a stone-floored corridor with one doorway on each side. I worked my tongue around my mouth to try and generate some moisture so I could lick my lips. Paradoxically, my palms were wet and I wiped them on a handkerchief as I tried to work out where I should go.

My cousin's office was on the first floor and evidently the only access was through the sun-filled open doorway at the far end of the corridor.

The spiral staircase vibrated with each step and I wasn't confident that the fixings held it fast to the crumbling rear wall of the building. The paved courtyard was enclosed on all sides and the walls, despite being hidden from general view, were ornately tiled in geometric patterns that created a disturbing 3-D shimmering effect. This, added to my concern about the stability of the staircase, brought a strange enervation to my legs. Holding tight to the metal rail, I heaved myself onto the upper platform and re-entered the building into a corridor corresponding to the one below. This time there was a murky-paned window at the far end. This would have looked out over Rua Sao Julião but for its impenetrable grime.

On my left, there was a brass plaque polished to a high sheen. The doorway on my right carried three yellow Perspex oblongs with black wording, *Agência de Investigação Escobar*. Should I knock? I took a deep breath and walked in.

It was a large room with two desks. The first was unoccupied and arranged to intercept visitors. Beyond it, at the second, a man sat in a wooden, leather-seated, tilt-and-roll chair. He stood to reveal his height – possibly approaching 7 feet. His head almost touched the beams that spanned the room. 'Mr Cross,' he said. 'You are very prompt. Please. Come in. Sit.' He pointed to a chair in front of the desk. He didn't wait for me to answer but continued, 'I'm not going to offer you a drink.' He nodded towards the empty desk that I hadn't yet walked around. 'As you can see, I am alone and this is a spartan office. Let us discuss the matters of a more personal nature and then perhaps we can adjourn to a bar for an apero.'

His words came out in an even tone. They were fluent but staged, as if he'd been rehearsing and I wondered whether the act was something I should be wary of. Or was he merely nervous like me? After all, this wasn't the usual client-needing-his-help meeting that was his quotidian experience. (Although, given the shabby and untidy nature of the room,

I wondered how much detective work actually came through the door.)

I shimmied around the guard desk and took my seat in the high-backed chair provided for clients. It was lower than I'd reckoned and my backside hit the seat hard. From this lowly position, I had to look up to my cousin, sitting tall in the saddle. Taking a tip from Mr Thurslow, I placed my Panama hat deliberately between us on Escobar's desk. However, the desktop was strewn haphazardly with files, typewritten sheets and two volcanically overflowing ashtrays so I'm not sure this had the desired effect.

Slightly behind me and to my right, a printer squatted on the floor alongside a computer station. The base had a port for a 5-inch floppy disk drive. Scotia had updated our computers to read 3.5-inch disks at least five years before.

'Well, Mr Cross. Or should I call you cousin?'

'Why not? For as far as I know, that is what we are.' While I told Luis about my discoveries I again searched for physical evidence of our shared antecedents. He was of a similar age to me, perhaps a few years younger. His dark hair was receding and his forehead high-domed. He sported tortoise-shell-framed glasses and when he smiled his snaggled teeth were stained by smoking. There was nothing to link him to me or the picture of my father.

Towards the end of the story, Escobar picked up a packet of cigarettes and offered me one. I shook my head. He lit up and took an exaggerated draw. I had nearly brought him up to date and finished with how Thurslow's agency had traced Luis's mother, Helen, to Lisbon and the discovery of her son. 'That's you, Luis Escobar.'

He smiled. 'Just to think if you had not seen your baptismal certificate naming my uncle as your father we would never had known the other existed. It is most exciting, yes? To find out that we are cousins; it is most exciting.'

I was surprised that he accepted my evidence so readily. 'My mother wouldn't have made the declaration for the certificate lightly, I'm sure. For her, a statement to a vicar would have meant more than testifying in court.'

He nodded. 'I am sure that you are right.' He sat back and steepled his fingers against his lips. 'I know about Anthony... your father... he was my uncle and he died in the war. As you say, a bomb.' He pronounced the last 'b'. 'But my mother did not mention that her brother was ever engaged to be married.' He spread his hands. 'But, then again, why should she? It was a long time ago.' He tapped his cigarette against one of the overflowing ashtrays, took another long drag, and pounded the stub into the mound that was already there. I shuddered as he flicked days-old ash from his fingertips. 'It is most interesting for me, Mr Cross, that you come here with this information about my family. You are filling gaps in what I knew. But I suspect that for you it means more – because you knew nothing of us – of my family. You thought you were alone. But didn't your mother have family – a history?'

I smiled and nodded. 'It's very perceptive of you, Luis. May I call you Luis?'

He nodded. 'Of course, and I will call you Steve.'

'You have your memories of family and I have nothing. Sadly, my mother was given up for adoption when she was a baby. She never knew her mother. No stability, no history.'

'And history repeated itself in your mother, in a way.'

'Not exactly. My father — your uncle — they would have married but for the war... and my mother didn't leave me on a doorstep.'

He held up an apologetic hand. 'Yes, of course.' He leant forward. 'But one thing is troubling me and I don't know how to say it. I don't want to be rude but—'

'But I don't look like somebody who could be related to you?'

He spread his hands in apology. 'Yes. I hope you—'

'I totally understand. My mother was mixed race. She believed that she was abandoned because her father was black. My hair, some of my features are from her.'

'I understand. Okay. This is what I suggest. We go for apero now.' He stood up. 'Over a drink, I will tell you about my family — your family. Perhaps we go on and have dinner later. You are alone in Lisbon, yes?'

I drew my hat back from his desk. It was done. Luis had accepted my story without demur. Only my instinctive reserve held me back from hugging him. Instead I beamed my widest smile and he responded with what looked like genuine affection. I turned towards the door so he wouldn't see me wipe away a tear.

Five minutes later, we were sitting in the sunshine outside the Café da Prata on the corner, yards from Luis's office. In the brighter light, I could see that his cream, cotton jacket was crumpled and frayed at the cuffs. He had a five o'clock shadow. This might not have been slovenliness. Men with his colouring probably had to shave twice a day. He had clipped dark-lenses over his glasses.

He had ordered without asking and two schooners of pale sherry sat in front of us. The sun floundered at the bottom of each glass radiating a warm glow. The drink's initial taste as we toasted each other 'To cousins!' was bitter and like a ball of blotting paper in my mouth. I wasn't sure I could finish it.

'Of course, I am my father's son first,' Luis said. 'Jose Escobar was a toolmaker. He worked in factories — actually, small engineering works — in the Bairro Chinês. This was an area on the river to the north of Lisbon – you would call it a shanty town – where people coming from the countryside lived to be close to where they worked. He was one of them, an incomer. He met my mother in a *Fado* bar. You know *Fado*?'

I shook my head.

'I will have to take you to see. Proper *Fado*. Not touristic. It is a music style of only Portugal. My mother came to a touristic bar where my father played the guitar as an accompany to the singers. They met before her father died... 1926. My father was ten years older than her. He died when I was twelve. The *Fado* bars – he had been a big drinker – I'm not sure my mother was happy with him in the later years after they came back to Lisbon.' The harsh sunlight made shadows in the creases at the sides of his eyes.

'When were you born; do you mind me asking?'

He took a sip of his drink. '1950'.

According to Mr Thurslow, Luis's parents had married in 1927. 'That's twenty-three—'

'Yes. You have a good head for figures. My parents were married for over twenty years before I was born. My mother was 46.' He shrugged. 'I was a mistake? She thought she was too old to have a baby perhaps? I don't know.'

I studied my glass, wondering whether to risk another sip. 'And you've always lived in Lisbon?'

'Yes. They moved to England to marry, but didn't settle there... then the war came. When they returned, there was no need to go back to Barrio Chinês. The money after my grandfather's... he was your grandfather too, right?... the money from his death was so much that my dad did not have to work in the factories no more. They had enough from his playing to get by. But his... boozing... is this the right word?'

I nodded and raised my glass. I took a tentative sip. The drink had warmed up and was less harsh.

'Yes... boozing... meant that there was nothing left when they died. It had all gone.'

'This was Kellie-Smith money?'

'Yes. From the plantations. From Malaysia.'

I recalled Thurslow telling me that my father had been

born in Malaya but I had inferred nothing from it. 'Plantations' meant horizon-stretching swathes of land, an army of labourers producing... something, money, riches. 'I'm sorry I know nothing about this. Can you start at the beginning?'

He finished his drink. 'Let us meet up for dinner. Not to be fancy. A little place around the corner from my apartment. This will be better, I think.'

I took another sip of sherry but left the majority as a pretext to stay at the table. I had a lot to think about. 'I have no plans. Yes, let's meet later.'

Luis paid the bill and left a scribbled note with the name and address of the restaurant and a rough map of how to walk there from my hotel. The breeze was now cooler and the table exposed. I regretted not bringing a jacket but I wasn't uncomfortable enough to move. It had been interesting to learn about my Aunt's marriage to a (presumably) tall, dark *Fado* guitar player.

Luis had implied that Helen's money was a problem in his parents' marriage. Was it so much? Plantations in Malaysia, he had said, plural. Had Luis's grandfather — our shared grandfather — made a fortune out there? If he died in 1926, as Luis said, it meant that Anthony would have been alive to have had a share of an inheritance as well. Where had that gone when *he* died? Was it this money that paid for the house in Aquinas Street? But who had been around to make sure that Mum was helped financially? Were there other Kellie-Smiths neither Luis nor I knew about?

7

The restaurant was cramped, barely bigger than my front room. Luis was already sitting at a table, the size of a large tea-tray, by the window. The others were all occupied. Had I not been in Portugal I would have said that the background music was Spanish – lots of guitars and sung *con vibrato*. The room smelled warmly as if one of Mum's fish pies was cooking. For a moment, I was there, in her kitchen. She in her housecoat spooning the mash over the golden-centred roundels of hard-boiled eggs, 'I've made your favourite.'

As I approached, Luis stood and we shook hands, He poured me a glass of red wine from a decanter. 'I knew you would be prompt,' he said. 'My powers of detection.'

'Deduction.' Immediately, I regretted correcting him. His forehead lined with disappointment. It wasn't a good start.

'Detection is good,' I said. 'But we would normally say, 'powers of deduction' like Sherlock Holmes.'

'Ah, yes! The great detective of Baker Street. I have read all the books.'

'You were right, you haven't been let down by your powers of *deduction*—' we smiled agreement '—I like to be on time. It's an important courtesy.'

He sipped his wine and offered his pack of cigarettes. I held up my hand and he slipped the packet back into his pocket. 'And you would prefer it if I didn't smoke – especially at the dinner table.'

What could I say? I merely nodded.

'So, this is a restaurant for local people, Lisbon people. We live in small homes and eat out very often. It is very cheap here. The cooking is good. I especially recommend the Dorada. Grilled simple with potatoes and salad.' He made no sign but the owner came to the table and took the order.

'Now it is time to tell you what I know about my family – your family—' he chuckled '—*our* family!'

I raised my glass. 'Let's drink to that. To the Kellie-Smiths!'

Luis responded and the other diners turned to look.

'It all starts with William Kellie-Smith,' he said. 'He was Scotch. Our grandfather. He was only a young man when he went to Malaya to seek his fortune. He invested the money he earned into land that he turned into palm oil plantations. This was in Northern Malaya. Soon he was very rich—'

'Your mother told you this?'

'Yes, from my mother. She used to tell me bedtime stories about when she was a child in Malaya. The big house in the sunshine, the rainfalls, the animals in the jungle. She told me about her father William like he was a prince and how he married the princess Agnes, who was his sweetheart in Scotland, and my mother was born quickly – in Malaya. Her year she was born was 1904.'

'Eleven years before my father.'

'I don't know it complete but she remembered taking care of her baby brother, so yes.'

'Sorry, go on.'

'William, our grandfather, wanted to live in a grand house on the plantation and he set about to build a copy of a Scotch castle. I remember my mother would always start her bedtime stories, "Once upon a time in a land far, far away, there was a castle".'

'A Scottish castle in Malaya. Crazy!'

'Yes. A Scottish castle. He started building and the First

World War is going on in the rest of the world but not touching Malaya. Your father had been born by now and the building is a slow job and it is still not finished ten years later. By then Anthony, your father, has been sent to school in Scotland and his mother is there with him. In 1926 William and my mother travel to visit Agnes and Anthony but come first to Lisbon because he wants to order elevator equipment for the house.'

'Why Lisbon?'

Luis shrugged. 'You have seen the *elevador Santa Justa?*'

The restaurant owner appeared carrying two plates. We picked up our knives and forks to make room and started in without ceremony. I was pleased to see that Luis treated his fish with reverence. He made a precise incision along the mid-line and separated the muscle segments either side of the exposed spine. It was surgical and exactly how I liked to operate on my fish. The white flesh tasted of the sea.

'Hmmm! Delicious!' I said. 'Elevador what?'

'*Elevador Santa Justa.* It is a big touristic attraction. You must visit. It was built in 1902. We are very good at elevators. Maybe we had the right companies to build such things. Perhaps this was why our grandfather came to Lisbon. While he was here, he caught the influenza and died. My mother had already met my father and fallen in love. She married him—'

'And you came along twenty-three years later!'

'Exactly so. But we are now ahead of ourselves. We should go back.'

'Of course. I'm sorry. I interrupted.'

'When William died, Agnes his wife inherited everything but she could not bear to return to Malaya so she sold it all.'

'Do you think that your mother would have had some money from her father when he died?'

Luis laughed as he pushed his plate away. 'It is a detective thing in Portugal when we try to solve a crime to say, "follow the money". You are being a good detective, Steve.'

I held up my hands. 'Guilty as charged. I'm sorry I was being rude.'

He shook his head. 'I was having the joke with you. No problem. There was an inheritance but it came later, I think. Not big monies. It came when my mother's mother died.'

'When was that?'

'Sorry, I don't know. Sometime after the war, I think. I was still not born, remember. Maybe the money comes at about same time as me. I know things not the same between my parents after the money.'

It made sense. When William died, his widow Agnes inherited the fortune. If my father died before her, my mother wouldn't have any right to it because they never married. Perhaps the money for the house in Aquinas Street had come from Agnes as some sort of recognition of me being her grandson. 'It's sad that your mother inheriting the money may have led to your parents' difficulties.'

Luis shook his head. 'I think maybe my father already tired of being in marriage after twenty years. Perhaps there were too many temptations for him when he was back in Lisbon. Then either me or the money happen or both... and my father stayed out of duty not because of love.'

After the meal, we walked around the corner to Luis's apartment. As soon as we were inside the small living room, Luis went to the kitchen area at one end and poured tooth-glass sized tumblers full of dry sherry. He had persuaded me to come back to see the view from his roof terrace. We accessed it using a narrow stairway, hardly more than a ladder, fixed along one wall. We pushed out through a Hobbit-sized doorway and there we were.

The sky was everywhere. Perhaps it was the poignancy of Luis's story about his parents or the strong perception that the light piercing the inky satin was from long-dead stars; either way, I had tears stinging my eyes as I looked around that Lisbon sky.

The roof was the highest in the immediate vicinity and there was a clear view south all the way to the river shimmering in the moonlight. Luis pointed in the direction I was looking. 'There on the right, you can see the top of the *elevador Santa Justa.* Do you see the lights?'

He was right. A lattice of metalwork resembling a pollarded Blackpool Tower peeped out over the surrounding rooftops, electric lights guttering like candles as they swung in the breeze. 'Yes, I see it.' William Kellie-Smith must have travelled on the Elevador, examining its operation like a potential buyer. Have you ever thought about going there?' I asked.

'Where?'

'Malaya – Malaysia – to see the Kellie-Smith land. Find out what happened to it.'

'Not until now. But since your phone call I've been thinking about that side of my family. Would my mother have wanted me to go there, to see the castle of her stories?'

'It would cost a bit. To travel all that way. Could you afford the time?'

He lifted his glass and studied the pale liquid as if it held the answer to my question. 'I have no family. No commitments here. Okay, the detective business is not making me a fortune of money. I do some divorce business from time to time. I follow husbands. It's enough. I live cheaply here. I have money.'

I didn't want him to think I was being pushy, 'Well if you decide to go you'll have to let me know what you find.'

'I will think about it.' He leant forward. 'I have had another idea, though, my friend – my new cousin.'

'What's that?'

'You should see your grandfather's grave while you are in Lisbon.'

He was right. I should.

'I will come to your hotel in the morning. We can walk there. It is not too far.'

It seemed that in Portugal's capital city, everything was in walking distance. I wondered whether Luis had ever escaped. 'Have you always lived here. When you served in the police force, was it in Lisbon?'

'When my father came here from the country, he worked and lived in the shanty town area called Bairro Chinês. In the police force, after I made detective, I was assigned to the same area. It was the most lawless. Friday and Saturday nights were crazy with the drinking, the fights. If there was a murder in Lisbon it would have been in the Bairro Chinês...' His voice drifted. There was silence except for thump of a nightclub's music. '... When I left the police force and started in this business, I had no fancy ideas about where my clients would come from – Bairro Chinês. It would always be – how do you say – grabby?'

'Grubby.'

'Yes, grubby end of the market. I could see how my business would be like the private investigator in my favourite film *Chinatown* – Jake Gittes. Do you know it?'

'I love that film. But, sorry. I'm being stupid; I don't get the connection.'

'You don't see it? It's a private joke for me. What was the name of the Los Angeles detective in Chinatown?' He chuckled. 'He gave poor old Jake Gittes such a hard time.'

I shrugged.

'You don't know? It is Escobar!' He tapped his chest.

I shook my head. 'Of course.'

'And the other coincidence of the film and my life, do you see it?'

'Sorry. You'll have to tell me.'

'Bairro Chinês, where I worked – in English you would say it *Chinatown*. Detective Escobar working in Chinatown!'

I laughed.

'Would you like another drink?' he asked.

I held up my glass still a third full. 'Did it bother you working in Chinatown?'

He shrugged. 'Not so much.'

'The reason I ask is you've just reminded me of a scene in the film – the bedroom scene. Do you remember it?'

The booming disco bass flared louder for a few seconds as if the sound had escaped momentarily from a carelessly opened door. The lights on the *elevador* jostled each other more vigorously. The muffled beat resumed.

Luis chuckled. 'Faye Dunaway with no clothes on. How could I forget?'

'I was thinking more about what Jack Nicolson said as Jake.'

'What was that?'

'Faye Dunaway – Evelyn Mulray – says, "Why does it bother you to talk about Chinatown?" and Jake says, "It bothers everybody who works there." When Evelyn asks why, he says, "In Chinatown you can't always tell what's going on." Is that what it was like for you?'

While I was talking, Luis had looked increasingly morose. He turned blank-faced searching over my shoulder for something in the past. I thought he might be wistfully picturing Faye Dunaway's breasts, but he said, 'Yes. That's it exactly. In Bairro Chinês nothing was what it seemed.'

Next morning, we walked up a hill to the west of the Avenida. It was cooler than the day before. The clouds bustled to obscure the sun with the regularity of London buses and their shadows were distinctly cold. Scented dust fell from the lime trees, thickening the air. I paused to remove my Panama hat and used a handkerchief to wipe my brow. Luis turned back, scarcely hiding his impatience. Clearly his liver was in a better state than mine. The dull headache I'd had since 6am, when I'd been woken by the need to pee, was now a full-fledged throb.

He smiled sympathetically as if he understood how I was feeling. 'It is not far,' he said, pausing to light a cigarette and allowing me to catch up. He coughed, doubling up and chuffing out the smoke like a steam engine. He straightened up and stubbed his cigarette out with the sole of his shoe.

We passed a row of antique shops and under an arch that used to be part of the old city wall. On the crest of the hill, blank slabs of pre-fabricated housing, with washing sprouting from narrow balconies, mixed with grander blocks of mansion-flats. These were clad in tiles similar to those at the rear of Luis's office building; either that or they had even more extravagant art-nouveau or art-deco plastering that swept up the corners or filled the spaces between the windows.

Another junction brought us to a wide and busy thoroughfare that stood between us and a lawned area about the size of a football pitch. The saltire of paths that joined the gates at each corner were bordered by exotic flower beds. The domes of a cathedral-like church on the far side dominated the right-hand frame of my view and, as I panned left, my gaze settled on the massive Christ statue in the far distance on the other side of the river. He held his arms outstretched in welcome.

Luis led me along the pavement that followed a high wall. We turned in through open wrought-iron gates: The British Cemetery. The sound of traffic hushed. A blackbird greeted us like a child trying out a penny whistle for the first time. The sun had emerged from cloud behind us, its light bounced from the white façade of the small church. I put on my sunglasses. We followed the wide gravel path that led to the church doorway. There were narrower paths to each side lined by memorials of all styles: statues of angels – plain and overwrought; cherubs – vibrant and etiolated; crosses – ornate and simple; sarcophogi – brash and diffident; obelisks – tall and stumpy; and at least one skull and crossed bones; all were shaded beneath the vaulted branches of heavy-leafed trees.

A sign pointed left to where we would find the grave of Henry Fielding but Luis passed the opening and turned right. He stopped by a tall Celtic cross that leaned into the embrace of a glossy-leafed bush. The grave that I stood alongside belonged to *Amy Elise Hirst of Leith* and I wondered whether this corner was reserved for expatriate Scots. Luis leaned forward, brushed a hand over the wording on the cross and I shuffled closer to him to read the inscription: *In affectionate memory of William Kellie-Smith who was born at Elgin on March 1st 1870 and who spent thirty-seven years of his life in the federated Malay states and died in Lisbon December 11th 1926 aged 56 years. At rest.*

Did *I* feel at rest in that moment? I didn't feel sadness. How could I feel sadness for someone I never knew? There was no rest for me here, only the turmoil of family. I was connected by blood to Luis, who had sidled away to leave me with my grandfather; to my aunt, whose grave Luis now knelt beside; to the man whose tilted headstone I stood before; to his widow buried somewhere in Scotland. All this made me part of a world way beyond the walls of the house in Aquinas Street. This is what I'd been looking for when I crawled around on the stained carpet of Mum's bedroom. Tears flowed from my hungover-heavy eyes and tracked down my unshaven cheeks – tears of relief not of sorrow.

8

Luis was loitering outside the restaurant. His cigarette glowed in the dusk of late evening and as I approached, he ground it into the pavement with his toe. He nodded and led me into a cramped, ill-lit room. It was more a bar than a restaurant. There were a few tables but they weren't laid out for eating and each was encircled by a group of men and women, in their sixties and older, who had drinks in front of them. Clouds of blue cigarette smoke rose into the forest of grotesque, wooden mannequins, in the national colours of green, red and yellow that were strung between the beams. It looked like a mass hanging of Pinocchio and his pals. Guitars were stacked haphazardly in one corner.

We climbed the narrow staircase at the back of the bar and entered the room above. It was no bigger than downstairs and already every table except one was occupied. The waiter intercepted us and he and Luis embraced. They conversed in Portuguese. Perhaps Luis told a joke because they both burst into laughter and clapped each other on the back. Luis signalled me towards the vacant table that was by the opening for the hatch to a dumb waiter. We sat down.

'Is it allowed for *me* to smoke?' Luis asked. He jerked his head back indicating that almost everybody else in the room was polluting the atmosphere.

'Of course,' I said.

'I hope you like rabbit. There is no menu. Tonight, we have

rabbit – a stew. It is the best rabbit stew in all of Lisbon.' He laughed. 'In all of Portugal even. If you like rabbit you will like rabbit stew here, I guarantee.'

'I like rabbit!' We had to shout over the hum of other conversations.

'Good! First we eat; then we listen to music.'

The rabbit stew was everything that Luis had promised, juicy and with the distinctive taste of the meat tantalised by herb-laden, spicy sauce. The red wine, from half-litre carafes, arriving, like the rabbit, without being chosen, was robust and fruity. We were the last to be served and the last to finish and, as our plates were cleared, the room swelled with anticipation.

Three of the ancients from the bar below appeared at the top of the stairs. They carried guitars and sat in a confined space by the banister. They started tuning their instruments and the conversations around the tables petered out. The lights dimmed, leaving the performance area in the arc of a single spotlight, and one of the guitarists embarked on a complicated riff – not a melody – using all his fingers on both hands to pick at the strings and strum seemingly at the same time. It sounded like two were playing but the others sat immobile, their heads bowed in appreciation.

In a moment, the waiter who had greeted us and who had served our food was standing at the soloist's side. The other guitarists joined in, playing chords, and the waiter delivered a song of desolation and longing communicated, not by words, but through the heart-rending sequences in the melody and the passion that the singer wove into the lyrics. When he came to a particularly plangent passage he wrought it so well that there were grunts of approbation from the elderly men at tables nearby.

A succession of singers took us through the next two hours: a young woman whose voice was fresh but whose heart had only recently been broken; a grey-haired man supported by a crutch who had the demeanour of a retired street-fighter; a beshawled, older woman whose voice was cracked by smoking but who knew everything about love and desertion; and, most memorably, a timeworn troubadour, linked up to a gas cylinder that fed his nostrils with oxygen through plastic tubes taped to his face, whose body shook with passion as he sang his songs of longing and loss.

The music entered my bloodstream; touched my soul. It was as if I was making discoveries about myself. Not about romantic love. No, my melancholy was about family. Not me and Mum. You couldn't call *us* a proper family. We were damaged and unnatural when she fell ill and our roles reversed.

No, the songs revealed an emotional void that should have been filled by familial love – from a father, brothers and sisters, aunts and uncles – cousins even. I glanced at Luis. The *Fado* singers touched the absence that was now in the past – the hollow at my centre. I had shared the vulnerability inherent in their singing. I wiped my eyes hoping that Luis wasn't watching me.

'Where does it come from?' I asked after the applause for the final singer had died and the guitarists had stumbled back downstairs.

'From the heart,' Luis said, chuckling.

'Obviously. Seriously, what is its history?'

He shrugged. '*Fado*, it means "fate". They are songs from the waterfront. Sailors, fishermen, their wives and girlfriends – who knows?'

'It's very emotional... powerful... and I understood every word even though I... didn't, if you see what I mean.'

'Of course. That's *Fado*!'

'That's *Fado*,' I whispered. It had triggered something in me. As if I had found my place in the world. I drained my wine glass and looked around the restaurant. I could envisage myself in the future as one of the old *Fado* aficionados murmuring 'Bravo!' This version of me, which I could assume with the ease of a man donning an overcoat, was there, waiting in the wings. If ever I wanted to renew myself, this city would be the place to do it.

Luis clapped his hands together in a gesture of finality. 'We finish our evening here. We must have one more sherry to nightcap.'

'I'd like that. I leave tomorrow. It has been a great visit. I hope we will stay in touch. Perhaps you can come to London?'

He raised his glass, 'To our family!'

'To the Kellie-Smiths!' I said and took a gulp – it wasn't an evening for restraint.

'You know,' he said, 'I might come to London, yes. Perhaps Scotland where our family came from. Your visit here has raised in my mind thoughts of my mother, her life in Malaya with our grandfather. I've never asked what happened there, what is left of the castle in a land far, far away – the plantations. You have made me think about these things – how much I don't know. Maybe this is my next detective work. I think I *will* go to Malaysia, you know. Go to the castle to find out.'

He looked at me expecting a response. Was he asking me to go with him? As much as I wanted to attach myself limpet-like to this new idea of *family*, was I ready to travel halfway across the world with a cousin I'd only just found? Such closeness so soon? Luis had welcomed me warmly but... 'If anybody can find out what happened there, you are the man.'

'But, what about you, Steve? You could go as well. Cousins together exploring our family history. Come with me.'

'I don't know.' As I said it, I realised that I was shaking my head. I had already dismissed the idea. It had been adventure enough for me to come to Lisbon. As much as the city's vibrancy and the music of *Fado* had captivated me, I felt vulnerable at the prospect of more travel, like a toddler waking in a night-time bedroom. Deep down he knows the darkness holds no monsters but he dares not look under the bed nor open a wardrobe. He hunkers down under the blankets.

The promise of a long-haul flight, the foreign-ness of a tropical country, the strange customs and food; logic told me that there was nothing to be afraid of, but my natural inclination was inaction – I too hunkered down.

Instead of embracing adventure, I conjured up all the objections: the renovation and refurnishing of my house; the exciting plans for starting a new independent life. Give it a couple of months, I thought. Let Luis do the legwork. Wait and see what he comes back with. I clasped his hand and pulled him to me in a hug. It was out of character and theatrical but I wanted him to know how grateful I was that he had accepted me so readily. I would see Luis again. I would be able to recreate this sense of belonging, to him, to his city and to its music. 'Yes, Luis. *You* should go. Go to Malaysia for both of us.'

9

My family then: a father who died in the war alongside my great uncle; my mother now deceased; an aunt on my father's side who, like her father, had died in Lisbon; and a cousin, *my* cousin Luis. There's no doubt about it, the Kellie-Smith's weren't great breeders. My grandfather, the man whose grave Luis had taken me to see, was top of the league. He had sired a son, my father, and a daughter, Helen, Luis's mother. But you couldn't call it unrestrained reproduction by the standards of his time.

Both Luis and I were only children. This wasn't surprising given his mother's age when he was born. Perhaps she and Jose had been trying for years by the time he came along. My mother devoted her best years to me. Where was the time or opportunity to think about marriage and more children?

Luis and I were both in middle age and single. Had we inherited a weak 'breeding' gene? After Mum fell ill, I accepted that my job was to look after her. Perhaps my readiness to adopt this role meant I wasn't as highly-sexed as men around me. In the last thirteen years, one thing I didn't need was the complication of a 'relationship'.

As for Luis, everybody knows that policemen make poor romantic partners; it's the nature of the job. He could also have been scarred by his father's mistreatment of his mother. Either way, he had his reasons for being single.

When I was back in London, I briefly thought about

leaving the UK and going to live in Lisbon. If I sold Mum's house there would have been enough money for an apartment there and to cover my expenses until I was able to find work. However, the Chief Clerk of the London branch of Scotia Mutual Life, although it doesn't sound like a big job, carried a certain responsibility, was paid well and promised a good pension. If, as had been planned, the company demutualised at the end of the year, I was in the right place, as both employee and bondholder, for substantial windfall payments. It made sense to stay put, at least for the time being.

The house in Aquinas Street suited me very well. Its location south of the river may not have been 'posh' but it had never been subjected to the low-rent, multi-tenanted influx that had blighted other parts of London. Younger professionals were moving in and energising the neighbourhood and the leisure developments on the South Bank promised a new vibrancy.

I consulted a builder and we made plans to modernise the parts of the house that hadn't been touched for nearly twenty years.

What about me? Could my love life be renovated? The office had provided romantic opportunities in the past but being part of the branch's management meant those days were over. I tried to imagine myself haunting the local nightspots, but all I could picture was a circle of laughing youngsters watching me uncle-dancing on the strobe-lit floor of Waterloo's infamous disco-nightclub *Southern Electric*. The answer, according to agony aunts, was always to 'develop new interests' and 'meet new people'. Easier said than done.

The 1990-91 football season was approaching its mid-point and I decided to resurrect my support for Chelsea. Not as a way of meeting the opposite sex, obviously, but more to create a fixed point on alternate weekends that would take me out of the house. Most boys adopt the same football team as their dads and they usually know which team it is before they go to primary school. I arrived on my first day handicapped by ignorance and unable to answer to the basic question, 'Which team do you support?' Most of my glory-hunter contemporaries had chosen Arsenal, the most successful London team at that time.

The more my peers pressured me to join them, the more I resisted, and in 1955, the year I moved up to the grammar, Chelsea won the Division One Championship. Knowing that, in the new school, I would be asked the same old question, I prepared by choosing the Champions as my team. It was an own-goal. Chelsea never repeated the 1955 success while I was at school and the club and I suffered the ultimate humiliation of relegation. I stuck with my choice even though it gave the playground bullies yet another reason to taunt me.

Chelsea were back in Division One in 1990. One Saturday, with workmen knocking seven bells out of the house interior, I joined the crowd for the mid-table clash against Norwich City. Despite an uninspiring draw, I decided I'd go back.

It's difficult to describe, but Luis's existence gave me the confidence to feel that friendship and even love might come my way. Loneliness begets solitude and this, in turn, begets exclusion and I felt that I had snapped out of that spiral. It was important not to lose touch with him. Consequently, I sent notes to his office email account from time to time using Scotia's system. I told him about the changes to the house and renewed the invitation for him to come to London. I suggested he come over in the spring so we could explore Scotland together and find our ancestral home in Elgin.

One of Luis's replies explained that he was preparing for his trip to Malaysia. He was very excited and described how his research had revealed that the family home – the Scottish castle – was near a city in the north called Ipoh. He had booked accommodation and had telephoned ahead asking for information.

A later e-mail said: *After our grandfather died in 1926, the romantic castle became the centre of rumours and mystery. The local people think it is haunted and there are secret rooms and tunnels underground that nobody knows about. These are where the ghosts are thought to dwell.*

I had started out wanting to know no more than who my father was. Thurslow had turned up a cousin and he, in turn, had revealed the existence of a castle. In my imagination, I recalled Mum's Christmas shortbread biscuit tin with a picture of Loch Ness and Urquhart Castle on the lid. This is the image I transposed into a Malaysian plantation landscape. The building's crumbling castellated walls loomed above, not the loch's placid waters, but rows of tropical trees.

Luis had given no clue as to whether our house was occupied but I could picture a very un-Caledonian verandah where the owner and his wife, both British and, anachronistically, sporting 1930s colonial safari-wear, sipped gin and tonics as they looked out over their demesne. I was beginning to regret my decision to stay in London and I made up my mind to see Luis immediately on his return so he could tell me all about it.

His last e-mail from Lisbon: *I leave for Malaysia on Friday. If the hotel has Internet connections I will send e-mails. If they do not I will send faxes to your office.* I replied, wishing him a safe journey and looked forward to hearing what he made of Malaysia and our family's connection.

On the following Monday afternoon, Tracy came into my office with the first of his handwritten faxes: *I am in Ipoh! It was a long drive from Kuala Lumpur. Malaysia has a strange* atmosphere with people of Malay and Chinese heritage. The hotel has found a local guide who will take me to the castle. The business centre has Internet but I am not able to access the company email account. Who knows why? It is most complicated. This is why the fax. It is best for you to reply by fax also. It is very interesting here. The castle is abandoned. The surrounding plantations are being worked and I am trying and find out who owns it all. Perhaps I do!

I set my files aside and pored over Luis's text looking for the meanings between the words. I had never heard of Ipoh. I looked it up in the office copy of Encyclopaedia Britannica and read that it was the capital city of the state of Perak in the north of the country. There was nothing about our castle. Now I knew it was abandoned, I updated my vision of it with a version based on the ruinous House of Shaws in Robert Louis Stevenson's Kidnapped. I answered straight away: It's good to hear from you. The house sounds interesting. I think you were joking when you said that we might own it! Excited to hear more. Every day now I looked forward to hearing from Luis, wondering what he might uncover next.

Later in the week, on the day the office was buzzing with the news that Margaret Thatcher had resigned as Prime Minister, another fax arrived after lunch – bed-time in Malaysia: Thursday: I have found out who owns the house and hope to have a meeting soon. I feel sad for my grandfather. He never saw his dream house become reality. I wonder if his wife in Scotland or my mother came back to see it after he died? It is very unhappy.

The handwritten reply I gave to Tracy said: I'm intrigued by your descriptions of the 'castle'. Let me know how your meeting goes. Its neutral tone far from reflected my mood. Hardly an hour went by without one of my pictured versions of our castle interrupting what I was doing. In all of them, whether he was negotiating the treacherously tumbledown spiral staircase of Shaws or striding across a cannon-scarred battlement in Urquhart, Luis, cigarette in mouth, was planting his Kellie-Smith feet and metaphorically reclaiming our birthright.

The next day's fax arrived later in the afternoon. Unlike the others, this one was typewritten, presumably at his dictation: *Interesting meeting with the family who own the castle land and palm oil plantations. They bought the land from our grandmother some time in 1930s. I'm happy that grandfather has such a fine monument. The owners will continue to maintain the house and will put up a memorial to him if I pay for it. Leaving for home on Monday.* He hadn't bothered to append his signature.

My flights of fancy could return to earth. There was no drama. It was comforting to know that the owners recognised their responsibility as custodians of our family connection to the place. I decided to work diligently for the rest of the afternoon and think of a response at home that evening. I would word something carefully so that Luis didn't think I was too disappointed by the outcome. Why had I invested so much in the news from Ipoh? Our family had built a grand house and now it was owned by someone else. What had I expected?

It was only on my way home that evening that I realised that it was Friday and that a fax from me on Monday wouldn't reach his hotel until after he'd left. I could have gone into the office over the weekend but I'm ashamed to admit that I didn't know how to work the fax machine. Any further news would have to wait until I could call Luis when he was back in Lisbon. I assumed this would be on the following Tuesday at the earliest.

In the weekend that followed, Chelsea, who had made a bad start to the season, unexpectedly won away at Old Trafford. It was always good to beat Manchester United and it served to take my mind off events in Malaysia. The match was broadcast live on television. I watched it at home, amid the smell of drying plaster, enjoying a bottle of Young's Special Bitter during each half.

When I hadn't heard anything from Luis by the Wednesday lunchtime, I picked up the telephone and dialled his office number. It rang and rang, the sound hollow. A recorded voice speaking Portuguese cut in followed by the beep to signify that I should leave a message. 'Hi Luis,' I said. 'I hope you had a safe journey and I'm desperate to hear how you got on. Call me.'

That day, the Conservatives, against the odds, elected John Major as leader of their party and he automatically became Prime Minister. Like me, John Major was a south London, grammar-school boy whose first job had been an insurance clerk. Watching him on television, it struck me that our voices betrayed that background in the words we used and the cadences of our speech. We both had an unassuming manner and it was hard to picture our new Prime Minister as a heroic figure. Indeed, he had once been described as the sort of person who tucked his shirt tails inside his underpants and was depicted this way by a cartoonist. Did people see me in the same light, I wondered.

10

I called Luis Escobar's office again on the Thursday. There was no answer and I didn't bother leaving a message. I sent an e-mail asking him to call me.

When he didn't respond, I could only assume that he was still in Ipoh. I re-read his last typewritten fax. Could it be he had learned something after his meeting that meant he decided to stay? If so, why hadn't he told me?

It was the memory of Luis's first fax from Ipoh that blew a hole in my easy acceptance of the outcome, the one where he had said something about him owning the house. Could he have been following up a lead that he didn't want me to know about? The fragile bridge I had constructed out of my world's few certainties cracked under the strain of Luis's lack of faith, betrayal even, and threatened to cast me into the river of self-doubt that always burbled beneath. I needed to confront him. Before I left for home, I gave Tracy a fax to send to his hotel in Ipoh demanding an explanation. She came back saying that it had not been accepted at the other end. Either the fax machine in the hotel wasn't working or the operator had declined the transmission.

It was easy to organise a few days break from work to deal with a 'family emergency'. In the wake of Mum death, the regional manager fell over himself to grant me a few days, longer if I needed it. My reluctance to take on the rigours of the longer flight meant that I had decided to go to Lisbon first. When London ground to a halt in an unseasonable November snowstorm that weekend, my flight was cancelled. There wasn't another until the Monday. I re-booked, still hoping that I would hear from Luis in those two extra days.

The taxi dropped me at the end of Rua Sao Julião and I covered the fifty yards or so with my umbrella tilted into the cold, driving rain. The ground floor passage was darker than before and any sounds from within the offices either side were drowned by the percussion of the rainfall and the gurgling of gutter pipes. My footsteps on the iron staircase sounded like the toll of a church bell. I ducked inside, shook and furled my umbrella and hurried to the door marked *Agência de Investigação Escobar*. I knocked. There was no sound. I looked for a letterbox to peer through but the door had no openings. I retraced my steps.

I directed the taxi driver east of the Avenida to the *Fado* restaurant and from there I was able to scramble on foot around the corner to Luis's door, the spine-ends of my umbrella nearly touching the walls on either side. The cobbles were loose and uneven and I had to dodge deep puddles where they were missing altogether.

At the house, with water streaming through the narrow gap between my umbrella and the wall, I rang the bell for the top apartment '*Escobar*'. There was no response. Should I return to his office? I buzzed for the apartment below. A woman answered and I could hear a child chortling in the background. We established who I was looking for and that she spoke English – a little. 'Mr Escobar not here.'

'Is he at work? In his office?' I was on tiptoes so I could speak into the microphone on the security panel and the water splashing off a ledge soaked my face.

'No, not office. Feriado... holy day.'

'He has not come back from his holiday?'

'Diga isso de novo?' The intonation in her voice told me she hadn't understood.

'His holiday is finished, I think.'

'No not finished. He is gone holy day.'

If this was true he'd either been away for three weeks or he'd come back briefly and I had missed him.

'Did he come back after ten days? He was supposed to be away for only ten days.'

'Diga isso de novo?'

It looked like I had exhausted the neighbour's English so I thanked her and turned back into the street. I looked at my watch. It was too late to return to Luis's office to see if anybody in his building knew where he was. There was nothing for me to do except return to my hotel.

The rain showed no sign of letting up so I stayed in the room scanning the television channels until I found one showing the movie *Crocodile Dundee* with Portuguese subtitles. I ordered a bottle of red wine and a burger and chips from room-service. Like a tongue that can't stop itself probing a broken tooth, I returned again and again to Luis's whereabouts. He wasn't in Ipoh and it looked like he hadn't returned home. Wherever he was, he was ignoring me.

Next morning, I left the hotel so that I would arrive at Luis's office shortly before 9 o'clock. There was a blue sky above and a chill edge on the breeze carried an ozone freshness from the Tagus estuary.

Half an hour later I was still alone by Luis's office door. I had expected somebody to arrive at the solicitor's office across the passageway, but they were clearly not early starters. Finally, a heavy tread on the stairway indicated that somebody was coming. When the man reached the top, his bulk blotted out the light through the doorway. He was as tall as Luis and at least twice the weight. An Orson Welles of a man. He said something in Portuguese.

'Do you speak English?' I asked.

'Of course,' he said. His voice was a bass growl emphasising the similarity with Welles.

'My name is Cross,' I said.

'I am Doutor Ardiles,' he said, indicating his name on the polished plaque. 'How may I help you?'

'Actually, I am looking for Luis – Luis Escobar.' I pointed to the nameplate on my side. 'It's a family matter.'

'Come in. Come in. Escobar is away.'

I followed him into a single room, the same size as Luis's and furnished in a similar manner with two desks and the usual office equipment. Here though the desks and chairs matched, were more modern in style and the teak was polished. The main desk by the far wall was clear and there were side tables for current files. The antique telephone was ebony with ivory detailing. It looked heavy. There was an oil-painting portrait hanging behind the desk and the sitter was none other than the gargantuan man who stood before me.

He placed envelopes he was carrying on the desk nearest the window and then lumbered across to a sideboard by the opposite wall. 'My assistant will be here soon. She will bring a pastry for me. I will ask her to go out and purchase the same for you if you would like it?'

I could tell from the tone of his voice that he expected me to decline. 'That's very gracious of you. But no thank you. About Mr Escobar – you say he's away?'

Ardiles started fiddling with the filter coffee machine. 'I'm sorry but I must make coffee while we talk. It is our routine, you understand. I like to have it ready when my assistant arrives.'

'Of course.'

He spooned coffee into the filter. 'Yes. Escobar went on holiday... two or so weeks ago.'

'Is this his trip to Malaysia?'

'To Malaysia, yes.' He switched the machine on.

'He's actually been away for nearly a month.'

The big man grunted back to his desk, opened the top drawer on the right-hand side and took out an A4 week-to-a-view diary. 'Let me see—' he flicked back three, then four pages '—yes, over three weeks. Time flies, I think you say.'

'Indeed. Do you know any more about his visit to Malaysia?'

He shook his head. 'Sorry. But you didn't say who you are.' He shifted his bulk back to stand alongside the coffee machine that had begun to hiss.

'I'm his cousin. I live in London.'

'I didn't know Luis has family.'

'Nor did he, until a couple of months ago.' I could see he wanted me to say more. 'It's a long story, to be frank.'

'Are you worried because you think he should have been back by now?'

'Yes, I am. I sent a fax to him at his hotel and they refused to accept it. I assumed that he had checked out.'

There was a flurry of activity behind me and I turned. A woman stood at the door with a handbag dangling from her shoulder. She held two paper bags, the pastries, in her hand.

Ardiles, suddenly light on his feet, sashayed across to where I still stood, relieved her of one bag and set it on his desk. He spoke to her in Portuguese including the word 'Cross'. The woman nodded. She went over to stand by the coffee machine and Ardiles settled himself behind his desk. He indicated the seat opposite and I sat down. We waited, neither speaking, while his assistant poured two mugs of coffee and placed one on a coaster in front of him.

'Are you sure...?

'No, I'm fine. Thank you.'

Ardiles sipped his drink, and held it high while he turned to one of the side tables to retrieve a coaster.

His assistant sat at her desk and opened the morning's post.

After another sip, Ardiles smacked his lips and gave a nod of appreciation towards his assistant. 'You could say that I am Luis's friend as well as his lawyer. He has been able to pass cases my way, usually divorce and, in my turn, I have been able to give him business. I have also looked after his affairs when he has needed legal help. It is my concern also that he has not come back as you expected. But if he has reasons to stay in Malaysia...'

'Yes. He may have good reason to stay there.' I was beginning to believe that he had discovered many reasons – paper ones in the local currency. 'But it would be good to be sure.'

He opened the brown bag and took out a white-dusted custard tart. 'Do you mind if I...?'

'Go ahead.'

He took a bite and icing sugar coated his lips. His words puffed out drifts of powder. 'As his lawyer, I can make enquiries.' He shifted his bottom lip forward to retrieve a fleck of pastry that was threatening to drop. 'Perhaps, Mr Cross, you will come back tomorrow at this time and I shall tell you what I have discovered.'

I looked at my watch as I stood up. 'At 10am?'

'Yes. At ten.'

11

There's no doubt about it, Nancy accepted as fact that Western men invariably thought she was one of the most beautiful women they had ever met. To her, it was a tired routine. As they said it, she waited for one of them to be honest and insert the word 'Chinese' as a qualifying adjective. It was no surprise to her when Luis Escobar said it and it affected her evidently less than he hoped. Was she to fall at his feet because he was a 'man of the world' from Europe and he had complimented her?

She attracted compliments from western men because she didn't look typically Chinese. She was thirty years old when Escobar came to Ipoh and, unlike many Chinese women he would have bumped into, she was tall and slim. In the privacy of her room she was proud of her curves. It wasn't part of her culture and certainly not in her upbringing to flaunt her body, but she found nothing wrong in dressing modestly in clothes that made the most of her figure.

When Nancy was in her early teens, her mother had taken her to see *The Flower Drum Song* at the movies; the scene in which Nancy Kwan sang *I Enjoy Being a Girl* had been a formative experience. It was then that she decided if she ever needed an English name it would be Nancy.

Despite her exceptional beauty, or perhaps because of it, she was still single when she met Escobar. Maybe it was her intelligence that scared away eligible men of her own kind.

In Nancy's experience, many Chinese men adhered to the ancient proverb: *ugly wives and stupid maids are priceless treasures*.

So, she was, back then, in her own words, 'a little part lonely'. But she had compensations: a serviced apartment in KL and a good job with responsibilities. She worked in the training department of Malaysia's largest bank. She had won awards for being the top salesperson on the counter in the main branch in *Negara Maybank* during the 1980s and, at the end of the decade, was transferred to sales training so she could pass on her skills.

It was only when she visited her home town of Ipoh that she played the part of her father's dutiful daughter, and duty called late in 1990 when she was enjoying a relaxed Sunday at home.

'Lai Ping, I need you here.' Her father always used her birth name.

She answered in his language, Mandarin. 'Has anything happened? Is it Mother?' Her mother was unwell with suspected breast cancer. Nancy was expecting a diagnosis anytime.

'No. The doctors have everything under control. Nothing is wrong.'

He continued breathing into the mouthpiece and she waited for more news of her mother's illness but he coughed, snorted back phlegm, and said, 'I have a job for you. It will only take a few days.'

'A job? What sort of job? Why me? What about all the employees there you could choose from?'

'I'll explain when you come. This needs a woman with education. One who knows the world. They may be as common as rats in KL but here in Ipoh there are not so many to choose from. Just you. When did I last ask you to help me with business?' He paused to let this sink in. 'And you can visit your sick mother.'

What he didn't need to say was that he had paid for his daughter's expensive education, initially in the English school in Batu Gajah, where she had first used her chosen name, and then at the polytechnic in England.

He required a small favour in payback and he knew she couldn't refuse, even though the word 'business' gave her a shiver of apprehension. Her father, Lee Song Yong – known to the locals as S Y, ran the Leeyate hotel chain that boasted properties in all thirteen Malaysian states. The Lee family was spread across the country and involved in many industries: palm oil, rubber, entertainment, import and export. The government's legislation to restrict the Chinese dominance of commerce had begun to bite and Nancy knew that the family would take any measures necessary to maintain its power.

One of the things Nancy liked about returning to Ipoh was that her beauty was not incomparable there. The city was famed throughout the Peninsula for producing tall, beautiful Chinese girls just like her. She no longer stood out. She was thinking as much in the car as it travelled along the North-South Expressway the day after her father's call. She slumped in the back seat watching the roadside plantations whizz by while Lang-ren drove.

Lang-ren was her minder in KL. He received his orders direct from S Y and kept his boss up to date regarding Nancy's affairs. Lang-ren and Nancy had known each other since they were children and for a short time, when they were teenagers, he was her secret boyfriend. When she realised that his highest aspiration was to work as a chauffeur for her father she finished with him. It was lucky for him that her father never found out.

Lang-ren's birth name was Ng Cho Sui but he was called

Lang-ren shortly after he was born because he had one milk tooth already in place and a full head of dark hair that ran all the way down his spine and across his shoulders. Lang-ren is Mandarin Chinese for 'wolfman'.

As they approached the Ipoh city outskirts, Nancy shrank further down into her seat while Lang-ren sat taller. In the city, he would be afforded the courtesies due to one of S Y's henchmen. She was the daughter of a man of the old school who still held to the saying, *unmarried, a woman obeys her father*.

The car pulled onto the forecourt of the *Leeyate Plaza Hotel* and Nancy waited until a uniformed flunky had opened the door before she stepped out into the immediately stifling heat. She hurried past the doorman who saluted and said, 'Welcome back to Ipoh, Miss Lee.'

She left Lang-ren behind to sort out her luggage, hurried across the cool lobby to the private lift and punched in the access code. The doors opened straight into S Y's office on the eighth floor. Her father stood waiting. He had watched her arrival on the security feed from the foyer camera. 'Daughter, welcome. Thank you for coming.'

They hugged.

'I've put you in one of the suites on the seventh floor. Lang-ren has the number.'

'Thank you, Father. What's all this about?'

'Awah! When did you become so western? Always straight to business. Say hello to your mother first.'

Nancy nodded and strode along the inner corridor, to her mother's room. Her mother lay prone in bed. A nurse sat reading and looked up smiling. Nancy looked past her. A machine delivered what Nancy assumed was a morphine-based drug through a cannula into the old lady's claw-like hand. Her face was grey and still as if carved from granite. She didn't respond when Nancy kissed her cheek.

Nancy turned to the nurse. 'How long has she been like this?'

The nurse frowned and cocked her head, 'Your father—'

'Forget it!' Nancy hurried back along the corridor her heels tap-tapping her anger on the marble floor.

'Why didn't you tell me!' she demanded as her father looked up from his desk.

'I didn't want to—'

'You must have had the diagnosis weeks ago. Why didn't you say?'

S Y shrugged and whispered, 'She didn't want to have chemotherapy. You know what your mother's like. She doesn't trust western medicine. She was worried you would have insisted... so she said not to tell you until you needed to know.'

'You could have ignored her.'

'And over-ridden *her* request in favour of you?' He shook his head. 'I fear she is failing fast. She left it very late before she told anybody and by then it had spread.'

'I don't think she was awake enough to even know I was there.'

'The doctors say it's weeks now rather than months.' He looked down as if the floor would help him come to terms with the prognosis.

Nancy's insides felt hollowed out. She loved her mother. Who doesn't love their mother? But she had never felt warmth or respect. Her attachment to her was no more than if she had been a family retainer – the nanny who had nurtured her but always under the command of the ruler in the house. After all, the full proverb that her parents both lived by was, *unmarried, a woman obeys her father; married, her husband.*

Nancy stretched her neck to ease the tension and fiddled

with the coil of hair at her nape. 'But this – mother's illness – isn't why you called me?'

'No, we have a... situation.'

'What sort of *situation?*'

A man from Europe checked in yesterday. Supposedly he is on holiday.'

'Supposedly?'

'Yes, he asked the concierge if he could arrange for a driver and guide to show him around Ipoh.'

'You have any number of people who could do that.'

'Yes, but he particularly wants to see the Kellas House – Kellie's Castle' – he spoke these words in English – 'as he calls it.'

'Why?'

'I had one of the Filipina girls – 'meet' him after dinner and make sure he had a lot of drinks. He told her his family owned the castle and all the plantations around it before World War Two. He wants to see his family home.'

'Is he from Scotland?'

'No. This is a strange thing. He is from Lisbon in Portugal. His name is Luis Escobar.'

Nancy had a natural affinity for intrigue. One of her boyfriends had once called her a 'drama queen'. He hadn't lasted long afterwards. She felt a flush rise behind her make-up. There was something significant in this moment. This man from Lisbon had been in Ipoh fewer than twenty-four hours and her all-powerful father was troubled enough to have her hauled in from KL. There must be more to it than a simple enquiry to see the house. 'What has he been doing today?' she asked.

Her father smiled. 'Well, first he had to lose the girl. That took most of the morning! He had brunch and asked the concierge about his guide. He's been told that there'll be somebody to help tomorrow. Somebody who can speak excellent English – as he does.'

'Me.'

'Yes, you. He's been kicking his heels around the city. We had him tailed. The usual tourist stuff.'

'And you want me to take him to the house and find out what he wants?'

'You have a very quick grasp of business, daughter. You're a credit to that expensive English education.'

'What has he been told?'

'Nothing more than that his guide, Nancy Lee, no less than daughter of the owner of this fine establishment, will act as his driver and guide while he stays here. You are to be in reception at 10am tomorrow. I'll have one of the white Mercedes ready for you.'

12

I imagine that the first thing that struck Nancy about Luis Escobar was how tall he was. The top of her head barely reached his breast bone. The second thing was the smell of him. Chinese men smoke. Awah! How they smoke. She expected the reek of tobacco to cling to them like a miasma, but she had never noticed it so strong on a European before. Despite this, Nancy smiled her sweetest smile as they shook hands. She delivered the line she had practised, 'Mr Escobar. I am your guide. My name is Nancy Lee. We are to converse in English, I understand.'

His eyes were all over her, sweeping from head to toe and back again like a radar scanner. She knew that he would be happy with what he saw. She had dressed to suit the occasion in a white, crisp, cotton shirt with a demure neckline. It was tucked into black ski pants and, in the cool hotel interior, covered by a black cashmere cardigan. The loops of her pants disappeared into matching flat shoes. She held a coolie-style hat at her side.

His cream linen suit was crumpled and his brown sandals, which he wore over pale socks, were scuffed. His teeth were nicotine-stained. He offered her a cigarette and put his own back in the packet when she declined. 'It's very nice to meet you. Should I call you Nancy?'

She cast her eyes down and nodded, conscious of acting a part. 'It is allowed in private if that's what you wish, Mr Luis.

But if other people are with us it is correct to address me as Miss Lee.'

'If I can call you Nancy, you must call me Luis.'

She nodded, knowing that she wouldn't drop the 'Mr'. 'Which attraction should I show you first? Come, my car is outside.'

It was already over twenty-five degrees despite being only mid-morning. The white Mercedes was waiting with its engine running. She would leave her cardigan on. The Malay doorman followed them from the hotel entrance and ushered them into their seats, first the passenger side for the European, while Nancy waited. The boy skittered round, careful not to run, and held the driver's side door to allow Nancy to lower herself into the seat and swing in her legs.

'Where to?' she said, glancing across to Luis's crumpled form, jack-knifed into the seat with his long legs stretching away under the dashboard. She had a momentary vision of his shattered kneecaps and compressed femurs following a head-on collision. She fussed with the rear-view mirror to wipe it from her mind.

'I'd like to see Kellie's Castle,' he said. 'Do you mind if I smoke?'

'Open your window a little to let the smoke out,' she said. 'Kellie's Castle – the Kellas House – is on the road to Batu Gajah. The house is worth a look but nothing else to see in that direction.'

He put a lighter's flame to the end of his cigarette and blew the smoke through a narrow slit above the lowered window. 'The house has an interesting story, though. Do you know it?' he asked.

They had already left the city centre behind and Nancy turned onto the main Batu Gajah road. 'I grew up in Ipoh. The story of Kellie's Castle is well known. It's romantic. Young girls swoon when they hear it the first time.' Her eyes were on the road but she sensed that he had turned to study her. With his window open, the car's air conditioning was struggling to keep the temperature down and she wished she had taken off the cardigan.

'The man who built Kellie's Castle was my grandfather.' Luis opened his window wider and flicked the unfinished cigarette out as if to punctuate what he had said. He pressed the button to close the window and settled back in his seat waiting for her to respond.

'But you are not English – Scottish,' she said.

'No. I'm from Lisbon. If you know the story, you'll know that my grandfather died there. His daughter, my mother, had already met my father. He was a Lisboeta.'

She nodded and turned the car off the road into a piece of cleared scrubland. 'Here we are.'

Although Nancy had been to the castle before, the broad sweep of its shadowed façade always made her shiver with apprehension. A solitary crow lifted from its perch on top of the circular tower and cawed its reluctant welcome.

She donned her hat and led the way, knowing that Luis would be admiring the view. It gave her pleasure to know that men couldn't stop themselves responding to the way she looked.

They crossed a wooden footbridge over a sluggish stream. The sloping path led them up beneath the sandstone wall. It was two storeys high for most of its length and boasted a tower at each end. The one furthest away, where the crow now circled in a proprietary way, finished level with the roof, whereas the square tower to their left extended upwards a further two levels. The dead-eyed windows – there were at least thirty of them – looked as if they had been copied from a Rajah's palace. The building was forsaken rather than derelict.

'Wow! It's impressive. But it's not the Scottish castle I was expecting.' Luis took a compact camera from his jacket pocket and clicked a snapshot that was followed by the characteristic sand-clogged whir of the automatic film-winding mechanism.

Nancy removed her sunglasses and turned to face him. 'I hope what you see is not disappointing you.' She didn't know why she was playing up to him. It wasn't as if she found him in any way attractive. 'Some say it's like film set. There is hardly nothing behind this frontage. None of the rooms is finished. There is the old building that was completed and lived in – the original Kellas House – but most of it was pulled down by the Japanese.'

Luis stood on tiptoe to look through one of the windows. 'It *is* just a shell.'

'The story is that it was nearly finished when your grandfather died. Local people looted the wood panelling and flooring soon afterwards. It's a rumour that many homes in Ipoh and Batu Gajah have panels and floorboards that were taken from this house. When the Japanese invaded, they needed stone and took what they wanted by destroying the older house. The sandstone of this house was not strong enough for what they wanted.'

They turned left, followed the wall under the square tower and turned into the building through an incongruously narrow doorway. Nancy pointed to the tiled floor. 'Be careful not to trip. The tiles are loose.' She pointed left. 'This leads to rooms – empty rooms, walls only.' She swept her hands in front of her. 'The grand staircase up to the top floor was here.'

Luis now had his camera's viewfinder up to his eye at every turn. Click and whir. 'What happened to it?' He strode to the gap in the ceiling where the landing would have been. Before she could answer, he turned to his right. 'What's this?' He peered into what seemed to be a brick-walled cupboard and craned his neck round to look up. 'It goes all the way to the top.' Another photograph, this one of the tower's roof three storeys above.

'It's where the elevator would have been... the lift. It was never installed.'

'The elevator from Lisbon... hmm.'

'We go along here—' she pointed to the corridor '— and up to the next floor using the servants' stairs in the round tower at the other end. That way you see everything in one round trip.'

He smiled. 'You're a very efficient guide. Thank you.'

She led the way, pleased that he acknowledged her competence, and listened for his footsteps to make sure he was following. They were in a narrow passage with the building's rear exterior wall on their left. The passage ran perhaps fifty metres from one end of the building to the other. Each room on their right was enclosed by brick walls. Some still bore patches of plaster lining. 'They never intended to put glass in the windows here,' she pointed to gaps on their left. 'It was always meant be open. They have constructions like this in England – in big churches – I think they're called cloisters.'

'Yes. I am familiar. In Portugal, we say *claustro*.'

'There—' she pointed out one of the openings to a bare patch of land with the ruined building beyond '—they planned for it to be a courtyard with the cloisters on all sides.'

Further along she turned right into a room twice the length of those they had seen before. The windows at the far end indicated that they were now at the furthest point from the entrance hall. 'I am sad when I come here. To think it was never used. Never lived in.'

'What was this room?' he said from behind the camera, tight against his face.

'I do not know. I haven't seen any plans. But I think that it must be a room for entertaining, so perhaps a dining hall or a grand reception room.' She removed her hat and uncoiled a dark pony tail. 'The servants would have come through here.' She passed behind a wall and they were in an anteroom beyond which was the hidden entrance to the round tower. 'See how the floors and walls are rough here. Less care was taken to make sure the steps are even, that the walls are smooth; this area was for servants.'

Nancy climbed ahead of him knowing that his eyes would be at the same height as her hips. They emerged onto a boarded floor and passed through a keyhole-shaped arch into the passage leading to the upper rooms. This time, as they ambled along, the abandoned rooms were on their left and the window openings to the right. Luis stopped. He took out a handkerchief and ran it across his forehead and down into his collar. He blew his out-breaths through pursed lips. 'I need a cigarette.' He took out a fresh pack, stripped off the cellophane and proffered it to her.

She shook her head.

'Do you mind if I do?' He flicked his lighter into life and satisfied that her lack of response meant she didn't object, put it to the end of his cigarette. He was about to toss the cellophane wrapper aside, hesitated, and stuffed it into his pocket instead. 'It's very tidy. It looks like this floor has been added; it is not neglected.' He looked into the room. 'There's no rubble, no litter. Who is looking after this place?'

Nancy felt the colour rise from her neck. 'I think the owners are the same people who run the plantation. They make sure everything is safe to visit. They don't stop people coming but officially the house is not open to the public.' She followed him to the window. Beyond the stream, the parked car and the road, a plantation stretched in regimented rows to the horizon.

'You can see more from the roof.' Nancy said, as she turned

into the square tower where polished stone stairs took them upwards. Luis followed, wheezing. The stairs were narrow but not steep. She turned back. 'Are you all right? Want to stop?'

'No problem,' Luis said. But he was dabbing the handkerchief to his forehead again and his face was red.

The stairs stopped and the tower above them was an empty shell with holes in the walls for the beams that would have supported two more floors. The only opening took them out onto the flat roof. It had been cemented over, presumably to make it watertight. On the courtyard side, there was a low wall but on the edge they went to, instinctively chasing the unfettered view, they could have stood with their toes hanging over the drop. Nancy put her hat back on after detaching her sunglasses from the brim.

'What an incredible sight,' Luis said, holding up the camera again. This time the film-winding mechanism whirred for all of twenty seconds. 'Damn! he said, looking at the back of the camera. 'That's the film finished. I've left the spares back in the hotel.'

'You have seen nearly everything,' Nancy said.

They turned back to the view. On the far horizon, beyond the ranks of palm trees, a ridge crossed from left to right.

'Those trees,' Luis said. 'Are they rubber?'

She shook her head, gazing out over the countless rows stitched into the slopes, marching away in all directions. 'No. It's palm oil. See the bunches of fruits in the tops of the trees. That's where the oil is.'

'What is it used for?'

'So many things. One I know of is soap. Do you have the brand called *Palmolive* in Portugal? It's palm oil.'

'Mmm. I should have thought of it,' he said. 'Who owns the plantations now?'

She stepped sharply back from the edge. What did her

father want her to say? It would be easier to dissemble. She waved a hand airily as if this would distract him from her answer and studied the horizon. 'All this? A big company from London or America. All the oil they produce here is for export. Maybe it's the company that makes *Palmolive* soap. Who knows?'

They turned to face the other way and Luis pulled his hat forward to shield his eyes. The ruin of the original house, built of a colder, whiter stone, stood joined to its younger, showier brother by foundations for later buildings that never materialised. The older house was roofless, its jagged walls sticking up like the enamel sides of a drilled tooth. Again, plantations ran away from them, broken only by the silver thread of a river, until the patterns broke down on the lower slopes of the blue hills of the Highlands.

He had moved to the top of the stairs. 'I have to get out of this heat.' He held out his hand. 'Do you need help with the steps?'

Nancy shook her head.

As she followed the tall man down, she wondered where he would want to go next. Normally, she would suggest visiting the Hindu temple only a short walk away but she deduced from his concern about the heat and his laboured breathing that Luis would prefer the air-conditioned shelter of the car. The basement would be cool but, while there was no hint of feeling unsafe in his company, she knew that standing close to Luis in the dark would make her feel uncomfortable.

Her mother had brought up Nancy as a Buddhist and she retained some connection with her childhood religion. So, by the time she had got into the car and turned on the engine and air-conditioning, and while Luis smoked a cigarette in the shade of the notice board, she had decided to take him to see Ipoh's largest Buddhist temple.

There was an uneasy silence as she drove and Nancy assumed that Luis was mulling over what he had seen. Perhaps, though, he was merely casting around in his head for something to talk about because finally he said, 'So you work for your father?'

'Not really.'

'This is not what you do? I thought they said something about public relations for the hotel?'

She drove deliberately as if she was adhering to a speed limit. 'Oh, that. No, this work is part-time. My proper job is in a bank.'

'Oh!'

'I am doing this as a favour for my father. There aren't many fluent English speakers in Ipoh.'

'There are a lot of people who speak good English, though. The people of local origin—'

'Here we call them Bumiputera – Bumis for short. But it is bad for you to say this. You call them Malays, I think.'

'I wouldn't want to offend anyone.'

'It's fine. You call them Malays.'

'All right. The Malays and the Chinese they speak English as a common language, right?'

'Sort of. Lots of Chinese like me also speak little of Malay. I need it for my job. The bank I work for is the biggest Bumi bank in Malaysia.'

'And it's all right between you, Chinese and Malays? The troubles of the 1950s are behind you?'

She smiled. 'Yes. That's behind us.'

They stopped for lunch at a street cafe in Menglembu on the southwest outskirts of Ipoh, where Nancy introduced Luis to her favourite curry – juicy segments of fresh pineapple stewed in an ancient pot over a gas stove. The fiery sauce had of such depth of flavour as could only be achieved by never quite emptying the pot and endlessly replenishing the ingredients so that some element of the sauce was as old as the pot itself. Luis expressed his enjoyment of the food but, tellingly, (and to Nancy's secret amusement) he didn't manage to finish the sauce.

He lit a cigarette and sucked the smoke deep down. 'I've been thinking. I hope it won't offend you but I'm not interested in seeing a temple.'

One of the reasons that Nancy had reached a management level in the bank was that she was naturally diligent. Her immediate desire was to show off what her city had to offer. She was disappointed but was determined not to show it. 'It is a very impressive cave temple with many big statues of Buddha. Are you sure?'

Luis nodded, exhaling blue smoke through an apologetic smile.

'It is your choice. Is there something else that you would like to see instead?'

'I think I'd prefer to go back to Ipoh,' he said.

'Of course, Mr Luis.'

'Does it have a library?'

'Ipoh? Yes, of course.'

'I'd like you to drop me there, please.'

'No problem.'

She glanced sideways as she drove. He took a blank sheet of the hotel's notepaper out of his pocket and wrote on it in a shaky hand as she negotiated the light mid-afternoon traffic on the outskirts of the city.

13

When Nancy went down to reception at ten the following morning, carrying a list of Ipoh's tourist attractions, I imagine she was surprised to discover that Luis wasn't there. Albert, the concierge, handed her a note: *Sorry, Miss Lee. I left early to check up on something. Shall we meet back here for lunch? 12.30? Luis Escobar.*

It meant she had to kick her heels for two hours and was still not in the best of moods when she went down to the lobby at quarter to one. Luis hurried to his feet spreading his arms. 'Miss Nancy, I'm so sorry. I wanted to do some boring research in the library. You wouldn't have found it interesting at all. I can make it up to you. Let me buy you lunch.'

He was wearing the same creased linen suit but had changed his shirt since yesterday. He still exuded his stale-ashtray reek. Nancy's outfit was as the day before except the ski-pants were charcoal grey and her blouse had a softer collar.

He ushered her through the doors and she waved away the waiting white Mercedes. Lang-ren, who had been loitering in the shadows behind the doorman's station, stepped forward, without acknowledging her, to take the limousine back to its parking place.

Nancy judged that she'd given Luis a cold enough hello and suggested that he follow her to the mall around the corner. He only had time for a few drags on his cigarette before they arrived. He looked at her quizzically and she pointed to the *No Smoking* sign. He threw the half-finished cigarette on the ground and stamped on it. He wouldn't last long in Singapore, she thought.

The mall's food hall sold upmarket street food in air-conditioned surroundings. Nancy put on her cardigan while she ordered Penang speciality noodle for them both and Luis fetched two Tsingtao beers from the drinks stall. When they had settled at the table, she showed him her typewritten list of local attractions. 'Which of these would you like to see?'

'What do you suggest?'

She ran her finger down the paper. 'The railway station is worth a visit. It dates from Queen Victoria's time. Tourists go to see the roof because it was built to the same plans as if in London. It could carry the weight of a six-foot-deep snowfall, they say.' She giggled behind her hand. 'It never snows in Ipoh!'

'Mmm. It sounds irresistible.'

She ignored his ironic tone. 'You could also see Gua Tempurung, a big cave not far from here in Gopeng. The central cavern has a lightshow. All very interesting. But we will need clothes for the cold because it is a long way down. No sun; no heat.'

He looked down at his thin jacket. 'I'm not really dressed for cold. Perhaps not for me – today.'

'There's an ancient tin mine with a museum.'

'It sounds underground again.'

'The museum is separate, in a house. It's not in the mine.'

'Even so...'

She sighed and folded the sheet of paper. When she slipped it into her handbag she closed its clasp with the finality of a slammed door. 'Ipoh is not really a tourist city.

Maybe you should go back to KL or go to an island with many beaches like Langkawi.'

'I was thinking that perhaps you have a museum dedicated to the World War Two period or the insurgency war with the British?'

'My family, all Chinese in Malaya, have hard time when Japanese came. The war with the British was for liberation. Both times the Lee family fought for liberation – against Japanese first and British second. But both times many Malays joined the other side. We have learned since to get along. It is difficult to make memorials to suit everybody.'

'Is there nothing to see from that time?'

'Not touristic or a museum.'

For a few moments, they ate in silence surrounded by the clamour of office workers on their break. The restaurant was crowded but nobody sat alongside them, even though their table had space for six.

'It's interesting. It's as if the country turned from Malaya to modern Malaysia without anything in between,' Luis said. 'Through all this time the house my grandfather built was standing there empty. A war and an insurgency going on around it and no records, no memorials. As if the time from the invasion by Japan to the end of the colonial war has been forgotten.'

'There is a National Memorial in KL. Bear in mind it was a difficult time with people on the same side against the Japanese and then enemies only a few years later.'

'Or the things that happened are best left unrecorded?' He looked at her intently as if searching for an imperfection in her eyes. 'Do you know what I do in Lisbon – my job?' he asked.

She looked away as if distracted by another table. 'No, should I?'

'I'm a private investigator.'

She still didn't look at him. 'That's interesting.'

He shrugged. 'Not really. It's mostly divorce work. I follow the cheating husband or wife, take pictures—'

She put a hand over her mouth and giggled – a reflex.

'—no... not those sorts of pictures. Assignations: dinners together, car park meetings... Anyway, very occasionally I work on an interesting assignment.'

She took a sip of her beer. 'What sort thing?'

'Take one case. A man came to me and he was trying to trace his family. This man was from England and it turned out that he was my cousin. We share the same grandfather—'

'The one who built Kellie's Castle?'

'Correct. You are quick to understand.'

Nancy placed her beer down carefully and focused on the stall's menu hanging on a wall beyond Luis's right shoulder. She needed to stay calm and pay attention. This could be what her father had wanted to find out.

'Only this man, my cousin, didn't know about my side of the family so I was able to explain all about how his grandfather – our grandfather – was born in Scotland, made his fortune in Malaysia and then died in Lisbon. It was his interest in this story that made me think I ought to know more, that I should trace the family background.'

'Did you go to Scotland? I have never been to Scotland,' she said. She wished she hadn't had the beer. It always made her cheeks glow red.

'No. It would have made sense chronologically – in time order – to go—'

'I know what 'chronologically' means!'

'—sorry, of course.'

'I think my English is better than yours, Mr Luis,' she said sharply.

'Of course. Yes. I'm sorry. As I say, it would have made more sense *chronologically* to go to Scotland first but I ended up coming here. And now I'm here I'm beginning to feel that my cousin, his name is Cross, somehow wanted me to come.'

'I don't understand. Are you saying *he* is the interesting assignment?'

'Oh no.' He chuckled. 'No, no, no. The interesting case is the one he's laid at my door. What's happening now I'm here in Malaysia. *This* is the interesting case.'

She pushed their unused cutlery together in a single pile. The high-pitched nasal chatter around them filled her ears.

'Now,' Luis said. 'I need to go outside for a cigarette.'

While he smoked, Nancy thought about what he had said. It was clear he wanted her to know that he was embarked on some sort of investigation. He seemed to hint that it centred on what happened between World War Two and the Insurgency. While he had been on his own, had Luis discovered that it was the Lee family that owned the castle and all the land around it? If so, perhaps he understood why she had been recruited as his guide. Unless he confronted her, though, she had no choice but to continue to play out her appointed role.

They spent the rest of the afternoon walking in the city. It was a route that her father took when he entertained family from out of town. They passed through the railway station, comparable, according to the locals, to the Taj Mahal and stopped to admire the nearby War Memorial. He noted tartly that, 'They *do* recognise there *was* a world war.'

She led him through Panglima Lane, a stubby backstreet that had in the distant past been the red-light district. Along its short length, eating places now outnumbered the dubious looking massage parlours. Outside a house displaying exhibits from the city's tin-mining past, she suggested he may care to look in but he declined.

Every so often, as they walked, Luis would seek the shade

of a tree and light a cigarette and Nancy would wait nearby drawing circles in the pavement dust with the toe of her shoe.

By the time they reached the Royal Ipoh Club, they were ready for a drink and Nancy didn't hesitate as the doorman ushered them inside even though she wasn't sure that S Y had maintained his membership. She strode up to the porter's desk.

'Can I help you?' The Malay porter looked at her over the top of his reading glasses. His demeanour indicated that she must have made a mistake entering his demesne. He had spoken English.

Nancy responded in Malay. 'I'm hoping that my father is still a member here and his membership will allow me to entertain this visitor to Ipoh, who has come all the way from Portugal.'

The porter tapped a few keys on his computer. 'And who is your father, dear lady?'

'Lee Song Yong.'

His fingers hovered over the keyboard. 'Mr Lee of the *Leeyate Plaza Hotel* and *Leeyate Holdings*?'

She bowed her head serenely. 'The same.'

He stood to attention. 'We are delighted for you to take drinks here; a meal perhaps?'

She waved the suggestion away. 'No, just drinks.'

He clapped his hands and a waiter scurried up. 'Please take Ms Lee and her guest through to the Verandah Bar.'

'Would you like me to sign in?'

He bowed. 'That won't be necessary.'

They looked out over an extensive lawn, with tennis courts behind a hedge to one side , as they drank gin and tonics. Luis told her that her services would not be required the next day – Wednesday. 'Haven't we done all the sites?' he asked.

'In Ipoh, maybe. You should take a walk along the river

promenade but we can do this when we finish here. It is best in the evening. But tomorrow we could go on a trip maybe; try a beach resort? Cross the new bridge to Penang.'

'No, not the coast. Is there anything we should see in Batu Gajah? Anything of historical interest?'

'No Batu is mining town. No history. Tin mining museum, though?'

Luis's face did not crack. 'Then I'll stick to my original plan. I want to do some research to find out more about my grandfather. Reading the books on local history in the library reference section, that sort of thing.'

'Are you sure you don't need my help? I could make sure you read the right... material. What about translation?'

'It wasn't a problem this morning. A lot of the old books are in English or have English translations. Don't worry; I can get by with the help of the library staff. You've been very generous with your time already.'

As Nancy had promised, their evening ended with a stroll along a promenade alongside the River Kinta lined, on the other side, by restaurants and food stalls. A loosely-hung string of white lamps, only about half of which were working, lit their way. The river flow was thick with silt and a cocktail of smells, three parts tar and two parts sewage, bubbled out of its sludge.

'Would you like to stop to eat?' Luis asked.

Nancy patted her stomach. 'No thank you. It's too early after lunch. I will eat much later tonight.'

Nancy's previous report to S Y, after her first day as the westerner's guide, had been perfunctory. Luis had requested no more than she would have expected from any tourist visiting Kellie's Castle. Now things were different; she hurried to S Y's office as soon as they had returned to the *Leeyate Plaza*.

There were no pleasantries. Her father spoke in Mandarin.

'I heard that he cancelled this morning. He spent it in the records section of the library. I'm waiting to find out what he looked at. Whatever he saw yesterday is making him act like he's injected with chicken blood. He is onto something. Couldn't you have stopped him?'

'Why should I have done?'

'Did you suggest you would go with him?'

'Of course! But he said he didn't need me.'

'And he's interested in local history? Researching the records.'

'Yes. I told you.'

'Awah, Lai Ping. I don't want this to get out of control.'

'He's just interested in the history of the house. He wants to know what happened to it during and after World War Two. I don't see what the problem is.'

He slammed his fist onto the desk. 'Records! Records are the problem.' He sighed and walked across to a chest and bent to unlock the shallow, bottom drawer. He slid it out and removed a sheaf of blueprint drawings. 'I have never shown you this before. Come here.'

She stepped up onto the dais as he spread the plans across his desk. She soon realised she was looking at an artist's impression of a renovated Kellie's Castle. The top line of a text box in the bottom right corner carried the plan's title: *The Leeyate Castle Spa Hotel.*

S Y caressed the sheet, smoothing it flat. 'This is *my* dream for the house. It will be first in Malaysia of a new type of hospitality that is growing in Europe called spa hotels – top luxury and guests are pampered with health treatments. This is the hotel of the future.' He jabbed a finger. 'Here in the main house on the ground floor you have the public rooms—' he moved his finger along the frontage '—lobby, lounge, bar, restaurant. Upstairs you have four grand suites for first class clients.'

Nancy recalled the shells of the rooms that she had shown Luis the previous day. There was more than enough space for what he described.

'On this side: kitchens, housekeeping, offices.' His finger travelled across to the right. 'Here the new block of standard accommodation. Three floors, ninety rooms, all en-suite.' The long fingernail on his little finger scratched across the surface of a blue-filled swimming pool that graced the old courtyard. 'Over here in the original Kellas House we have the spa: treatment rooms, steam rooms, saunas... everything like that. Who knows, here—' he swept the back of his hand across the smudged representation of plantations at the rear '—in time, we have an 18-hole, championship-standard golf course with a top-class clubhouse.'

Nancy leant heavily on the desk almost giddy with enthusiasm for what he was describing. She had never expected this of her father. It was so dramatic, so... exciting. She imagined herself at the centre of the complex directing the minions as they attended to the cream of Malaysian society. She would be the queen of this castle. The air buzzed with possibilities. *This* was why she had been born into this family. 'When, father. When will it start?'

His shoulders slumped. 'It's money. It needs a big investment. Lee money is stretched across all our businesses. New Chinese money is difficult in this political situation. The new laws say we should have Malays on the board. I need to find the right people to come in with us. It's not easy. We are risk takers. Malays don't understand our ways.'

'But it *will* happen? I *love* it. Can I be part of it? I can help you negotiate... in KL.'

S Y shook his head slowly. 'Not so fast. I don't trust the Bumis who *want* to come in and... let's just say we don't make a deal by spitting on our hands and shaking. The Chinese know what it means to make a deal with S Y Lee –

commitment on *both* sides. The Bumis...' He shook his head and stared through the window to the floodlights illuminating the railway station, as if he was seeing beyond it to the castle. 'The old ways don't work anymore.'

'What has this got to do with Mr Escobar?'

'We can't afford there to be any doubts when we ask people to put up their money. Your Mr Escobar *shouldn't* find anything but we—'

'He *is* suspicious. Are you worried that he might find out we don't own the land? Is that it?'

S Y smoothed back his hair and took a long, controlled in-breath. 'Don't rush to conclusions. Let's just say that doubt has been cast on this in the past but the family is satisfied that it's all watertight. We don't want this westerner kicking the sleeping dog.'

'He talked about another relative – an Englishman called Cross.'

'Cross?' S Y shook his head. 'Escobar has been sending him faxes. He is in England. But there's nothing in what Escobar has told him to trouble us... yet.'

Nancy sidled round the desk and, in a gesture she didn't know she had in her, covered the back of his hand with hers. 'Perhaps it's because he doesn't know anything and everything *is* watertight. *Don't let the birds of worry build a nest in your hair.*'

He smiled. 'You're right, daughter. But I would like to be certain that he and this Mr Cross don't cause us problems.' He nodded decisively. 'I think you should have dinner with Escobar tomorrow night.'

'What if he doesn't want to?'

He smiled. 'If *you* invite him, will he say no? Honestly?'

'I'll do as you ask, father. But I don't like the man.'

'That's not the point. I'm only talking about dinner. You can leave the other stuff to one of the Filipina girls—'

She felt the blood rush to the tips of her ears. 'Father!'

He sighed. 'Don't act so innocent, Lai Ping. Do you think I believe you have reached your age without having a man? Phah! Now go and see your mother.'

14

I picture Nancy wearing a cheongsam for the dinner with Luis, her hair pinned up and clipped with a fresh, white lotus-flower – traditional and sending a correct, neutral message.

Luis stubbed out his cigarette and stood as she approached the table. 'You look lovely,' he said.

She lowered her eyes. 'Thank you.'

He had changed into a dark-blue, linen suit and a blue shirt with a pink and grey striped tie. The hotel tables for two were big enough to keep her clear of his cigarette smoke. Perhaps, she thought, the evening will be tolerable. A waiter hovered and pushed in her chair as she sat down. She ordered a Champagne cocktail and saw the blood drain from Luis's face. She smiled. 'Don't worry. You dine with me. Everything is on the house. Would you like one too?'

He nodded and asked her about her day. She said that she had gone to work in the local bank. It was easier than telling him what she had really done, which was sit at her mother's bedside, talking about her childhood and receiving no response.

She was still angry with her father for landing her with Luis when she should have been spending time with her mother, but the excitement of their possible joint enterprise with the house had softened her towards him and now she was again focused on the job in hand.

She spun Luis a story about running some ad hoc individual training sessions with the counter staff until the drinks came and she had helped him order.

Nancy raised her glass, 'Gān bēi!'

'Saúde!'

'So, how was *your* day,' she said.

'Very interesting. I learned a lot more about my family home here in Perak.'

'Excellent. Do you now know the whole Kellie story?'

'I think so. Are you interested?'

'Is it much more than I told you?'

'I think it is.'

'Then I'm interested.' She hoped that whatever Luis said now would signal whether her father's fears were justified. She was the picture of innocence, eyes lowered over her glass as she said, 'It will be useful for next time I show client around the castle.'

Over three courses and a glass of port, he told her what he had learned from his day in the library. She wasn't sure whether he was trying to inject a romantic theme into the evening but he focused on the love story; William Kellie-Smith had built the new Kellas House – the castle – as a testament of his love for his wife Agnes just as a Mogul King had built the Taj Mahal for his wife. (Luis commented that a guide book had compared the railway station to the Taj Mahal. 'What is it about Ipoh people and the Taj Mahal?') As he recounted the story, Nancy wished that she could take notes without inflaming his suspicions. How much would she be able to recall when she reported to her father? When they had finished their meal, Luis suggested coffee in the bar. Nancy declined and hurried to the exclusive penthouse lift.

S Y stood at his desk tapping his fingers. 'Well?'

Nancy poured herself a glass of water from the carafe on the sideboard and sat down. 'He's certainly been doing his research. He must be the world's authority on the Kellas Houses.'

S Y turned to the window so that he had his back to her. 'What does it mean for us?'

'He knows about the origins of the house back as far as 1890 when his grandfather came here to seek his fortune. How he made his money on other plantations and used it to buy the land here.'

'Before our time. What about us?'

'Most of the time Luis talked about his family. How his mother was born in Malaya and a brother some years later. It was after the boy was born that old man Kellie decided to build the house.'

S Y waved his hands like a conductor encouraging the orchestra to gather speed. 'Anything about how the land was divided?'

She shook her head. 'Understandably, he spoke about his grandfather's death in Lisbon – in 1926, I think. His widow was in Scotland at the time with the son. She never came back to Perak and sold the house to a company in the UK called Harrisons and Crosfield.' Nancy had worried she might forget the company's name.

Her father turned. 'That's it?' His head wobbled from side to side as he spoke mimicking her, '"She sold the house to Harrisons and Crosfield!" What use is that to me? What *exactly* did she sell?'

Nancy's mouth was dry. She tried to understand how she had fallen short of her father's expectations. She took a gulp from the water glass. A dribble escaped her lips and fell onto her lap. She brushed it into the fabric. 'The house. The house. That's all Luis said. She sold the house.'

S Y nodded. 'If that's all he knows...' He stepped down from the dais and leant over her. 'There's something else, isn't there?'

She shook her head. 'Only what he said before I left him in the bar.'

'What? Tell me!'

'When he got to the bit about the house being sold to the English company, I said, "Is that the end of the story." He smiled at me as if he had a secret and said, "No, it's only the start of it."'

S Y slammed his fist on the desk. 'And you left it like that?'

'I was tired. I was tired of his company.' Her eyes were filling up but she was determined not to cry. She bit her lip.

'Silly girl! He's hiding something. I know it. What happened next?'

'He said he has an early start tomorrow.'

'Why?' he demanded.

Nancy squirmed in the seat. It was if they had gone back twenty years and she was her father's little girl caught out in some misdemeanour. 'I asked him where we were going. He said, "I'm going to Batu Gaja again."' She looked up at S Y wide-eyed. 'Only for the morning. We're meeting for lunch.'

S Y stood over her jabbing his words home with a pointing finger. 'Look here, my girl. If he's going back to Batu Gaja, he's on the trail of something. Something that could be bad for us. You'd better find out what he knows tomorrow. And this time don't let him give you the slip.'

I imagine Nancy's father shook his head when she returned to the table from the breakfast buffet with only a dish of fresh fruit and yogurt. 'Is that all you're going to have?' He pointed at his own plate of eggs with beef sausage, turkey bacon and hash browns. 'Haven't you heard about the saying that we should breakfast like kings?'

She poured herself some coffee and raised her eyebrows. He nodded and passed his cup. 'The saying continues, Father,' she said as she poured his drink, 'that you should lunch like a prince and dine like a pauper. Your problem is that you dine like a king at every meal… and between.'

His face crinkled into the smile she knew so well – the one that could equally lead to more light-hearted banter or a stinging rebuke. She could never predict his reaction. He patted the belly that pressed against the material of his loose safari shirt. 'Lai Ping, if you had known hunger as I knew it before we had all this—' he waved a hand at the panelled walls of the penthouse dining room and the panoramic windows with their view across the infinity pool towards the railway station, '—you too would eat your fill at every opportunity. Now tell me, you know what to do with Mr Escobar?'

'I have to focus on the time before our family comes into the story of the house. From when the land was sold to the British company.'

S Y said the name: 'Harrisons and Crosfield.'

She put a hand to her mouth and suppressed a giggle. He had mangled the r's and l's as if he was in a cartoon.

He ignored her and stroked his chin. 'It's too bad that he's going to that piss-and-wind town Batu Gaja on his own. You should have gone with him.'

'I did ask.'

'Awah! What man in his right mind would give up spending the morning with you?'

'Thank you, Father. I *think* that was a compliment. We *are* meeting for lunch.'

One of the staff came in to clear the plates and S Y waved away the offer of pastries. 'He's probably going to tell you that he knows the family business – Leeyate Holdings – owns the castle and the Kellas plantation. It will be difficult for you unless you tell him that you didn't know. Why should you? Tell him I am old-fashioned and would have told you if you were my son. Yes, that should convince him. You must find out how much he knows about how we acquired the property.'

'What do you mean?'

'It was all done properly... after the Japanese left... but the records... let's just say some important legal documents were lost during the liberation.' He chewed a thumbnail. It was a sure sign that he felt vulnerable.

'Are you saying that he might think he still has an interest?'

'He's mistaken if he does! You must find out what he knows and call me as soon as you leave him.'

Nancy stayed in her chair waiting for more guidance. She needed to know whether her father was telling the truth. Was he as certain of the castle's ownership as he would have her believe?

'Go!' he shouted. 'Go off and sit with your mother.'

Luis was back in his cream linen suit, now even dingier after its further exposure to the tropical air. He stubbed out a cigarette as she approached. He had secured a table under a striped awning and he stood as she took the seat opposite him.

'Pineapple curry?' he said.

'And boiled white rice, please.'

'Off course. And to drink?'

'Coca-Cola.'

'Do you mind if I have a beer?'

'Of course not.'

Across the road from the street stalls, customers filed in and out of the Ipoh branch of *Maybank*. She wondered how many of its tellers she had trained. Probably most of them. She imagined the upselling conversations they should be initiating about the advantages of *Premier Banking* or the better interest rates from such and such an account.

Luis returned with the food and drink on a red plastic tray. She didn't offer him money. The cost of everything would have been less than he would have paid for a sandwich in Portugal. He lit a cigarette, took a deep drag and perched it on the edge of the ashtray. With his mouth still full of smoke, he took the first spoonful of curry.

She couldn't resist. 'You should cut down your smoking, you know.'

He shrugged. 'Of course. I know. But it's an addiction. Knowing it's bad for you isn't enough. Anyway—' he indicated the traffic that buzzed past only feet away '—I could try to cross the road after this meal and not make it to the other side. The number of cigarettes—'

'Sorry! It is not my concern.'

'But it makes people think I must be stupid to still smoke in spite of the evidence against it. Sometimes... in my job... it is a good thing for people to think you are stupid.' He looked up from his food, his eyes trying to fix on hers.

Nancy focused on her plate. Was this a warning that she shouldn't under-estimate him? Did he expect her to confess to being part of the family that owned the Kellas land there and then? Nancy busied herself by fishing a particularly fibrous chunk of pineapple from her curry and placing it on the side plate.

'Aren't you interested in the rest of the story about Kellie's Castle?' Luis asked.

She looked up. 'Yes, of course.'

'Where was I?'

'William Kellie Smith was dead and his widow had sold everything to the British company.'

'Correct. And the British Company ran it well until the Japanese invaded and appropriated all the production. None of this was legal. I don't know what happened to any British people who worked there. From what I have read they either fled before the troops arrived or were interned. But that's the story of the people not the land.'

She finished her meal and pushed the plate to one side. The coke bottle perspired in the heat and she wiped it down with a paper napkin before picking it up.

'The Japanese weren't interested in the palm oil so the Kellas plantations reverted to jungle. The land had lost value by the time the war was over. It was taken over by a Chinese family. This family had behaved very honourably during the war. As you know, there is no love lost between the Chinese and Japanese at the best of times so it was the Chinese who were on the end of Japanese atrocities; it was the Chinese who led the resistance. The family that led the resistance in the area around Batu Gaja was your father's family – the Lee family.'

'We were resistance heroes against the Japanese? I didn't know this.'

'Your family should be proud of their actions in the war. But afterwards,' he shook his head, 'the family kept its band of fighters together and, as far as I can tell, they operated on the edge of the law under the post-war government. The Kellas estate was among the assets they acquired.'

'What do you mean *acquired*?'

He pushed his chair away from the table, leaning back and extending his long legs almost into the road. 'They bought it – or rather your family did. That what the records show.' He suddenly took an interest in the traffic passing by as if he was waiting for her to respond in a way that incriminated her.

'You mean my father owns Kellie's Castle?'

'The whole estate. Not him alone though. Your father has brothers and together they own a company called *Leeyate Holdings* and it's the company that is the registered owner of the Kellas Estate. I'm surprised you didn't know.' His body language – the studied nonchalance – screamed that he knew he had caught her in a lie. On the roof of the house she had said the owners were British or American.

She followed her father's line. 'It's strange my father never told me. Maybe if I was a boy... a son...' The fakery of each word shone like a KL-market Rolex. She picked up the napkin and dried her upper lip.

He seemed to pick up the hint. 'Mmm. Look, do you mind if we move? I need to get out of this heat and I can smoke another cigarette as we walk.'

They crossed the road, his hand on her back, ushering. She wondered what he thought of her. He knew she had lied about her family's connection to the land but he didn't challenge her. Was it because she was a woman and he was acting out of old-fashioned chivalry? Did he think it was a cultural thing that it would be grossly offensive to confront her in a lie? Was it merely that he, like most Western men, felt attracted to her and threatened by her at the same time and didn't want to do anything to endanger the delicate balance of what he thought was a relationship?

Mercifully, when they reached the safety of the other side, he needed both hands to light his cigarette. 'You didn't know?' he said after he had inhaled as if his life depended on filling his lungs with smoke.

'I'm not really involved in father's business.'

'Do you have any brothers or sisters? Sorry, is it all right to ask?'

She marvelled again at the way Europeans had such strange ideas about what offended people from East Asia. It wasn't as if he'd asked whom she had slept with! 'I don't have any siblings. My mother had illness, women's problems. Only me.'

He pulled his hat down to lower the brim over his eyes. 'Will you inherit your father's share of the business?'

'I suppose so. I studied business management in England with this in mind. When my father dies, I suppose I will run the hotels part of *Leeyate Holdings*. Unless some other member of the extended family steps forward – a man.'

'Your father's involved only in the hotels?'

'Yes.' She wondered where this was going.

'But he knows the Holdings Company's affairs?'

'With his brothers, I suppose he must.'

'Then he's the man I ought to speak to. Can I see him this afternoon?'

'If he's not too busy. I could try to arrange it. What do you want see him for?'

'Look, I have to buy some cigarettes. I'll meet you back in the hotel lobby...' he looked at his watch '... in half an hour. Can you try to speak to your father before then and arrange something for later?'

She nodded.

He dropped his cigarette on the ground, stamped it into the pavement and went into the mall.

S Y was in his office and he looked up from examining spreadsheets as Nancy approached. 'Awah! My spy in Mr Escobar's camp! How is he today?'

'He's well but he's *very* suspicious.'

'Suspicious!' He made big round eyes and his mouth gaped. 'Of what?'

'Well, Mr Innocent, he's suspicious of me not knowing that it's *Leeyate Holdings* that owns the Kellas Estate. And he seems to be suspicious about the way the estate ended up being owned by the Lee family after the war.'

Her father washed his face with his dry hands and then swept them back over his sparse greying hair. 'Mmm. Perhaps it was a tactical mistake not to say about your connection from the start, Lai Ping.'

'I did what you told me, Father.'

'Yes, yes,' he said, dismissing it with a wave of his hand. 'The big question is, what does he want now?'

'That's easy. He wants an appointment to see you. This afternoon.'

S Y flipped open his diary to an empty page. 'I think I can fit him in. What time?'

She looked at her watch. 'If we say 4pm it will give me time to find out if there's anything else you should know in advance.'

'Good girl.' He pushed the diary to one side, drew the spreadsheets towards him and looked up sharply. 'Well, get on with it.'

She took the penthouse elevator to the lobby and spied Luis cramped into one of the deep sofas by the window. He was looking at a sheaf of what appeared to be faxes. They had a just-come-off-a-roll unruly bounce to them. 'Hi!' she said. 'You're in luck. My father can see you at 4pm.'

He flipped his left wrist. 'Mmm. Just over an hour.' He stood up and hesitated.

'Shall we have some tea?' Nancy suggested.

'I'd prefer coffee,' he said.

She signalled for the lobby boy and ordered the drinks. Luis resumed his seat and she sat alongside, perched on the edge so that she could face him. She crossed her legs and tucked her right foot behind her left ankle. 'You were going to tell me why you want to see my father.'

'Yeeess.' He stroked his chin.

She looked through the window at the passing traffic. Men and women hurried by in front of buildings that shimmered in the heat rising from the asphalt. European men were notable for the dark sweat patches that spread across their backs. She could almost see the air, it was so heavy. An afternoon rain shower was in the offing. She waited for Luis to speak.

He leant forward but, at the same time, the waitress appeared with the tray of drinks and afternoon cakes. He waited while she poured. When everything was set out in front of them, he said, 'It's a pity that the business centre here has had technical problems and I have not been able to send e-mails.'

'Has it? I didn't know. You should have told me. I can make alternative arrangements for you.'

'Mmm. I'm not sure that you could. No matter. I've managed with faxes.' He waved the sheaf of curling paper. 'The issue I want to discuss with your father is that there are questions about the ownership of the Kellas estate.'

She felt the ground shift beneath her feet. Her chest constricted, compressing her heart. 'I promise you,' she said, 'this is first I have heard of this. It is news for me.'

'You didn't know?' he said. 'Well, the library has copies of the northern edition of the *Straits Times* since the occupation. Stories with relevance to Perak and Ipoh in particular have been cross-referenced – which must have been a very labour-intensive task—'

'Labour is the *cheapest* thing in Malaysia.'

'Just so. Anyway, there is a record card for the Kellas estate and from this I was able to read everything that's been in the paper since 1945 about the plantations and the Castle.'

'Was there a lot?'

'No. Mostly reports from the *Leeyate Holding Company* about profits, changes in senior personnel – that sort of thing. All very straightforward.'

'Good!'

He smiled and bowed his head. 'But... in 1974 an investigative reporter with the *Times*—'

'*Straits Times* not *London Times*.'

'Yes. The reporter was worried that Kellie's Castle was falling into disrepair and he saw its potential as a touristic attraction. He researched the history of the house and it's his work that is the basis for much of what we know about it today. He wrote a story back then about the transfer of the Kellas Estate to Harrisons and Crosfield before the war. He had seen William Kellie-Smith's will and discovered that my grandfather had left the estate to his wife but he bequeathed – do you understand "bequeathed"?'

She nodded. 'He left it in his will.'

'Exactly! This reporter discovered that my grandfather had left the houses and their grounds to the two children. His widow only owned the plantations, not the houses and the lands they stood on. She only had the capacity to sell the plantation land not the houses – not the castle.'

Nancy quickly worked out what this meant for *Leeyate Holdings*. If Harrisons and Crosfield only owned the plantations before the war, even if her family had acquired everything legally after the Japanese left, her family's right to the buildings was flawed. No buildings meant no spa hotel. Her father's secret dream, their shared dream, was in danger of being snatched away. She gripped her arms across her chest as if assailed by a sudden blast of cold air from the air conditioning. 'Was he able to prove anything?' she asked, determined her voice stay calm.

'It doesn't look like it. He failed to get the Perak government interested in taking the house over – which was all he wanted.'

'Did he write more about the house?'

'The later stuff about the estate was all by different reporters.'

'Do you think he was right?'

'It looks like he may have been. I looked at the copy deeds when I went to Batu Gajah. Even if the Kellas estate was properly transferred after 1945 there's a question about the houses. The estate boundary is clearly marked on the deeds and doesn't change. But there's another line marking the parcel of land within it that the houses stand on. This line appears for the first time on the transfer from my grandmother to Harrison and Crosfield. It's not there on the post-1945 deeds.'

'Is there anything to say that the houses were not in the first transfer?' Nancy could see how crucial this would be to her father. If there was a line of text in a contract that specifically excluded the houses, when Luis's grandmother sold the estate, the spa hotel would never be more than a dream.

Luis drained the last of his coffee and placed the cup down slowly. He appeared to be taking pleasure from her discomfort. 'In fairness, it's not clear either way. There's nothing specific to say the houses were included. But there's nothing to say they were *excluded* either.'

Nancy poured a second cup of tea and offered to pour more coffee for Luis. He shook his head and looked at his watch.

'I understand what you are thinking, Mr Luis,' she said. 'If you can prove that the houses – the castle and the original Kellas House – were not included in the first transfer, it means that Harrison and Crosfield never owned them. It was not theirs to sell after Japanese left. If the houses were passed by your grandfather's will to the children, your mother and your uncle, you could be real owner of at least half of Kellie's Castle.'

'Exactly. This is what I want to see your father about. It's a ruin. It's worth nothing to him. But for me... who knows.' He looked at his watch again. 'I just have time to go for walk and a cigarette before the meeting.

And I have enough time to warn my father, Nancy thought. 'Be careful,' she said. 'Don't get caught in the rain.'

Later, from her seat in the hotel lobby, Nancy watched the puddles, from the afternoon's heavy rain, steam under the early evening sun. From time to time, she glanced at the indicator above the private penthouse lift. It was resolutely fixed on '8'. She checked her watch again. Luis had been up there for nearly an hour. When she had told her father what the foreigner knew, she asked if she could stay for the meeting but he had banished her downstairs. All she could do was wait.

The hour point passed and just as she was steeling herself to go up and interrupt them, the illuminated number turned to '7' and then to '6'. She stood and moved around a corner so that she could watch Luis leave. She had no wish to talk to him until she knew what had happened with S Y.

Luis's tall figure ducked out of the lift. He paused momentarily to get his bearings and headed towards the exit, presumably to light a cigarette. She emerged from her hiding place, pressed the elevator button and stepped forwards as the doors slid open.

At the top floor, her father was sitting behind his desk finishing a telephone call. 'Make sure it does!' he said before returning the handset with his characteristic firmness.

'Make sure what?' she said as she took the low seat facing him.

He smiled. 'Awah! Lai Ping. Nothing to concern your pretty—'

She sighed. 'I know – man's stuff, nothing for my pretty little ears.'

He ignored her testiness. 'Presumably, you're here to learn how things went with Mr. Escobar.'

'If you think you can share such information with a mere woman.'

He ignored her tone again and merely shrugged. 'Escobar talked about the ownership of the house as you warned me he would. He wanted to know whether we knew that our title was unclear. I told him it was very clear as far as we were concerned. It had been brought up before when the

Japanese cleared out. But the records of those events had been lost during the emergency. There is no dispute about *Leeyate Holdings* owning the houses as well as the estate.'

'Did he *really* accept it?'

'He was a bit angry at first. It is understandable. He had hopes that he might own a substantial piece of real estate. But he accepted that he only knew half the story. He left me quite satisfied.'

She had second-sight as far as her father's lying was concerned. Was it the way he pulled at an ear and stroked a palm back over his head? Was it the intonation in his voice? Whatever it was, it had happened while he described the meeting with Luis. 'But he was here for an hour or more.'

S Y spread his hands. 'What can I say? He presented a case. That took up most of the time. I listened patiently. But as I explained to him, the only evidence for his doubts about the houses' ownership was based on supposition by a journalist. This was refuted at the time.'

'Are you saying he went away convinced?'

He shook his head. 'More *persuaded* than convinced. But he's happy not to pursue anything. I've said that we'll carry on maintaining the house. I even said that we would erect a memorial to his grandfather.' He smiled. 'But I did say that he'd have to pay for it!'

'What happens now?'

'He said he'd go and take one last look at the house and then he'd go home. On Monday, I think.'

'What about me? Does he want to see me again?'

S Y shrugged. 'Who knows? I can't imagine he wouldn't want to. Why not wait until tomorrow? I'm sure he'll want to talk to you then.'

I imagine a bedside telephone sounding in the curtained darkness of the next morning and intruding into a dream that had snagged the delicate weave of Nancy's sleep. Her voice was groggy. 'Hello?'

'Lai Ping—' it was her father '—come and see me straight away.'

'What's wrong? Is it Mother?'

'Your mother is fine. Come now!'

15

When I returned to Doutor Ardiles's office the day after he had agreed to find out what had happened to my cousin, the door was opened as soon as I knocked and the assistant ushered me in silence to the visitor's chair. Opposite, on the other side of the desk, Ardiles squatted like a Buddha. There were two mugs of coffee sitting on slate coasters. Two of the pastries I had seen the previous day perched on paper plates.

'Please, take one. The coffee is black but we have milk.' He pointed to a small refrigerator beneath the window. I looked the other way to check that I wasn't eating his assistant's breakfast. Hers was in front of her and she raised her mug.

'Thank you. It's very kind. No milk, thank you.'

His face was solemn. 'It's the least we can do. We have bad news for you, Mr Cross. Very bad news.'

'What do you mean?'

'We found out yesterday that Luis is dead.'

My stomach lurched.

Ardiles's voice was muffled by the sound of my blood pumping. 'There was an accident.'

The walls of the room shrank as if my eyes were pulling a focus lever zooming me out.

'Let me go back to the start. This is a shock for us all. We liked Luis. Very much. Unfortunately, it didn't take long to find out this news. I called the Portuguese Embassy in Malaysia and explained that my client had not returned as expected. They took details and called me back very quickly. He had died in the north of the country two weeks ago. He had been exploring a ruined building there and must have slipped and fallen. His body was found at the bottom of one of the walls. It's being kept in a city called Ipoh. The police in Malaysia passed the information to the Embassy. His passport lists no next of kin. The Embassy contacted the police here in Lisbon but it seems they have sat on the information.'

His voice echoed around me as the office faded in and out keeping time with my pulse. I reached for the coffee and nearly fumbled it over. I took a gulp. I was alone again.

It was only later that it struck me that Luis's death had happened exactly three months after my mother's. I had gone to Doutor Ardiles' office anticipating the news that my cousin was still in Malaysia, trying to find out about our connection to the castle. Although I had known him only briefly, he was my only family. Now, as I listlessly wandered the squares of Lisbon's waterfront, I was in a daze, not merely engendered by disappointment, but also by grief. Back in my hotel, I rearranged my return to London.

During the flight, I tried to work out what could have happened. He must have gone to the castle – perhaps for a last look – and been climbing on one of the walls. A slip, and he was dead. His carelessness had snatched my family away.

At Heathrow Airport, banks of snow, which had been ploughed from the runways, punctuated the airfield's perimeter. A thin drizzle drifted in the cold breeze. I made it through baggage and customs in quick time needing to get home and regroup. After a quick visit to the gents I would join the queue for a taxi.

Giant Christmas baubles hung in the arrivals hall and the shop windows were decorated with fake snow. Plastic figures of Father Christmas stood in every doorway. A nativity scene with life-size mannequins of the adoring host had been set up alongside the Bureau de Change. Shepherds, kings, Joseph and the animals elbowed each other for a view of the empty manger. The Virgin Mary, with a serene look on her face and a strangely empty tummy, awaited the babe's arrival.

Inside the toilet, I put my holdall down alongside the row of urinals and took the one nearest the wall. I unzipped and started to pee, taking care to aim slightly off centre of the plastic contraption that stopped cigarette butts and chewing gum from blocking the drain hole. It released a lemon perfume from the deodorant cake inside its central cage. The manufacturer's logo and a telephone number were stamped on the plastic. Absent-mindedly I read the manufacturer's name: *Kellie's Janitorial Supplies.*

PART TWO – 1995

1

There's no doubt about it, I went into a tailspin after Luis Escobar died. No sooner had I found the one surviving member of my family than he was snatched away. My work deteriorated, but luckily it came at a time when Scotia's management was preoccupied with readying the company for privatisation. It took a while for them to notice me falling apart in the London outpost.

Tracy was the first to spot my problem in the days after I returned from Lisbon. She was sitting opposite my desk taking dictation when Doutor Ardiles called.

'Mr Cross, I thought you might like to know that we have brought Luis back from Malaysia.' I pictured his bear-like head beneath his portrait, the telephone handset held to his ear in a giant paw.

'You have his body?'

Tracy's eyes widened in alarm and she half stood up. I signalled her to resume her seat.

'Yes. We didn't think it was right for him to be incarcerated out there. I am thinking that he should have a ceremony before a disposal. Do you have an opinion on this?'

I shook my head. 'No! I only met him once.'

'Was he a Catholic?'

'I have no idea.' I stifled a sob. Tracy studied the empty page in her notebook.

'Perhaps a humanist ceremony and a cremation. This is

what we had in mind. You will want to come of course,' Ardiles said.

I closed my eyes tight shut and teased through the frizz of my hair with the fingers of my free hand. 'No! I don't want to come. I'm sorry.'

Ardiles was silent for one, two, three beats... 'Of course, I understand. His ashes? Do you...'

'Talk to the people who run the British Cemetery. Perhaps they'll allow you to put his ashes with his mother's grave. I'm sorry. I can't talk about this.' I pressed the handset down on its cradle to prevent it echoing with Ardiles's silent recrimination.

Tracy's eyes were full of tears as well. 'Are you all right, Mr Cross?'

I nodded and tried to reassure her but from that day she could tell I was struggling. 'Would you like me to check the adverse underwriting and claims decisions from Head Office, Mr Cross?' and 'Shall I draft the letters to the brokers, Mr Cross?' I coasted along on two or three-pint lunches and in the afternoons, giving them only a perfunctory glance, I signed Tracy's letters.

After a month or so of this, one mid-afternoon, not long after I'd stumbled in from a pub-lunch, I was jerked out of my doze by a knock at the door. My head had been resting on a pile of files and I pushed them away, selected the one from the top and wiped a dribble of spittle from its cover. I tried to focus on the paperwork as I called for whoever it was to come in.

Peter Dell approached the desk, his wide, brown eyes shining with concern. 'Everybody can see what's going on, old chap,' he said.

'What do you mean?'

'Since your mum died. You're going to have to pull yourself together.'

'Dear old Peter. Such helpful advice,' I said, my tone as cold and flat as a nun's rebuke.

'I care about you. I understand. I'm no bloody good in circumstances like these but that's why I'm suggesting you see someone.'

I straightened up. 'A shrink, you mean.'

'Yes, and not just about how you're reacting to your mother's death. Your drinking is affecting your decision-making. It's driving business away.'

'So, your visit is, in fact, to bleat about your sales figures, Peter. Now, if you don't mind, I have work to do.' I turned back to the open file.

He gave out a long sigh. 'You need help, old chap. But have it your own way.'

As the door shut behind him, I had never felt so alone.

On my arrival at the office mid-morning a few days later, Tracy, snuffling into her handkerchief, gave me the message that the regional manager, wanted to see me. A weight lifted from my shoulders. The summons to the headmaster signalled that I would no longer wake each morning dreading discovery.

I made sure Tracy was in the clear. My dereliction wasn't her fault. 'To be frank,' I said. 'I don't think my heart's in it. I've been here for nearly thirty years. What with Mum dying and everything; I'm tired.'

They gave me a good send off. The management organised a dinner in the room over the *Golden Fleece* and we went there from the office on my last Friday. I was very drunk indeed when Tracy bundled me into the back of a cab and jumped in after me. She called out through the open door, 'I'll see he gets home safe.'

Scotia was generous and worked out a redundancy-style package. I had invested wisely, mostly in Scotia bonds that qualified for privatisation windfall payments. I sold Mum's house and sat on the cash. I had enough to not have to worry about earning money – not straight away. Given my state of mind, I only narrowly escaped sleeping on the streets.

My grand plan to go out and meet people never happened. I lost the habit of going to football matches. I went into my shell. The things that had once seemed to be important like having the spice rack in alphabetical order didn't matter a jot. I rented a flat in West London and it became a bit of tip, to be honest. I didn't bother to get my hair cut and I don't remember showering or bathing that often. I ate out: fast food and pub grub; or I brought takeaways back to the flat. My energy levels slumped and my paunch expanded.

I became as dependent on my video-player as an addict is on their drug of choice. At opening time every Wednesday, I stood on the doorstep of my local library like a Methadone user at the midnight Boots, so I could choose first from the new batch of films that came in, watching at least one a day; sometimes bingeing on two, three or more. I bought the classics for my own library, chief among them was *Chinatown*.

There were so many things to admire in that film but my reason for loving it was mine alone, as if I had a personal stake in it every time I clunked the cassette into the video player's breach and sat back for the opening credits. The fizz of the chemistry between Jack Nicholson and Faye Dunaway energised one of the best scripts ever and gave their director, Roman Polanski, a gift of a film.

My take, though, was that the secret of its success, topping even the contributions of its stars, is that the protagonists: Private Eye Jake Gittes and Faye Dunaway's Nancy Mulray were not the driving force that propelled it to its catastrophic denouement. The nitro-glycerine that exploded metaphorically in all their faces was smuggled in by a snake-like character played by John Huston, called Noah Cross. Cross – *my* mark, *my* cipher.

Chinatown's opening is all about deception. In the first scene, Jake Gittes is duped by the 'Mrs Mulray' who employs him. This sets the tone for the whole film in which, by its end, Noah Cross's manipulation of the Los Angeles water supply is of lesser concern than the fate of his grand-daughter.

Every time I watched it, I thought about my cousin Luis who, like his namesake, had worked in Chinatown. In those moments, I'd try to view it through his eyes so I could work out the links to *his* life, *his Chinatown*. Even as I wallowed in my bereavement for lost family, I understood that I should *snap out of it* because the film only accelerated my spiral into depression. Easier said than done.

My lack of *get-up-and-go* meant that I couldn't be bothered to follow up the name on the plastic disc I saw in the toilet at Heathrow Airport. So what that there was a company called Kellie's Janitorial Products? So what that Kellie, ending 'ie', was an uncommon name? So what if this could have led me to another branch of the family? My ennui was so all-encompassing that I drifted through the weeks and months frittering away my capital and not even thinking about what I might do next.

It was in this low mood that I found myself one day ambling along a side street off the Fulham Road in Chelsea. I stopped at the window of a run-down antique shop, called *Artiques*, that could have been lifted from a Dickens novel. I stepped inside and was drawn to a heavy-framed, bleak monochrome print that exactly suited my mood. The engraving depicted a death in battle. Based on the clothes and situation I wondered whether it was the death of Horatio.

I must have spoken out loud because a voice from behind the counter said, 'It's called *The Assassination of LS Dentatus*. He was a Roman consul.' The owner moved stiff-limbed around the counter and shuffled up to me in his carpet slippers. 'It's not that old but it is a print of an early 19th-century wood engraving. Are you interested in it?'

'There's something about it.'

'There certainly is.' He pulled the two wings of his moss-coloured cardigan together. 'It's quite a famous picture because of its size. It doesn't look much, does it? The work is no bigger than an A4 piece of paper but being a wood engraving makes it special. In its time, it was one of the largest and most labour-intensive woodblocks to have been cut. It was William Harvey's masterpiece.' He ran his fingerless-gloved palm over the glass and removed a film of dust.

I examined it more closely. The lines were fine and at times very close together. There were areas of detailed cross-hatching to give shade and depth. 'I can see it must have taken ages. God knows what it would have done to his eyesight.'

'That's a good point. He would have needed good light to achieve such detail. Imagine Harvey's workroom, a dingy outhouse behind one of the streets in Seven Dials – at the time one of London's worst slum areas – and you'll appreciate he could have only worked in the hours each side of midday. I can do you a good price.'

'I don't know.' I tried to decipher the engraved description. 'I can't see the artist's name.'

'It's definitely William Harvey. It's a well-known piece in the art world. The scene is based on a painting by his mentor, a fellow called Benjamin Haydon.'

'And these are famous names, are they?'

He shook his head. 'As I say, this picture is well-known in art circles but the artists aren't household names.' He adjusted his spectacles. 'There is a coda to this that may interest you, however. The engraver, William Harvey, is buried not far from here in Richmond. There is an ancient alley between houses there called Vineyard Passage. If you can find it you'll be walking alongside a burial ground and that's where Harvey is interred.'

I bought the print and hung it on my wall. It looked incongruous in my modern flat but I liked the way it dampened the cheeriness of the decoration around it. One Saturday I took the bus to Richmond to see Harvey's grave.

At the bus station, I was directed to a flagged path opposite a church and, sure enough, it ran alongside a burial ground. It was a quiet oasis in the bustle of the town; birds sang in the shrubbery while sparrows flitted in the dusty urban soil. The graves and mausoleums were laid out in no order that I could see and I soon tired of searching for William Harvey. I had come on a whim and wasn't bothered when I hadn't found what I was looking for.

Nevertheless, I was now intrigued by Vineyard Passage itself. Where would it lead? There was only one way to find out. I stepped back over the low wall that separated the graveyard from the alley and followed it, with the back gardens of houses on both sides, for a hundred metres or so to the end.

It emerged where an unremarkable residential street called *The Vineyard* joined another at an offset crossroads. There was a newsagent's shop on the corner and I went in for a Kit-Kat. Outside once again, as I was running my thumbnail along the groove in the foil, I glanced up the road and there, sticking out like a rusty tramp steamer in a row of millionaires' yachts, was the frontage of a light-industrial factory sitting dowdily in a row of Victorian dwellings. Above the factory gates the faded sign read, *Kellie's Janitorial Products.* Judging by the heavy padlocks securing the gates, the business had gone bust.

It was a quiet road and I wandered across it to read a letter that had been laminated and tacked to the Judas gate. I had expected something about bailiffs and unpaid bills but instead it read: *These premises are closed following the sale of the business. These buildings have not passed to the new owners and we are currently considering how to utilise them for the benefit of nearby residents and the community at large. If any local residents have suggestions as to how to make best use of the premises, please contact me. Mick Kellie.*

It gave an address in Richmond and a telephone number. I re-crossed the road and, with my back to a converted school building, contemplated the silent factory. I can't recall how the revelation came to me but an electric buzz ran up my spine as I imagined the building with a new glass frontage and two queues of people, one to each side, waiting to be admitted so that they could watch the latest movies in arthouse surroundings. I've never taken drugs so I can only imagine that what I felt then was akin to how a heroin user feels after having a fix – like iced water flushing through my bloodstream. My fingertips itched with energy. My brain fizzed with new opportunities.

I crossed back to the gate and made a note of Mick's details. In that moment, I saw two possibilities: the first, a thriving cinema complex; the second, simmering beneath, my resumption of my search for family.

2

I imagine Mick Kellie would have been thinking about the past when he turned the key in the padlock that secured the family's business premises for the last time.

He had been a perfumed child. He and his parents had lived on top of the factory. There was no garden, front or rear, so Mick played in the factory yard. It was home to the delivery van, outbound cartons of perfumed blocks and incoming supplies of raw materials. Mick would hide behind the exotic, green-glass carboys containing perfume oils and pick off patrols of German soldiers with his wooden-stick rifle as they passed across the open sliding-doors that fronted the road. The scent of lavender blocks attached itself to everything. Had Mick not been an only child, perhaps he might have been better equipped to cope.

The first lesson he learned at school was that he ran a high risk of being disappointed if he followed his dad's example and envisaged a future replete with benign opportunities. He was a gap-toothed, big-smiling five-year-old skipping on sturdy legs to keep up with his mum as she hurried him to the arched entry marked *Boys*.

But being perfumed, carrying the smell of the factory about him, made him different and difference is, of course, shunned. One of the boys at the sand table commented on the exotic scent that Mick Kellie brought with him. A moment later, the boy's synapses connected, his eyes gleamed with joy and a light of discovery beamed out to cast a shadow that would blight all of Mick's schooldays. 'Smelly Kellie!' He puffed out his chest and encouraged another boy to join in. 'Smelly Kellie. Smelly Kellie!'

Mick stood, fists clenched, with tears dripping from his trembling chin, bewildered by a world that had put him in that place, at that time, with those boys, when, for so long, he'd been dreaming of school as the place where he would find his very first friend.

Thanks to the same boy, who also passed the eleven plus, the nickname 'Smelly' followed him to grammar school. The boys would have said that they used it affectionately but, when one of them shouted, 'Oi, Smelly!' across a crowded bus, it didn't feel that way to Mick.

When his teenage face erupted in pustules, he suffered further abuse, his only consolation being that the violence was verbal rather than physical.

Mick's father, Robert, persuaded him to join the company as soon as he could leave school and started him at the bottom in the packing shop. That occasion had been the first when his dad had mentioned the family's business motto handed down by *his* father: 'There's money in micturition'.

Grandfather Kenneth had spotted the business opportunity in overpowering the "stench of men's pish" and had moved south from Scotland to start a company called 'Kellie's Perfumed Tablets' in the early 1900s. He had bought the livery yard with its black-cobbled harnessing area separating the stable buildings on either side. Kenneth converted them into the two factory shops: one for mixing and drying, the other for pressing and packing.

Even Kenneth couldn't have predicted how demand would take off during the First World War when wives and mothers included Kellie's lavender-perfumed tablets in the parcels that shipped over to the trenches in their millions. The women believed that the scent of lavender would aid their loved ones' restful sleep. Their menfolk hoped that the tablets would deter lice and rubbed them into the seams of their uniforms. When this didn't work, the tablets were their only weapons in the war against the stench of the trench and they sent home for more.

Mick's dad, Robert, had joined the business from school and took over from his stepmother, who ran it after Grandpa Kenneth died some time during the Second World War, another conflict in which Kellie's tablets played an unremarked role.

Luckily for Mick, his dad was an inspired businessman and he was spared being the third generation to run the company. One brutally hot afternoon in 1973 Robert came into the office, tossed his jacket across the back of the easy chair and announced, 'I've had enough of this, Mick. Look at the sweat on me.' He raised his arms. Dark patches were soaking both sides of his shirt from armpit to belt.

Mick leaned back in the swivel typist's chair. In the confined space of the office, a man of Robert's bulk, sweating as he was, would have given off a repugnant fug but here Kellie's perfumed products conquered all.

'I'm killing myself, Mick. Look at me. I'm 51. I spend my life in that damned Cortina and I drive up and down every High Street in Greater London and beyond getting orders. I must know every bloody corner-shop from Luton to Leatherhead; from Southend to Slough. There's got to be a better way.'

This started a conversation that continued into their traditional Friday after-work drink across the road in *The Duke's Head* pub. It culminated with Robert's decision that the future direction of Kellie's would be 'business to business'. 'I'm going to go nationwide, selling only to people who can buy in bulk. No more piddly, one-carton orders. We're going to sell to supermarket chains and local authorities. It's still micturition, Mick. But it's bulk micturition from now on.'

Within two years, perfumed blocks were flying out the factory as fast as they could make them, working twelve hours a day. They'd expanded the line to include new perfumes: lemon and pine. Mick decided it was time to take the initiative one early winter's evening in *The Duke's Head* as they huddled in the snug at the table nearest the open fire. Their faces glowed in the warmth of the flames and from the effects of the first beer of the day.

'We can't go on like this, Dad. The old works is busting at the seams. Everybody's suffering. If anybody gets sick we fall behind. The machines are over capacity. When we stop over Christmas we'll need to get everybody in Saturday and Sunday afterwards for two weeks to make up. We need new machines, maybe even a new factory.'

Robert drew his palm back across the top of his thinning hair, flattening the stray long strands into place across the dome of his head. 'You're right, Mick. I've been thinking the same. We're too big for this place. Leave it with me. I'll see what I can do. The last thing we need now is more orders. I'll scout around and see what I can find.'

The strong order book and the capital that had accumulated over the years enabled them to build a purpose-fitted factory unit in Reading. Mick's parents moved into a new four-bedroom house not far from the river in Maidenhead and Mick and Mary, his wife of three years, moved from a rented flat into the house where he had grown up. Even though the old factory was redundant, other than as storage space, it held too many memories for them to sell it.

There was room for expansion in the Reading premises and business kept growing. When Robert began to slow down, he assumed the role of Managing Director. The works manager took over the day-to-day production and Mick, who was 26, became Sales Director. He was now the one on the road.

The business-to-business formula meant that Kellie's was immune to the demise of the corner shop. The firm had relationships with buyers for the major supermarkets and the decision-makers responsible for supplying the lavatories in every type of public building; schools, hospitals, offices, transport terminuses, restaurant and pub chains: everywhere. At that time, if you were the sort of man who liked to aim at something in the urinal, the chances were one in three that it was a Kellie's block you were pissing on.

Mick realised that the business couldn't stand still; he became an innovator in the field of urinal accessories. He designed the first disposable trap with integral perfumed tablet. The company manufactured the moulded plastic containers and completed the whole assembly process. They argued long afterwards about which of them had designed the tri-corn trap (as Robert called it) that fitted snugly into wall-mounted urinal basins. With this wider range of products, they became *Kellies Janitorial Supplies* and had the major share of the specialist market.

Having established Kellie's as *the* top brand that now boasted the perfumed, anti-spray, plastic mat as its latest innovation, Robert was ready to retire and hand the business over to Mick. However, a multinational, with interests in everything from cake-mix to drain-cleaner came along with an irresistible offer and the Kellies decided to call it a day. The company name survived as another brand in the conglomerate's stable but Mick was made redundant.

He would always remember the scene, in *The Duke's Head*, when his dad told him how much was being deposited in the bank for his share of the sale. His smile was as wide as a motorway bridge, 'What did I always tell you, Mick? There's money in micturition.' The moment had added poignancy because Robert was spared no time to enjoy the proceeds. When he had his massive stroke and died, Mick, who, by now, was single again, inherited everything.

He'd looked round half-heartedly for another job but couldn't find anything that interested him. Maybe he needed those two years of doing nothing for his skin to lose the taint of lavender, lemon and pine. He acknowledged that he was drifting as he tacked his laminated letter to the Judas door, hoping that whoever responded would be able to come up with a project that would give him a new zest for life.

After turning the key in the padlock, Mick crossed the road in the direction of Vineyard Passage and turned to look back. He could hardly see the old place through his brimming tears.

3

I wrote to Mick Kellie at the address on the notice, suggesting that we meet over a cup of coffee in the new Starbucks in Richmond. He called me two days later and we made the arrangements. I went to the library and read a book called, *How to Run a Successful Independent Cinema*.

A cappuccino and a chocolate muffin sat untouched on the table in front of me. When I ordered them, I had told the server my name and that I was waiting for someone. I positioned myself where I'd be the first person Mick would encounter after collecting his drink.

He breezed in with the swagger of a man wearing a £10,000 watch – which, I later discovered, he was. He wore a dark business suit over a soft-collared shirt with no tie. He engaged the barista in conversation as she made his coffee and, when she pointed in my direction, he turned and smiled. He held up a hand to signify he'd join me shortly. I searched his face for a family resemblance. His eyes were very blue, the polar opposites of my brown.

My own appearance worried me for a second. Since I had left Scotia, I'd abandoned business suits but, not wanting to throw away perfectly good clothes, had developed the practice of teaming the jackets of one suit with the trousers of another. That day my jacket was dark blue and the trousers striped grey. Perhaps my scuffed trainers were a bad choice. Should I have smartened myself up? But I looked everything

I wanted him to think I was – a film nerd who had once been in business.

As Mick approached the table, his eyes were fixed on my hair. I had allowed it to twist into dreadlocks and for the meeting had bunched them together into a thick ponytail. I could see that this disconcerted him. His hair was sandy, short and well-groomed. The contrast between us worried me. I skulked in corners; he commanded the room. Me dark and unkempt; him pale-complexioned and dressed to make deals. Me hunched and stocky; him straight-backed and lean.

I'm not sure whether it was during that meeting or later, but I developed the theory, from the scant Eastern philosophy I'd picked up in the sixties, that I was the Yin – the shadowed, negative, while Mick was Yang – the sunny, positive. Rather than putting us in opposition, our differences made us complementary. If he took up my idea, this reciprocity of the opposites would work to our advantage. We could make a dynamic team.

I stood and we shook hands. We exchanged a few pleasantries before he said, 'Okay, then. About the premises. What's your idea?'

'Yes.' I licked at the foam on my spoon. 'I only came to Richmond to look at the burial ground by Vineyard Passage. You may know it.'

Mick tapped his fingertips on the table top.

'I was looking for a tomb. An artist from the beginning of the 19th century. He was an engraver who—'

'Did you find him?'

'Who?'

'The artist – engraver.'

'No.'

'You saw the premises when you came out of Vineyard Passage.'

'Yes. I saw the premises.'

'And you saw its potential as what?' He clearly wanted me to stop dithering.

'Let me tell you a bit about myself first and you'll see where I'm coming from.'

He looked at his understatedly expensive watch – this was no surreptitious wrist turn as if he was straightening his cuff. 'I don't want to be rude but I'm afraid the letter on the factory door has attracted lots of time-wasters. Why don't you tell me about your project and then we'll go into the backstory? If the idea appeals we'll keep talking. Is that okay?'

I took a deep breath. 'Okay. Here it is. I see your premises as a two-screen multiplex cinema showing the latest movie releases on one side and arthouse cinema on the other. A new local independent cinema to serve the residents of Richmond. A cinema to walk to.'

Mick stroked his chin as if he was testing the closeness of his shave. 'Mmm. Well at least it's different. It isn't sheltered accommodation for old people, a women's refuge, or a needle exchange and drug-abusers' drop-in centre which are the best I've had so far. Tell me more.'

I told him that I had been in finance but had become disillusioned and was looking for a new challenge as I approached my 50s. I wanted to do something different with my life. I said that I had always been a film enthusiast and, embroidering the story somewhat, added that I had been looking for work as a projectionist or independent cinema manager. 'It's a pretty small field with hardly any vacancies, so I was giving up hope when I came upon your building and had my vision in The Vineyard.'

He laughed. 'Have you any idea how much it would cost to convert the premises?'

'None at all, I'm afraid. But I do know that, with cinemas being up-graded into mega-complexes, auditoriums are getting smaller and there's a lot of furniture stock – seats and stuff – going cheap.'

He waved a hand. 'Money's not an issue if it's an idea that appeals. Something that gets my blood racing. Do you know about Kellie's?'

'No,' which was a lie because I had looked up details of the business in the library's reference section.

'It was an old family firm that made the scented blocks you find in public toilets? Kellie's developed and patented most of the hygiene innovations that you'll have ignored in forty-odd years of peeing in public urinals. My dad sold the business two years ago. He died not long after.'

'I'm sorry.'

He waved my condolences away. 'I took the old factory here out of the company's assets for sentimental reasons. I grew up in the house. I've been waiting for somebody to come along with a good idea. Yours is the best yet – different... positive. Let me have a think about it.'

It took a year. We set up a 50/50 partnership. I put no money in, only expertise and manpower. I argued that he was being too generous but, as he said, both he and the premises would have fallen into decay if I hadn't come along. We commissioned an architect and applied for planning permission. Everybody agreed that a cinema was better for the area than a factory.

True to his word, Mick didn't scrimp. Despite the availability of second-hand cinema seating in perfectly good condition we went for the most luxurious cinema seats available (they came from France) and even put in a two rows of sofa seats at the back of the smaller auditorium.

Mick had his bachelor pad by the river and the house attached to the factory stood empty. Once it was refurbished, originally with the idea of letting it out, he persuaded me to sell up and move in there, rent free. We both saw the advantage of being able to live over the shop and avoid late-night trips home.

I became an expert in the theory of cinema projection. My financial spreadsheets included the employment of a full-time projectionist but before he or she could start, it was my responsibility to see that we had the latest equipment. Films arrived from the distributors on reels but we invested in the latest platter system that allowed continuous screening without needing two projectors, one switching to the other when the first reel ran out. Mick and I both remembered the hoots of derision and cat-calls directed towards the projection booth when the screen went blank in the middle of a film and the embarrassment (for the cinema) when the new reel spooled through the lead stills.

When we opened for a dry-run to an invited audience of local residents, we showed *Forrest Gump* in the main house and *The Smallest Show on Earth* on the arthouse screen. We were lucky to find one of the few prints of this old monochrome Peter Sellers film on up-to-date film stock. Its grainy, benignant images reflected the affection we both already held for *The Film Factory*.

There's no doubt about it, at some level the Kellie name over the door of the premises before we converted them had been part of my motivation for writing to Mick. Almost every morning in those early months, while we were busy developing the site and then running the cinema, I would wake thinking that this is the day when I would talk to Mick about our possible family connection. I imagined that he would be sceptical at first, but as I described how my father had died in London with his uncle, Kenneth, which was Mick's grandfather's name, he would accept that we were cousins. It wouldn't affect *The Factory* but we would learn to treat each other as family rather than business partners.

Two things stopped me: I didn't want to expose myself to

rejection and I had the memory of Luis. His death had set the black dog on my heels and, though rationally I couldn't envisage anything that might put Mick in danger, I feared that history would repeat itself. Despite steeling myself almost every day with the thought that *today's the day*, I said nothing until early 1995 when he showed me the picture of the man on the horse.

We were in the *The Duke's Head* having our last pint before I had to go back to *The Factory* to close up. I placed two pints of Young's bitter on our usual corner table. 'You said something about a photo?'

'Yeah. I'd like to see what you think,' he said, holding out a playing-card sized, black and white photograph. I wiped my fingers along the seam of my jeans before taking it. It showed a man sitting astride a horse that stood in a dried-up river bed. A metal pipeline rose from beneath what, in times of flood, would have been the river's surface and disappeared into the sandy bank like a burrowing animal. In the background, a line of trees smudged the far horizon. It was a hot day; the man wore a straw hat and a thin shirt. He was shading his eyes from the sun.

I turned the picture over and read the inscription – *The family land*. My knee trembled involuntarily and the beer in my stomach soured. Flipping the picture again I could see in the far background – too indistinct for a casual observer to notice – the parapet of square tower. It was the castle where Luis had died. I recognised it from a picture in a travel magazine I had bought after Luis's death because of its special feature on Malaysia. Among the articles was a panel about the romantic story behind a ruined castle near Ipoh.

'Where is it?' I said, stalling for time, handing the photograph back. Was this the time to say something?

'That's the point. I don't know. I found it going through some of my dad's old papers. "Family land"...' he made the rabbit's ears sign with his fingers '... it's intriguing, don't you think?'

I shrugged, perhaps a bit too theatrically. 'You think it's *your* family land?'

'Could be. Dad once said something about us having a branch of the family in the Far East.'

'And you're showing it to me, because?'

He rubbed his chin. 'I don't know. The cinema is up and running. All very smoothly thanks to you. I'm thinking I need something new... maybe get away... travel. I remembered this picture, looked it out and now...'

'The Far East is a big place. Don't you know any more?'

He shook his head and considered his half-empty glass. 'Not really. But what would you say if I took off? Would *The Factory* be okay—?'

'Hell! You don't need to worry about *The Factory*. Look, why don't you sleep on it. You'll need to make some sort of plan. You can't just head off to "the Far East" on your white charger like Panzo Sanchez.'

Mick straightened himself up and threw back the last of his pint. He held his fingers close to my face. 'One, it was Don Quixote who rode the horse. Two, it was a decrepit old black horse called *Rocinante*. Three, Quixote's squire was called Sancho Panza. And four—' he put his fingers to his temples '—and four... are you sure the cinema will manage if I go off gallivanting?'

'We'll be fine.'

Mick stood to leave. 'I know how it looks. I've got too much money and itchy feet. But I genuinely feel I should go to the Far East and find out what this picture is about. But I'll only do it if you think the cinema will be okay.'

I replayed the conversation and its possible ramifications as I tried to sleep that night. Mick's revelation about the family land in the Far East almost certainly confirmed that he and I were related. I had missed the opportunity to reveal everything I knew; I resolved to say something the next day.

4

I imagine Mick felt vulnerable as he tottered along *Vineyard Passage* towards the town centre and his converted loft apartment in Water Street. His shadow leapt ahead of him as he passed in and out of the protection of each streetlamp's glow. It was an hour after the midsummer sunset and he could hear furtive giggles and snuffling noises from behind the larger tombs where groups of lads had collected to sniff glue and quaff strong cider at the night's close.

He looked at his watch. The screening had finished and his customers had either dispersed to their cars, walked across to *The Duke's Head* for a nightcap or were following him down the alley towards the town. He turned and, sure enough, there were three couples walking down, holding hands or arms linked, from the top of the alley.

The thing with the photograph had gone well. He had introduced the idea of taking off somewhere. He didn't want Steve to think he was bored with what they had built together even if it was a little bit true. He had discerned that Steve needed *The Factory* more than he did and the last thing he wanted to do was upset the life that was running smoothly. But he craved adventure. He had happened upon the photograph in his father's old paperwork and the idea of finding *the land* had seeded itself into his unconscious and germinated the need to act. Was it that irrational? The family land was out there – who wouldn't want to know what it meant? Admittedly, he couldn't fly off to the first country in the 'Far East' that took his fancy. He'd have to be more scientific than that. But if he could pin it down to one country why not do something crazy? He could afford to travel first class all the way if he wanted, thanks to Kellie's.

As he trudged thoughtfully homeward he considered the life that the micturition business had brought him. He had more money than he knew how to spend but he was single again, because he had put his work before his marriage. He was a partner in a cinema that was making enough to cover its running costs. His loft apartment had a balcony that, if he leaned out far enough, allowed a partial view of the river. A seldom-driven, restored Alpha Romeo Series 2 Spider occupied his space in the basement garage.

Why the hell would he want to literally chase a dream to 'the Far East'? Then again, why the bloody hell not? It was the *family* land and family was the one thing he didn't have.

I imagine Mick was proud of his apartment that (very nearly) overlooked the river. He furnished it minimally and didn't sully the effect with curtains. Shortly after 7.30am, when the first light entered his bedroom space through the floor-to-ceiling windows and crept across the bare boards, he lay with his eyes tight shut trying to recall how many beers he had drunk the previous evening.

The radio alarm that had woken him now recounted news reports about the alleged mass killings by Serb soldiers in and around a supposedly safe United Nations area called Srebrenica. He had tried to follow the conflict in Yugoslavia because, when he was a boy, the family had taken a summer holiday there in a resort town called Poreç. However, his attempts to make sense of the different factions and the fragmented, illogical geography of the various ethnic groupings made his head hurt on the best of days. He reached out gingerly and pressed the off button.

He twisted out of bed and strolled across to the window wearing only boxer shorts. His top floor apartment – he liked to call it a penthouse – was level with the roof of the building on the opposite side of the lane and his balcony floor obscured him from prying interest. He contemplated stepping outside but was deterred because of the light summer drizzle that pricked the puddles in the cobbled street below.

During some half-hearted stretching, he remembered talking about the photograph that sparked his idea of going to the Far East. Despite the effects of the previous night blurring his thinking, he could see that the proposed trip based on the photograph alone made limited sense. But if he could pin down the location...

In the kitchen area, he brewed coffee in a *Moka* pot, put two croissants in the oven and spooned out a measure of jam onto a plate – all without conscious thought. His mind was still turning over the idea of travel.

It was not as if he had ties. He *should* have ties. It was his own fault that he didn't. He went over the excuses for his wife's decline into into addiction. They'd married too young. He'd spent all his time on the road building sales, creating the growth that led to what should have been *their* fortune. If they hadn't broken up she could have shared in it. Maybe she wouldn't have felt so alone if they'd had children but neither of them... with him away so much... latterly it was him fighting the vodka bottle for her attention. He was never going to win that one.

He munched the thickly jammed croissant, keeping the creeping fungus in his head at bay with mental jogging. Married at twenty, divorced at thirty and here he was nearly forty. He shook his head to suppress a thought that was rising like a molehill in the otherwise pristine lawn of his contemplation. Perhaps it was time to put some effort into finding a life-partner. Was he thinking that he'd like kids? If it *was* what he was thinking he'd have to find a permanent relationship with a woman who was still young enough.

And to even think that he might want children; where did that come from? If his future was a choice between fatherhood and the madcap trip east, the latter seemed like a sensible course of action. Time for a shower.

5

The venue for the monthly management meeting had recently been switched from the Starbucks in town to the new coffee shop on the corner opposite *The Film Factory* where the newsagent's used to be. It should have started at 10.30am but, as usual, I was ten minutes late. From behind his morning paper, Mick said, 'I'll have another Americano.'

'Will do. Sorry I'm late.'

We had a set agenda for these meetings, I would give a brief overview of the financials, size of the houses, net receivables, costs, and then a review of the relationship with the agency that helped set the programme and organised the courier delivery and collection of the reels.

We moved on to discuss the forthcoming screenings and my ideas for the 'clubhouse' programme. Mick, who didn't know his John Huston from his John Boorman, was always happy to nod through my suggestions.

'Anything under AOB?' he said.

My dreadlocks had fallen forward and I flicked them back behind my shoulders. 'No. It's all on-plan.' I put the spreadsheets back in my shoulder bag. 'You okay, Mick?' I said, 'You seem a bit down.'

He shrugged. 'It's like I was saying last night. Maybe I've got itchy feet. Everything with *The Factory* is going so well, thanks to you but I need... I don't know... just to get out of Richmond would be a start.'

The time had come. I took a deep breath. 'So, you've decided. You're offski to Saigon or wherever?'

He nodded. 'It looks like it. I'll probably throw a dart at a map and see where it takes me.'

'And another when it lands in Bognor!' I said.

'Bugger Bognor!' he exclaimed in basso profondo.

'Now!' I said. 'You know that photo you showed me last night – the one that was meant to be a relative of yours from the past? He was on a horse?'

Mick's cheeks flushed. 'It's what started me thinking.'

'Well I found something. It was in this travel magazine, a special about Malaysia, and on one of the pages I saw your name—'

'Mick?'

'No, you plonker. Kellie. Not just any Kelly but spelt 'ie' as in your weird name. Did you know there's a big house in the north of Malaysia called Kellie's Castle?'

Mick leaned forward. 'Okay. Now I'm interested.'

'This—' I mimed speech marks on either side of my head '—castle *was* built by somebody called Kellie-Smith, though. Do you know of any Kellie-Smiths, not just plain Kellies, in your family?'

He shook his head.

'Anyway, this article was about beach resorts in Malaysia and this castle place was in the side bit. It had a picture and everything.'

Mick straightened and shifted forward in his chair. 'Have you got it with you?'

My bag was by my feet and I leant down, took out the magazine and flipped it onto the table with an imagined ta-dah! 'Have a look at this and I'll get another coffee.' I needed to be away from him. My armpits were pumping.

As I stood at the counter, I watched Mick flick through to the correct page and start reading. The article was about a resort island called Langkawi but one of the quirky pieces in a box to the side was entitled *The Castle of Doomed Romance*.

I put the coffees on the table. Upside down I could see the the ruins of the building and the paragraphs that described how William Kellie-Smith had built Kellie's Castle as a grand romantic gesture for his wife who, because of his death, had never even seen it.

Mick looked up and tapped the page. 'Have you read this?'

I nodded feigning nonchalance. My knee was in spasm and I gripped it with my right hand.

'It says here that the man who built the house, William Kellie-Smith, originally came from a small hamlet in Scotland called Kellas. He named his first house after it. I don't know much about my grandfather, Kenneth, but one thing I do know is that he was born in Scotland. William and Kenneth could be related. It could be another branch of the family.'

'I'm pretty sure it is.'

He looked at me askance. 'What do you mean?'

I took a sip of coffee. 'It's something I should have told you right at the start. I kept this magazine because my father's name was Kellie K-E-L-L-I-E Smith—'

'But your name is Cross and you're...' he pointed at my hair.

'Cross is my mother's maiden name. You're right, yes, my mother was mixed race. My father was white. They never married because he was killed in the war. He was with his uncle when he died. His uncle was Kenneth Kellie-Smith. When you told me about your family business being founded by your grandfather – Kenneth, I put two and two together. We're related. We're cousins.'

Mick's mouth opened but no noise came out. I wasn't sure whether he'd taken in all I'd said. He snapped open his wallet and slipped out the black and white image. 'What you're

157

saying is that this is Kenneth Kellie-Smith, my grandfather, and he's related to you and this is Malaysia? Hang on. I can't get my head round it.'

'No. The man in the picture is probably the man who built the castle. He's my grandfather *William* Kellie-Smith. If I'm right, he's your grand-*uncle*, although I think the proper word is *great* uncle like in Great Uncle Bulgaria.'

Mick looked up, his brow furrowed.

'Sorry. Never mind,' I said and pretended to study the photograph closely, glancing between it and the image in the article. 'Look!' I pointed to the smudge on the tree-line in the photograph. Couldn't that be the tower there?' I pointed to the end of the building in the magazine picture. 'Your photograph could be the castle from the other side of the plantation. It shows the extent of—' I did the finger thing '—*the family land*. The man on the horse is probably your father's uncle. It's the Kellie family land. It's your great uncle's land. It makes us cousins.' I jabbed a finger at the picture. '*This* is where you should go.' I waited. My heart was thudding.

Mick took the photograph and held it alongside the magazine. 'Mmm. It could be, I suppose. He turned the photograph over. 'Why the bloody hell couldn't they have written *Malaysia* on the back?' Wide-eyed he shook his head. 'And this makes us cousins? How long have you known?'

'I suspected it right from the start because of the name on the factory, but I didn't want to say anything because it would have complicated the whole pitch to get you to accept the cinema idea. Then, afterwards – I don't know – I was happy that I knew you were probably my cousin and it was enough.'

He seemed to take what I'd said at face value and re-scanned the article. 'Look, it says this place in Scotland, Kellas, where William came from, is only a hamlet. Maybe I can find out there whether he and my grandad were brothers.

Rather than going on a wild-goose chase to Malaysia, I should go there.' He nodded. 'Thanks, for this, Steve. Yep! That's what I'll do. I'm going to Kellas.'

He was immediately preoccupied by the land thing and the prospect of a trip to Scotland. He was already making plans. If he had asked me to go with him I knew I would have had to decline because one of us had to stay behind for the *Film Factory*. I had still wanted him to ask me, though.

As soon as Mick had returned from the coffee shop, I picture him taking a magnifying glass to the photograph of his great uncle and, sure enough, spying the top few feet of what appeared to be the square castle tower over the tips of the trees. It was merely a ghost of a smudge and he marvelled at how I had been able to make out such detail.

He checked his AA Book and found Kellas in north Scotland. The name marked an area of green that didn't have even a speck of grey to denote habitation. The nearest town of any size was Elgin and next morning, Mick called to book a room in the Laichmoray Hotel.

He drove up in the Alfa Romeo at the end of the same week. It took the best part of fifteen hours including breaks and, after checking in, he unlocked the door to his room and fell onto the bed in one movement. Later, in the small hours, he roused himself sufficiently to change into his pyjamas and brush his teeth before snuggling under the duvet.

Next morning, after a full Scottish breakfast, he drove out to the hamlet and discovered that it consisted of a few bungalows strung along a country lane with a sign at each end bearing the legend 'Kellas'. Despite driving up and down the deserted road twice he couldn't find anything or anyone to help him.

The nearest habitation he could see on the map was a village called Dallas, and after driving in that direction for three miles, the main road took him between two terraces of one-storey stone houses. Signs by a war memorial pointed him south to Bridge of Lossie and St Michael's Church. The bridge was an unprepossessing structure crossing a tame rivulet that didn't seem worthy of special mention on the road signs, but it did lead to St Michael's Church, which, though only four walls and a roof, lifted Mick's mood. It promised answers. It was set back from the road behind a square cemetery with neat rows of gravestones separated by grass paths. He pulled the car into the lay-by opposite.

The drizzle that Mick had cursed during his drive was turning into sleet as he ducked inside the porch and tried the door. It opened. Mick didn't frequent churches but he was immediately struck by the absence of a centre aisle. The pews were set in three blocks separated by two aisles so that neither led to the middle of the altar. The smell of freshly applied emulsion paint hung in the air and, when Mick paused and looked up, he saw that the buttercup yellow on the ceiling was fresh. It contrasted with the cracked and flaking distemper that covered the walls. He was approaching the rood screen along the nearest aisle when he was stopped by the sound of a door opening behind him.

A young man emerged from a doorway opposite where Mick had come in. The clergyman was dressed in a black cassock. Shined black toecaps flashed at the hem of his skirt. 'Can I help you?'

Mick cleared his throat. 'I don't know. I'm trying to trace some relatives who came from round here. From Kellas to be exact.'

'Then you've come to the right place. This parish covers Kellas. It's a very small place.'

'I've seen.'

'I assume that's your Alfa parked opposite.' He nodded towards the south wall as if he could see through it.

'Yes.'

'Nice car. Have you driven far?'

'I came up from London yesterday. Stayed in Elgin.'

'Good. Come back here and we'll look at the books. Tell me, if I find your relatives in our register would you mind letting me have a quick spin in your motor? Just up the lane and back.'

'What about the insurance?'

'Don't worry about that. The only police hereabouts are in Lossiemouth. Who'll know?'

Mick was tempted to say, God will, but stopped himself. He didn't want to antagonise the man.

The vestry was a combined changing room and office. There was a monitor on the desktop wired into an IBM personal computer set on its side in the knee space. The priest saw what Mick was looking at. 'Sadly, I haven't been able to even think about transcribing our records onto a computer.' He pointed to a bank of red leather-bound registers. 'That's where we'll be looking. Our past clergy kept records of all the births, deaths and marriages in the parish – members of the church or no. Any idea of what date you're looking for?'

Mick had worked it out before he left Richmond. 'Births around 1870, I think.'

'Well, it gives us a starting point. And the name?'

'Kellie-Smith.'

'And are you a Kellie-Smith?'

'We only use Kellie now. It's Kellie I E not Y.' He held out his hand. 'Mick Kellie.'

The priest's handshake was dry and firm. Mick was reassured that, should he allow the priest to go for a spin in the Alfa, it would be in safe hands.

'Fine good it is to meet you, Mr Kellie. I'm Rodney Sullivan. Call me Rod.' He took down one of the ledgers,

June 1863 – February 1874 and flicked though to six months into 1869. The vicar at the time had meticulously entered the details of every event in date order, births, marriages and deaths mixed together. Mick wasn't sure how big an area was covered but the population couldn't have been large because the events came at a rate of one or two a month. Some months nothing happened.

They found what they were looking for on the first page of entries for 1870. Kenneth Kellie-Smith and William Kellie-Smith had been born on the same day, 1st March. They were registered in the book seven days later.

After copying out the entry word for word and watching as the vicar returned the book to its place on the shelf, Mick tossed his car keys into Rod's hand. 'Be careful.' He followed Rod to the porch and they both paused. The sleet was feathering down in soft-edged, heavy drops.

Rod looked up. 'I'd like to take the roof off if it's all the same to you.'

On the drive back to Richmond, broken by an overnight stop in a hotel outside Edinburgh, Mick recalled his parting conversation with Rod as they sat in the car after it had been spun up and down the road mostly at something like 70 miles an hour with the top off and the sleet skidding over them.

Rod had asked whether he intended to visit the Kellas House Farm – the address given as the Kellie-Smith residence. Mick admitted that he was going back to Kellas in the hope of finding it.

'I wouldn't trouble yourself,' Rod had said. 'The original Kellas House was pulled down forty or so years ago. The existing property is modern thing.'

Drinking a nightcap whisky in his Edinburgh hotel room, half watching a film on television, Mick went over what he knew: everything pointed to the family land being in Malaysia. The twins, brought up on a farm in a sleepy little hamlet, had spread their wings and done so well. His grandfather, Kenneth, had gone south and founded the factory in Richmond; his grandfather's twin, William, had travelled to Malaysia and made his fortune.

There were two branches to his family; he was on one side and strangely, his business partner, Steve was on the other. He wasn't ready to get to grips with what this meant for them and *The Factory*. He needed action and his path was clear. He would follow his great uncle William to Malaysia and the city called Ipoh.

On the night of his return from Scotland, I imagine Mick slept fitfully. He woke often and his first thought was always of the house and the land. He reached into the recesses of what he knew about the family to make a connection. Robert, Mick's father, had schooled him on the timelines of their company's product development from simple lavender-perfumed blocks to anti-splash, fragrance-infused, plastic mats but hardly anything about the family origins. He vaguely remembered being told that his grandfather, Kenneth, founder of the perfumed-block dynasty, had died in an air raid during the Second World War. Or was this merely prompted by what Steve had told him?

His mind a pre-dawn jumble, Mick put in place the few jig-saw pieces of his family tree. His trip had placed William and Kenneth, twin brothers, alongside each other at the top. Each had a main stem and on Kenneth's side there had been a mysterious 'aunt' Siobhan who was Kenneth's second wife. She had run the business in the immediate aftermath of her husband's death until Robert was old enough to take over, which would have been around 1960 – when Mick was five and starting school.

As far as Mick knew, there had been no communication between the two arms of the family after his grandfather died. He and his father, Robert, were only children; he was the only Kellie on Kenneth's side.

He knew that Kenneth's twin, William Kellie-Smith, was married because, according to the magazine article, he had built the castle for his wife. They may well have had children. Steve had said that one of them was Anthony, Steve's father, who died alongside Kenneth. But wouldn't Robert, his own father, have told him if he knew there was family somewhere? All he had was the photograph of 'the family land'.

He had no reason to doubt Steve's father was Anthony Kellie Smith. If he accepted it, Steve – the strange, mixed-race, film enthusiast with unkempt hair and mismatched clothes – was his cousin. He could accept it as a theory – a genealogical fact even – but what did it *mean*? Should Steve mean something more to him because they shared their grandparent's DNA? He attempted the calculation. Twenty-five percent or maybe half of that. It's not a lot to have in common.

A week later, Mick sat in the business-class lounge at Heathrow Airport waiting to join the flight to Kuala Lumpur. Assured that *The Film Factory* would survive without him, his only concern was how he would use his time during his fourteen days away. The travel agent had arranged for him to spend the first two in KL, as he had learned to call it, and booked nothing for the rest of the time. Mick planned to travel north by rental car on the third day and find a hotel in Ipoh, the city nearest to the castle. He was then in the right part of the country to head to the coast for a ferry to Langkawi where he could start a beach holiday. The big question at this stage was whether the three novels he had brought with him would last two weeks.

He had enjoyed spending the money. He had told the travel agent that he wasn't constrained by cost and was already pleased with his decision not to fly economy. There was something calming about the lounge where his companions dressed in business attire and studied broadsheet newspapers and magazines. The business centre was equipped with computers so that they could contact their offices by e-mail and he even spotted one passenger ostentatiously holding one of the new wireless telephones to his ear and talking into its built-in microphone.

After the first in-flight meal, Mick consulted the menu of films and chose *Groundhog Day* and, it was only when the woman who sat next to him nudged his elbow, he realised that he had been laughing out loud. She too was wearing headphone; he mouthed an apology.

She signed back that she wanted to know which channel he was watching.

Half-looking at the screen he removed an earpiece and waited for her to do the same. 'It's *Groundhog Day*,' he said. 'You know, Bill Murray.'

'I love that film,' she said. 'I didn't see it on the list. How long has it been on?'

'Only about twenty minutes...'

She twiddled with the handset control and nodded vigorously at him with her eyebrows raised as she replaced her headphone. For the next hour or so, Mick was aware of her right arm trembling in unison with his laughter.

At the end of the film, Phil Connors woke and, miraculously so it seemed, it was the day after Groundhog Day. He had accomplished the perfect 24 hours. How many hundreds of days had the weatherman committed to achieving contentment? Life was more random than that, Mick thought. Perhaps his fate – his happiness – could be determined by something as arbitrary as... he glanced to his left, as arbitrary as the allocation of business class seats by Malaysian Airlines.

The woman's hair was pulled back tight from her scalp

and scrunched into an extravagant ponytail that fell over her shoulder and down her chest. She was wearing a loose, pullover top and pale, cotton trousers. Dressing for comfort rather than style was the hallmark of the seasoned traveller, he thought.

He turned to her. 'I'm sorry about earlier. I've seen that film over and over and I still find it hilarious.'

'Me too,' she said, and proffered her right hand, her elbow crooked awkwardly into her waist. I'm Amy.'

'Mick.' He wanted to say more but his mind was blank. When he was in the perfumed tablet business these conversations could be so excruciating

'What takes you to KL, Mick?'

It was such an obvious conversational gambit; why hadn't he thought of it? It was a relief simply to say, 'It's a sort of holiday.'

'In KL?' Her eyebrows added the question mark.

'Not exactly. I start there – just for a couple of days. Then I head north and probably end up on a beach in Langkawi.'

The hum of the engines that underscored the conversation made them watch each other's lips as if they were hard of hearing.

'Lucky you.'

'And you? Why are you going to KL?'

'Work, I'm afraid.'

'What sort of work is that?'

'It's a funny old job, actually.'

He settled his backside deeper into the seat. It was comforting to find the other person being evasive about what they did for a living. He smiled. 'Sounds interesting.'

The lights in the cabin dimmed and they were illuminated only by the screens that showed the progress of the plane somewhere over the Middle East.

She frowned and a movement of her head indicated that

she'd summed Mick up and decided on an action of some sort. Or was this wishful thinking on his part? 'I'll show you.' She leant down to a briefcase by her side and rummaged through the contents. When she sat up again she was holding something in her closed fist. 'I shouldn't really share this with you – with anybody. It's *so* totally a secret. If you tell I'll have to kill you.'

It was a joke, but she *was* going to share a business confidence. This much was clear. It implied complicity and who knew where it might lead? He turned on his seat's reading light. Amy had handed him a plastic figurine of a woman with an impossibly inflated bust and tightly corseted high waist. Her solid plastic hair was jet-black and rolled down to her shoulders like breakers on a rocky coast. Her hyper-long legs, which must have been as anatomically impossible as her bosom, were covered in a purple, swirling skirt beneath which flashed the white of a petticoat. 'You make these?' He immediately regretted how negative he sounded.

She pulled away from him as if he had raised a hand.

'Sorry. That came out wrong. She's... I'm sure little girls will love her.'

'We hope so.' She held out her hand and took the doll back. 'Boys too. It's top secret. You mustn't tell anyone but I work for a company that does *Happy Meal* promotions for McDonalds...'

She was evidently waiting for a signal of recognition. He knew what *McDonalds* was, everybody did. But where did this grotesque figure fit in?

She sighed. 'The company I work for designs the *Happy Meal* promotions. You know, the box packaging and the free gifts.' She held up the figurine. 'Esmeralda here is part of our big Disney-linked promotion for the middle of next year.

I've got Quasimodo, Captain Phoebus and Judge Frollo in my bag.'

'I get it. Sorry! I've been so thick. *The Hunchback of Notre Dame*.'

'Exactly! The *McDonalds* promotion runs alongside the release of the next *Disney* blockbuster.'

'And your company designs all the freebies. Brilliant!'

'It's not exactly making the world a better place.'

'It *is* for the kids who go to *McDonalds*. Why KL, though?'

'It's my job. I go around the world to all the franchisees to let them know the details of the promotion. They have to keep it under wraps until the release date.' She looked at her watch. 'I must be tired. I shouldn't have told you all this. You will keep it under your hat, won't you?'

'Of course. What an amazing job. Where do you go?'

'All over. Wherever there's a *McDonalds* – even Moscow and Beijing.'

'Wow! This is the first time I've flown like this – business class. If you do this all the time, you're very lucky.'

'It's like everything. You get used to it and it becomes –' she shook her head '– everyday. And it's not exactly what I had in mind when I left college.'

'We all make compromises.' He was unhappy that this, apparently confident business woman had such a low opinion of her worth. 'You'll never guess what my company did,' he said. And for the next hour they discussed the relative merits of perfumed urinal tablets and *Happy Meal* toys as far as the advancement of mankind was concerned, each taking the other's part. They only stopped when one of the cabin staff squatted by their row and said that the other passengers were complaining about their loud conversation and could they tone it down, please?

When the attendant had gone, they shrugged and scrunched up their faces like children who'd been discovered doing something naughty. They wished each other goodnight. She turned away from him, let the seat-back fall almost flat, pulled up a blanket and was soon making the regular breathing noises of sleep.

The morning brightness of the cabin and the calm efficiency of the breakfast serving made Mick feel foolish about the encounter of the previous night and he was sure Amy felt it too. The vagaries of Malaysia Airline's booking system had forced them into a conversation that was perhaps more familiar than either intended and now they looked set to resume their separate lives.

They barely acknowledged each other. He was tempted to start up a conversation along the lines of how much he'd enjoyed sleeping with her, but knew this was ill-advised. But what *should* he say? There was something about last night's darkened cabin that encouraged indiscretion. The magic had been driven out by the dawn.

After the plane landed, as they scrabbled together their possessions, they said a perfunctory goodbye and he wished her well with the *Disney* promotion'.

'Have a lovely holiday,' she said and, lugging her sample briefcase over one shoulder and dragging a wheeled suitcase with her free hand, she disappeared from his life. Why hadn't he asked for her business card at least?

7

I imagine Mick would have found it difficult to sleep even without his scrambled sense of time. His body clock told him that it was early evening but his watch said three in the morning. Four hours earlier he had turned off the air-conditioning because its roar stopped him from falling asleep. Now he tossed in the sweat-damp sheets, his head bursting with the repercussions of his encounter on the plane.

The only way to find Amy would be to contact *McDonalds* when he was back in London. But she didn't work for them; she worked for a consultancy company that worked for *McDonalds*. Even if he could trace her company, he didn't know her last name. 'Amy who does the travelling with the *Happy Meal* promotion stuff.' How lame did that sound?

'Why do you want to speak to her?' he asked himself out loud.

'Because I met her on a plane and now I want to ask her out,' he admitted. He sounded like a stalker.

He rolled over, pummelling his head deeper into the pillows, praying for sleep. Unbidden, Amy's unadorned night-flight face with the freckles each side of her nose appeared in front of his closed eyes. Her hair was now jet black and obscured a cantilevered bosom. He groaned and rolled out of bed.

The cold from the floor tiles leached deliciously into the

soles of his feet as he padded across the tiled floor. The mini-bar fridge cast a beam of light across the room as he reached in for water. He stood, his naked body glowing in front of the open door, and drank from the bottle. He reached to the window and pulled the blind's wooden slats apart to look outside. The twin spears of the Petronas Tower, which, when finished, would be the tallest building in the world, pierced the purple, night sky half a mile away. He caught his reflection in the glass, noticing that his hair was snarled and spiky. The pallor of his skin emphasised dark circles around his eyes. He decided that maybe a swim would help.

Emerging from the lift on the top floor, Mick was pleased and mildly surprised to find the entrance wasn't locked. He made his way up the stairway and his feet, still bare, were prickled by the resistant tufts of the Astroturf in a way that heightened his anticipation of the cool water. When he reached the roof, the fresh zing of the chlorine fumes wiped Amy from his mind.

The sky was a dark canopy pegged to the white walls surrounding the pool. Pinprick stars burned their ancient energy alongside a moon that glowed with the luminosity of a paper lantern. Mick could make out the craters on its parchment-like surface. He stood awed; they don't have moons like this in England.

The lamps at the bottom of the pool created an arc of brightness that flooded into the warm air. As he swam he floated at the misty margin that marked the mini-horizon between the liquid below and the humid air above. His arms chopped into the water without tearing its surface; the drips from his hands sparkled as if he was swimming through mercury.

The meeting on the plane with Amy, the magic of this rooftop swim were auguries – what did they portend?

Next morning, after he had eaten a solitary, late breakfast,

Mick went to reception and conscious that this was his only full day in the city, asked which tourist attractions he should visit before he left for the north.

The Chinese concierge bowed, his intelligent brown eyes shining from behind thick-lensed glasses. Using a felt-tipped pen, he marked the King's Palace, the National Mosque, the telecommunications tower and the railway station on a map. 'These are main things to see in KL,' he said. 'Where you heading tomorrow?'

'I'm travelling north. Eventually I'll go to Langkawi.'

'Where in north, you go?'

'Ipoh. Do you know it?'

The concierge nodded enthusiastically showing off his teeth. 'Yes! Ipoh fine town. Chinese town.' He looked around and leaned forward. 'KL now all Malay. Bumis everywhere. Ipoh better – more Chinese. Not much for tourist though. Why you go there?'

'Have you heard of Kellie's Castle?'

The concierge nodded.

'Well my family name is Kellie. I think my grandfather's brother built it – the castle. I'm going to take a look at it. What can you tell me about it?'

The concierge looked at the floor. 'I not know castle. Can't help you. Sorry!' He pushed the map across the desk to signify their conversation was over.

'But—'

The concierge looked over Mick's shoulder as if another guest was waiting but, when Mick turned, there was nobody there.

'I thought you said—'

The concierge's eyes were wide and a line of sweat appeared below his hairline. He turned away to rummage in a drawer and for a moment Mick wondered whether he was ill. 'Sorry, can't help you. Anything you need more for trips in KL? I know good karaoke lounge for tonight – *very* pretty hostesses.'

Later, while Mick sweltered on the tourist trail, he found himself unable to concentrate on the buildings and on what the guides were saying. Remembrances from the previous night kept intruding: the sight of the tropical pre-dawn moonlight; the smell of the swimming pool; the feel of the enveloping morning mist. Then there was the concierge's strange reaction. Something about this overheated city was shifting his mental cargo, affecting his equilibrium.

When he stood on the viewing deck of the Menara KL, looking out over the tops of tall buildings but only eye-to-eye with the middle of the Petronas Towers, or sat among locals eating Chinese-style seafood in the crowded Jalan Alor, he wanted to turn to one of the strangers alongside him and share his impressions of the exotic city. The alien bitter-spice smell of it. The clamour of its traffic. The way hundreds of mopeds, driven by young men in back-to-front zippered jackets, weaved dangerously between the cars. How the riders' girlfriends, perching side-saddle on the pillion seats – modesty being more important than stability – clung limpet-like to their beaus. The city's obsession with a strange fruit called a durian that apparently smelled like sewage but tasted of honey. The dank, deep gullies that ran beneath the pavements, tunnels that he imagined were thoroughfares for the city's rat population.

The unsettling nature of his encounters with Amy and the concierge had primed him for something. Events lay in his path. His future was preparing to ambush him. When his chance came – in whatever form it appeared – he would be ready to embrace it, not brush it away.

At around 5pm, Mick, back in the cool of the hotel, watched from his window as a rainstorm passed over the city. The streets became torrents and the deserted square out front turned into a lake deep enough for a pack of strays to have to doggy paddle their way across. Within an hour, the rain stopped and the pavements steamed. The square's drainage system coped (those cavernous rat-runs) and the floods were no more.

That evening, Mick went to a restaurant recommended by the afternoon concierge. It was set back between high buildings alongside one of the main six-lane routes across town. The food was unremarkable and he'd washed it down with Tsingtao beer. The tables were outside on a series of wooden decks that cascaded down from the rear boundary marked by high palm trees and stands of bamboo. He imagined a sign: *The Jungle Starts Here.*

While he ate, Mick had listened to a family group at the next table. One of them was soon to appear in court on drugs charges. It was another example of the bubble of the uncanny that encased him. Were they really talking, in English, about intimidating – no liquidating – witnesses? Was one of them naming members of the judiciary who could be bribed? Was the family patriarch targeting police officers who would be persuaded to revise their statements? Should they have discussed these subjects so openly when it must have been clear that Mick was eavesdropping on their competing boasts of graft and corruption?

When the family left, Mick ordered a brandy. It came in a balloon glass big enough to give a goldfish agoraphobia. The 'tot' was generous but merely lined the bottom of the bowl. As he sat back, once again contemplating the unsettling other-worldliness of the East, the lights dimmed and the remaining diners departed tables on the other decks. He was alone on the middle stage and below him the waiters talked together by their station, glancing at him: silent entreaties to pay and leave.

Something fluttered past his left ear. Given the lateness

of the hour, Mick assumed a tiny bat had flown close to his head and he watched it skid to earth beneath a table on the lower deck. It scuttled a few paces and the strangeness of its movement made Mick lean forward for a closer look. It had two antennae, six legs and an armoured body. Mick jerked back and watched squeamishly as more cockroaches flew in. They were careful to avoid his table and soon the surface of the lower deck resembled one of the city's multi-highway junctions with the invertebrate traffic avoiding collisions only narrowly as it darted that way and this.

The first of the rats came tentatively, peering around the corner of one of the decking posts on the highest level, then more boldly as it was joined by others until four of them plundered crumbs under the tables farthest from him.

It was time to leave. He looked over to the waiters. They were oblivious, or more likely inured to, the invasion. He would have to negotiate the area where the cockroaches were most populous. As he pondered his route, he heard a chattering call and a monkey landed with a thud on a table behind him, beneath the palm trees. Two others followed. They were grey and mangy with yellow teeth that they bared at each other as they fought over scraps.

Mick hurried for the exit, not caring what he would have to tread on to reach it, and he was relieved when his Moses-like presence caused the scampering masses to part. This was confirmation of something else that he had been dimly aware of; the jungle was out there primed to take over.

And as he hurried back to the hotel, ignoring the man-girl prostitutes who loitered by the entrance, he was again aware how welcome it might have been to have been able to say to someone – almost anyone: 'You'll never guess what just happened.'

Early next morning, Mick collected a *Proton Mira* and drove up the main highway to Ipoh. All the way, he was reminded of the lesson he had learned the night before. The word 'tropical' signified rampant nature, restrained by man but never totally controlled. The road took him to the west of the central highlands where, he had read, the British had built summer homes to escape the worst of the heat. On the lower slopes, regimented rows of trees spread in every direction. The ranks were so precise that, when the angle was right, he could see the diagonals were as neat and straight as the parallels.

This was his view for scores of miles until the road continued north in the company of a river, sharing the valley as it twisted through high outcrops of rock. The river ran only as a trickle before the afternoon rain and fleetingly Mick saw the man from his photograph – or thought he did. He was riding bareback along the riverbed with his mount carefully selecting safe spots for its hooves among the dry, rounded stones. The image flashed by. Mick looked for a place to stop but there was nowhere and, before he could think any more about it, he was taking the slip road to Ipoh where he had booked a room in the *Excelsior Hotel*.

The drive into the centre was a nightmare. Traffic came at him from every direction. The moped riders in their back-to-front tops zoomed about him like Kamikaze pilots. Despite the car's air-conditioning, Mick was wired and sweaty when he pulled the car onto the hotel's frontage. A valet-parking assistant took the keys from him and the doorman called a bell-hop for Mick's bags. Three people. Malaysia was proud of its 100% employment rate but so many of the workers had meaningless jobs.

After check-in, while a porter took his bag to the room, Mick sauntered across the marble-floored atrium to the concierge's desk.

The badge on the man's lapel told Mick that he was addressing Anwar. 'I wonder whether you can help me. I'm only in Ipoh for a couple of days and I'm very keen to see Kellie's Castle while I am here. Do you know it?'

The man nodded in a way that could have been interpreted as a respectful bow. 'Yes, sir. Of course. Do you have a car?'

'I do. But is it close enough for a taxi?'

'Yes. It's 20 clicks out on the Batu Gajah road.'

'Clicks?'

'Sorry, sir. 20 kilometres. Possibly 10 miles or so?'

'I think I'll take a taxi.' He looked at his watch. It was approaching 2pm. 'Is it open this afternoon?'

'It is always open, sir. It's a ruin. There is nothing to see. Just an old building.'

'So I could see it this afternoon?'

'Any time.'

After a quick visit to his room to freshen up, Mick returned to the ground floor and went out onto the forecourt. After the air-conditioning in the hotel, the heat hit him as if he'd walked into blast furnace. He took off his sweater and carried it over his arm as he approached the taxi rank.

A Chinese man was leaning nonchalantly on the bonnet of his black Mercedes. As Mick approached, the driver stubbed his cigarette out on the sole of his trainers and deposited the stub in the breast pocket of his vividly coloured Hawaiian shirt.

'Kellie's Castle?'

'Sure, boss. Jump in.' He smiled through misshapen yellow teeth.

The interior of the car smelled of stale cigarettes, body odour and something rancid, indeterminable, as if someone had recently been sick. Mick was torn between opening the window for the fresher air outside and keeping cool. He opted for the fresher air, sitting in the sagging leather bench seat, leaning forward so his forehead could rest against the interior above the window opening.

'You been Kellie's Castle before, boss?'

He shook his head. 'No'

'You feeling okay?'

Mick turned back into the interior. It was the faded vomit stench, rather than anything emanating from the driver, that was making his stomach lurch.

The driver grinned into his rear-view mirror. 'Some damn Bumi smuggled durian into car one night. Had car fumigated since but that damn durian smell it don't go way. They say it taste like heaven and smell like shit!'

'I wish you had said.' Mick muttered and resumed his nose's vigil at the window.

The driver was looking in the mirror again. 'Not much see Kellie's Castle. But I show you round. I show all tourists. Take you temple. See Kellie-man's statue. You know story of Kellie-man?'

They were now leaving the city and Mick realised that he wasn't going to be able to stay in the car for the full journey. If, as the concierge at the *Excelsior* implied, the castle site was deserted he would have to rely on this cab to get back. Another half an hour in this fetid atmosphere was a prospect he couldn't contemplate. He was irritated with the driver for using the car when he knew that it was so rank. 'Yes, I know the story. The man Kellie was my grandfather's brother...' At that moment, they passed a hotel on the edge of the city and he spotted a taxi rank with two cars. 'Stop! Stop here, please.'

The driver evidently thought he was going to be sick and swerved to the side of the road. 'You okay, boss?'

'Yes. Look I'm going to take a walk.' Why did he feel the need to explain? 'How much do I owe you?' He paid and gave the driver a generous tip that he immediately regretted.

'Thanks, boss!' The wheels of the Mercedes squealed as it

performed a U-turn and headed back to the city centre. Mick waited for it to be out of sight and strode across to the cab rank. The driver of the front car wore a turban. 'Where to?' he asked.

Mick sat on the back seat and consulted his watch. Perhaps he had been too ambitious to want to see the castle on his first day. He didn't know what to expect there and he realised that if he went now he'd probably feel constrained by the driver's waiting time. No, despite the awful prospect of driving in the traffic once again, he thought it would be best to drive himself there tomorrow morning. He'd seen the route he'd have to take. He'd have all the time in the world tomorrow.

The Sikh driver was looking over his shoulder expectantly. 'Where to?'

Mick sighed. 'Back to Ipoh, please. *The Excelsior Hotel.*'

8

When Mick arrived in Ipoh, he had been primed for romance by his encounter with Amy on the flight to Kuala Lumpur. His introductory days in Malaysia had disoriented him (if such a thing is possible in the orient) and heightened his isolation. That first morning in Ipoh the stench-memory of yesterday's durian-defiled taxi was still lodged at the back of his throat but he was fated to undergo one more trial before his salvation.

At the restaurant, Mick discovered that his room rate did not include breakfast. He would have to pay extra. Undeterred, he found his way to the long buffet cabinet of local items spread on banana leaves: various types of curry, dishes of noodles, rice dishes mixed with various meats. These all appeared to be cold. There was a small plate with a few slices of cheese that appeared to have dried out from exposure to the cabinet's lights. Further along there were bains-Marie: he lifted the lids, bacon in one, pale sausages in another, tomatoes, and hash browns. A sign caught his attention: *English Breakfas: Egg at choice with beef bacon, turkey sausage, hash brown's and toast.* The price was insanely low compared to what he would pay in the UK, even in a greasy spoon.

'Can I help you, sir?' The man on the other side of the counter had the name label 'Tifanu' and appeared to be a local Malay.

'I'm going to have the English Breakfast, please. No egg.'

'How would you like the egg?'

'I don't want egg.' Mick had an aversion to eggs cooked by others. More often than not, they were either undercooked, so that he had to negotiate near-raw embryonic fluid, or they were overdone to a consistency that made them bounce. For as long as he could remember he had only eaten eggs he had cooked himself.

Tifanu took a plate and used tongs to compile Mick's breakfast: beef bacon, turkey sausage, two hash browns and a slice of white bread, toasted. He placed it on a tray and slid it along to the pay point.

Tifanu himself appeared behind the till. 'That will be...' and he quoted a price 5 Ringitts more than was advertised.

Mick checked the sign. 'No, it's...' pointing to the figure written there.

Tifanu drew himself up to his full height. 'That's for the *English Breakfas*, sir. You have chosen items separately.'

'But it's *less* than the English breakfast. I haven't had an egg.' The difference of 5 Ringitts meant nothing to him but he baulked at the absurdity of being charged more for less.

'Sir, you haven't had an *English Breakfas*.'

'If you put an egg on this plate I would pay the price on the sign, right?'

'Yes, sir. What egg would you like, boiled, scrambled or fried? It will take a few minutes, of course.'

Mick automatically looked at his watch. He wasn't pushed for time but the food on his plate was going cold and a queue of other guests was building behind him. 'Just put an uncooked egg in its shell on the plate, charge me for the English Breakfast and I'll give you the egg back.' He smiled the smile of a man who had beaten the system.

Tifanu shook his head. His expression changed to that of a vet about to tell Mick that his dog had not long for this world. 'We can't sell you a *raw* egg, sir. I'm sure that would be against our health ordinances. Now, how would you like the egg cooked?'

Mick put up his palms and admitted defeat. 'Okay I'll pay for what's on the plate.'

As he picked at the assortment of Halal meats and the hash browns that he now wished he hadn't ordered, Mick felt again the loneliness that had gripped him since arriving in KL. How much better would his life be if there had been somebody waiting for him at the table watching this ludicrous pantomime? Being able to recount the details of the interaction between him and the man at the till would have been so much fun. He might have dressed it up to make it even more ridiculous: perhaps extending the interplay further before he gave up. What was the man's name? Tifanu. That was it. *Breakfast at Tifanu's!* He laughed out loud, much to the consternation of the Chinese gentleman at the next table who was noisily slurping up the gelatinous contents of a savoury noodle bowl and following each mouthful with a bite of a sugared doughnut.

Because Mick had slept in, because he was still battling the effects of jet lag, and because he had followed his breakfast with a leisurely coffee while he read a couple of chapters of *Captain Corelli's Mandolin*, it was approaching midday when he left the restaurant. In truth, he had been procrastinating: he wasn't looking forward to the drive out of the city. Nevertheless, now steeled for the fray, he intended to go to his room, freshen up and then drive out to the castle. He was heading for the lift when he became aware of somebody approaching fast at an angle. It was a woman hurrying to pass in front of him but, as he slowed, she appeared to change her mind and with it her direction. They collided shoulder to shoulder and she spun round spilling a carton of leaflets.

They scattered across the polished floor, skidding under the coffee tables and easy chairs that lined the lobby.

'I'm so sorry,' Mick said, even though he was sure that it was the woman whose late swerve had caused the crash.

She was already squatting, gathering leaflets together. 'No. I am so sorry,' she said. 'It was my fault. I wasn't looking where I was going. I was too much in a hurry.'

Two things occurred to Mick in this moment. Firstly, that the woman was Chinese but, uncharacteristically in his limited experience, her face was thin with impossibly high cheek bones beneath wide brown eyes that had a limpid, depthless quality. Secondly, her ease with the English language. The few words she had spoken were said without hesitation and were easily understood. He knelt beside her and scrabbled around for her leaflets.

'No,' she said. 'Leave this to me. It was my fault. I'm always in such a rush.' She was now looking at Mick full in the face and something about him appeared to fluster her. She put her fingers over her lips as if to stop herself saying more. A red colour spread up her neck from the collar of her cheongsam.

They both returned to rootling on the floor for leaflets. Other guests joined in and when the job was complete she stood alongside Mick with the carton at her feet. She was tall. Her slender height brought to Mick's mind a drift of bamboo swaying under the influence of a warm breeze. Perhaps she was a dancer – her body had a relaxed ease of movement that made him think of Ginger Rogers gliding across a dance floor and sighing like a fainting damsel into Fred Astaire's arms. The woman was waiting for him to say something and held out her hand for the leaflet he was still holding.

He looked at it. *The Top Ten Attractions of Perak* and there on the front page at number three was a picture of Kellie's Castle. 'Sorry, the last one,' he said, passing it across. Her fingers were long and tipped by crimson nails.

'Thank you.' She looked down as if to check the shine on his shoes.

Her dark hair was tied at the back in a bun and held in place by a flower. 'That's very pretty,' he said. 'What flower is it?'

She touched it and the action straightened her back, emphasising her figure. 'It isn't a real lotus. It's just for show.'

'Your English is very good.'

'Thank you. I need it to be. You've worked out from the leaflets, I suppose. I'm a tour guide.'

'In Ipoh? It's not exactly a tourist resort.'

'You think so? Actually, Perak has many touristic sites. You should enrol on one of my tours.'

She's flirting with me, Mick thought. 'Would *you* be my guide if I enrolled?' He hoped that she would not be offended by his being so obvious.

'Sad to say, I can't guarantee it. But...' She looked down at the carton and then across the lobby as if she was late for an appointment.

'Sorry. Of course, you're in a hurry. Another time.' As he said it he recalled his conversation with Amy on the plane. Was this what it had prepared him for? He tried to think of what to say to keep her there. Would it be too forward to invite her to lunch? What would be acceptable in her culture?

'Look,' she said. 'I'm only here to restock the hotel's shelves with leaflets. I have no tours booked today...' she raised her eyebrows. Her full lips parted slightly and the tip of her tongue was there briefly. If ever there was a signal...

'Perhaps,' he said, 'we could have coffee...' he looked at his watch '... or is it too early for lunch?'

She consulted a gold wristwatch. 'Coffee?'

He nodded. 'Coffee. Let me give you a hand with that box.' He bent to pick it up. 'Shall we stay here?'

'No, my car is around the corner. There's an excellent coffee shop in the mall there. Shall we go?'

'Yes... excellent.' He felt as if a Texas tornado had twisted him round and spat him out. He tucked the box under his arm. 'My name is Mick... Mick Kellie.'

She nodded. 'It is so nice to meet you, Mr Mick.' She held out her right hand. 'My name is Nancy Lee.'

9

After Luis Escobar's death in November 1990, Nancy Lee was disturbed more by the way her father had used her than she was by her acquaintance's demise. I imagine that when she arrived in the penthouse the morning Luis's body was found, her father was in the dining room eating eggs and beef bacon. Through the open screen doors behind him, low sunshine was bouncing off the swimming pool. He didn't greet her or give her time to sit down. 'The police called the hotel. First thing this morning your Mister Escobar was found dead by one of our gardeners out at the Kellas House.'

She was unable to process anything beyond the word 'dead'. It was if her brain was running in too high a gear and an obstacle had made its engine stall. She was aware that she was lowering herself onto a seat but it wasn't anything she willed.

'Lai Ping? Are you all right?'

Her hands trembled. Why should this be? It wasn't as if Luis had meant anything to her. 'How? What happened?'

'The police say he must have had an accident. It seems he was on the roof, possibly in the dark, and fell.'

A sob rose in her constricted throat and she covered her mouth, not to stifle a moan of despair but rather, she realised, there was a danger she might fall into a fit of giggles. Anything now could tip her into a state of collapse, sniggering like a schoolgirl. If any man ever was destined to die early it was the chain-smoking Mr Escobar. But not like this.

'Look, Lai Ping. You're going to have to pull yourself together. The police are coming to see me. They'll want to talk about his meeting with me yesterday afternoon.'

'What happened?' Different thoughts rolled round her head like clothes in a tumble drier but one kept appearing at the front making itself distinct, set apart from the tangle: was her father responsible?

'It's like I told you. He fell from the roof of Kellas House. That's what it looks like.'

'No. I mean what happened when you met him?'

S Y stood up, sidled round the table and sat alongside Nancy taking both her hands in his. 'You're shaking, Lai Ping. This must be a shock. You have spent a long time in his company and now...' He placed a knuckle under her chin and lifted it so that they were looking directly into each other's eyes. 'Daughter, when the police come I'm going to say that my discussion with him *was* about the house but it was merely a conversation between a man who had a family connection to it and the owner. A *discussion of general interest.* There is no need to complicate matters by mentioning that nonsense about Harrison and Crosfield, is there?'

She didn't answer. She was thinking about why he should be saying this.

'Is there!'

She pushed his hand away from her chin. 'No! There's no reason to tell them the truth.'

'Lai Ping, you know how things are. The police... the situation with the Bumis. We don't want to tread on a sleeping dog.'

She snatched a napkin from the table and wiped the tears from her cheeks. 'You want me to say that I just took him round and that we didn't talk about anything other than the usual tourist things.'

'You're a very smart girl. A real *chip off the old block.*' He used the expression in English.

'And when he wasn't with me, when he went off on his researches, I—'

'—you didn't know what he was doing.'

'Are you going to tell me what really happened?'

'It's like I said. We discussed the house, I pointed out that he had no hard evidence to back up any claim he might be considering and I agreed that we would put up some sort of memorial to his grandfather.'

'But why would he go back to the house—'

S Y's patience was stretching thin. 'He said he was going for one last look. I have no idea why. Perhaps he was thinking of where to put his father's memorial.'

'But I'm to lie to the police and tell them that, as far as I know, Luis Escobar had no reason to talk to you about the house in anything but general terms.'

He put her hands to his lips. 'Not lie exactly. You are merely not telling the whole story.'

'And I'm doing this for *you*, Father?' She dreaded his response. If he said 'yes' it would be a tacit admission of some level of involvement in Escobar's death.

He smiled as if he understood what she was thinking. 'No, my child. You should do it because it's the most certain way of keeping our dream for the new hotel alive. We can't allow anything to put it in danger.'

A Perak police investigation into a case that might negatively affect the Lee family was never going to be rigorous. By the end of the weekend, it was agreed that, triggered by the knowledge that S Y Lee had agreed to put up a memorial to Luis's grandfather and perhaps to select a suitable site for it, Luis had returned to the castle. The police hadn't been able to locate the taxi driver who had driven him there but it would only be a matter of time.

Escobar had probably gone up to the roof to watch the sunset over the plantations. What westerner would be able to resist the opportunity if it presented itself? Perhaps overcome by the intensity of the experience, he had not noticed that he had strayed close to the unguarded edge. He lost his footing and fell approximately ten metres onto the gravelled, cement path below. The autopsy revealed that death had come instantaneously; Luis had broken his neck.

It appeared from his passport that the victim had no relatives and the police contacted the Portuguese Embassy in KL for guidance. The body was to be kept in the mortuary until its repatriation.

Nancy didn't go to see his body. Why would she? She had spent part of four days in his company. She had overcome her initial revulsion for the stink of spent cigarettes that polluted the air around him and she had learned to make allowances for his unkempt appearance but she held no trace of affection for him.

By the following Tuesday she had returned to KL, to her work in the bank. I imagine that by the end of the week she was well into the process of forgetting that he had ever come into her life.

When she went home the following Christmas, Nancy was shocked to see how much her mother had deteriorated. She was bedbound, mostly asleep or semi-conscious because of the pain-killing drugs. S Y Lee had arranged for her to have nursing care night and day. Her mother's presence at the end of the corridor on the eighth floor of the *Leeyate Plaza Hotel* laid a blanket of sadness over what would normally have been a celebration and Nancy couldn't get away quickly enough. She left before the western New Year's Day.

Chinese New Year had come and gone before Nancy's

father called with the dreaded news. Her mother's time was near. Lang-ren had been told to pick Nancy up from the bank and drive to Ipoh with all speed. As it was happening, Nancy recognised she was living a cliché, but it *was* as if her mother was holding out for her arrival.

A Buddhist priest was in attendance and Nancy interrupted him mid-prayer when she was ushered into the room. Her mother's head was barely heavy enough to make an impression on the pillow. Her cheeks were hollow, her thin lips blue. Her breathing was so shallow that there was no discernible movement of the bed covers that lay flat upon the wisp of her body.

Nancy's father hovered beside the bed as if he had an important appointment elsewhere. The blinds were shut and light was provided by candles set around the bed. A censer swung from a tripod stand with smoke trailing from its belly. Nancy looked at her father and raised an eyebrow.

He shuffled towards her but stopped before he was close enough to make physical contact a possibility. 'It's what she would have wanted,' he whispered. He nodded towards the priest who resumed his low chanting.

Next day, S Y arranged for his wife's coffin to be moved to one of the hotel's conference rooms where the priests from the Temple Kek Lok Tong set up an altar and a scale replica of the Tian Tan Buddha. It was there that the Lee family from all the Malaysian branches and the workers in its various businesses filed past to pay their respects.

The day after the funeral, on the morning that Nancy intended to return to KL, she was summoned by her father. He sat behind the desk, his back to the window with its panoramic view over the cloud-clothed, distant highlands.

Come in, Lai Ping,' he said. 'Tea?'

She refused.

'Coffee, then. Something before you travel south.'

'No. Nothing, Father. Thank you.'

'It's been a sad time.'

Nancy nodded, half smiling. 'But she is out of pain. If all that mumbo-jumbo has done its job, her spirit will have found a better home.'

He shook his head. 'Awah, daughter, you should show respect for our traditions.'

'I know you don't believe that stuff any more than I do, Father. Don't pretend.' She indicated one of the easy chairs. 'May I?'

S Y stepped from behind his desk. 'Of course,' he said and sat opposite her.

'What did you want to see me about?'

'It's a delicate subject and I couldn't raise it while your mother was suffering so—'

'But—?'

'But now I think the time is right to talk about your future. It is time for you to come back into the family.'

Nancy's instinct was to leap to her feet and protest; instead she settled her backside deeper into the seat.

S Y patted the air with his palms. 'I can see you don't like what I'm saying, daughter,' he whispered. 'Please don't overreact.'

'I'm not—'

'Please don't interrupt.'

She gritted her teeth and the muscles in her cheeks pulsed in protest. She had kept herself in check and yet he was accusing her of insolence.

'How old are you now – 32? It's time for you to settle down. I've been very lax and allowed you to have your own life in KL. But now it's time for you to come back to Ipoh. It's time for you to take your responsibilities to me and to our company.'

She stood up. She was a helpless teenager again. In her

frustration, there was only one course open to her. She stamped her foot. 'Sorry, father...' she completed the sentence in English as she made for the lift entrance. '... there's fat chance of that happening.' She stabbed the call button and had to wait, fuming, with her back to the desk, while the lift doors moved agonisingly slowly apart.

By the middle of the year Nancy was living in an Ipoh city-centre townhouse in one of the Lee family's compounds and was lined up to be married. She had stood her ground for two months after storming out of her father's office. The threat of losing him counted more than his threats to cut off her allowance and make her, as he put it, 'dead to the family'. When S Y introduced the idea of arranging her marriage, it had given her a reason for returning to Ipoh even if it was only to remonstrate with him.

The man the family had lined up for her was her second cousin Lee Zhi Bo. He'd originally been given the western name Simon and it told her everything she needed to know about him that he had chosen Tommy as his a *nom de guerre* after he had watched *Goodfellas* and seen Joe Pesci's turn as the psychopath, Tommy DeVito. Although he was four years Nancy's junior, he had already established a reputation in KL as a womaniser. This was facilitated by his position as manager of the city's chain of *Leeyate Karaoke Bars*. He could be seen cruising in his top-of-the-range convertible BMW with the roof down, transporting a bevy of giggling Filipina bar girls – 'lounge hostesses' – from one of his clubs to another.

Nancy, bowed to pressure and agreed to consider the possibility of the engagement but stayed in Ipoh to keep a distance from her prospective husband. She took up the position of running the European export arm of *Leeyate Holdings*, the previous post-holder having been summarily dismissed to make way for her, and enrolled for English elocution lessons so she could be a more effective communicator with the Leeyate world-wide subsidiaries.

S Y still held on to his vision of an expanded hospitality business with the *Leeyate Castle Spa Hotel* as the jewel in the crown but, during those years, the company's cash position never grew to the critical mass needed to turn the dream into reality. Nevertheless, he would summon Nancy to his office, show her the plans again and entrust her with the sacred duty of turning her father's dream into reality should anything happen to him.

With her in Ipoh and Tommy in KL, Nancy could bemoan their lack of opportunities to meet and further their relationship. Luckily for her, Tommy was as reluctant to settle down as she was. As engagements go, hers didn't and this was fine by her.

Nancy acknowledged that her body clock was ticking and at some time she would have to accept her fate as decreed by her father. She was old-fashioned enough to know that she would do her duty by her husband and this would result in children. Their presence would force her to settle down. She knew Tommy would be unfaithful. Here again her complex relationship with her culture confused her. She knew that she could live in the comfort of the Leeyate business family, making compromises, accepting her lot, but she also knew she could never be entirely happy.

Over the next two years, she and her fiancé spent some weekends together. When they weren't anticipating sex, having sex or resting after sex she would read or watch television while he went to the gym or played *Pokémon* on his *Nintendo Game Boy*.

As far as Nancy was concerned, the sex was not fulfilling. Foreplay consisted entirely of preparing her man to perform. The concept of Nancy deriving pleasure from what was happening was as alien to him as the idea that he could make his *Game Boy* orgasm if he pressed the buttons in the right order. Being older, Nancy felt some responsibility for tutoring him in the finer arts but even broaching the subject caused a frown to appear on his forehead and his eyes to cloud.

She didn't tell him that she was taking the contraceptive pill and he never asked. To suggest that he might wear a condom was akin to asking him to operate his *Game Boy* wearing boxing gloves.

To Nancy's surprise, the unsatisfactory nature of her impending marriage troubled her less as time went by. She foresaw a day when she would stop taking the pill and, if it happened, her pregnancy would mean that her relationship with Tommy would be forced to move to the next stage. She was not yet 35. There was plenty of time.

This is how it was when, in September 1995, her father called to ask if she would act as guide for another westerner who was asking about Kellie's Castle.

'The castle is on the tourist trail now, Father. What's so special about this one?'

'He arrived in KL and yesterday, according to our informant there, he mentioned that he's coming to visit Ipoh and see the house. His name is Kellie. He told the taxi driver who picked him up this afternoon that he's related to William Kellie-Smith.'

10

After dropping the carton of leaflets in the boot of Nancy's modest *Proton* saloon, Mick followed her to the mall entrance where a doorman pressed the button that activated the power-assisted doors. I imagine Mick shaking his head at this example of the country's full employment policy but being quickly distracted when his gaze homed in on the taut, but not stretched, silver material that encased Nancy's hips.

When they were through the door and she turned to him, her face was almost a caricature; flawless skin, razor-sharp cheek bones, large almond eyes and full lips.

'There's a coffee shop I go to, down there.' She pointed from the balcony to the floor below. The *Windsor Tea Shoppe* was guarded by a rank of tables along its frontage, each set with a lace edged white cloth over red and white gingham. 'I would prefer inside if you don't mind. It will be cooler,' she said.

The air-conditioning in the mall had already forced Mick to don the sweater he had carried during the walk from the hotel. Nancy conjured a cashmere cardigan from her shoulder bag.

Once inside, she led him past the front ranks of tables to the rear wall where there were four cubicles. She chose the one farthest from the counter and indicated he should sit opposite. It was a bench seat with a cushioned back. A female server came and they ordered cappuccinos. Mick was relieved to see that they were produced from an Italian machine on the other side of the counter.

He turned back to Nancy sitting opposite, smiling expectantly. He couldn't quite believe how this had happened. 'So, you're a tour guide,' he said.

'Some of the time, yes. I work in an office but I do some tours to help out a friend. It is sort of part-time.'

'Your English is very good.' The compliment echoed. 'Sorry. I've said that already.'

She put a hand up to her cheek. It seemed to be a reflex response; there was no evidence of her blushing. 'Thank you. I lived in England for three years for my education.'

'Oh? What did you study there?'

'Business Management at Kingston Polytechnic.'

'Kingston in Surrey?'

'Yes, why?'

'Because I live in Richmond just down the road.'

'Of course. I know it. It is very posh, Richmond. The river there is beautiful. I remember Hampton Court and Richmond Park.'

Hampton Court was west along the river but he decided it might be bad form to correct her. 'When were you there?'

She waited while the waitress served the two coffees. Her eyes reminded him of a fawn and now, perhaps surprised by the directness of his question, they took on a startled look that accentuated their size and the pitch-black, deep pools at their centres. 'I was at Kingston in the early 1980s'

He calculated: if she had been in her late teens fifteen years ago, she would be in her early 30s now. He could be as much as ten years older than her.

'Anyway, that's enough about me,' she said, smoothing the silk of her cheongsam along her thighs and crossing her legs at the ankle. 'What brings you to Ipoh?'

'I only arrived yesterday. I want to do a bit of sightseeing. One sight in particular, actually.'

'Which one?'

'Kellie's Castle. Out on the Batu Gajah road.'

Nancy nodded. 'I know it. There is a romantic story attached to it, you know, about the man who built it – William Kellie-Smith.'

'He was my grandfather's brother.'

'Who?'

'William Kellie-Smith. His brother, Kenneth, was my grandfather.'

'Really! You're a member of the Kellie-Smith family? That's amazing!'

'Not really. I didn't know anything about the family's connection to Malaysia until a few weeks ago. It was a total coincidence. My business partner who's actually my cousin, had a travel magazine article that mentioned the castle and the romantic story of how it was built but never lived in. I didn't know of it or the family's connection to Malaysia until then.'

'Well, you're in luck, Mr Mick Kellie-Smith.'

'Our branch of the family dropped the 'Smith' part. I'm just a plain 'Kellie'. What makes you say that – I'm in luck?'

She spread her arms and sat back, accentuating the line of her body from her ankle to the lotus in her hair. 'Who better to guide you on a tour of the castle than me? I know its history. I can tell you about the rooms, the secret tunnels, the temple—'

'The statue of William?'

'Of course, the statue. Yes, but it is not exactly a statue. It is more what you'd call a statuette. It is on the temple roof.'

He shook his head. 'I don't—'

'I will explain it all when we get there. Now, when do you want to go?'

'I was heading out that way when we bumped into each other...'

'This was very lucky for you, I think. How about this afternoon?' She consulted her watch. 'I need to change first, grab a sandwich. We'll go in my car. I'll call for you at your hotel at 2.30pm, okay?'

She was rushing him into a decision that conflicted with his original plan. Would he feel more relaxed on his own, communing with his long-dead relatives? He remembered how he had felt sightseeing in KL. His own company hadn't been enough. Had he learned nothing from his encounter on the plane?

Nancy leant back against the cushions and watched him expectantly. There was a secret smile on her lips and her eyes were wide. She was evidently not used to being refused by a man. This woman, incredibly, was trying to persuade him that they should spend more time together. The first opportunity presented by this uncanny trip had slipped by and he wasn't going to let it happen again. 'Yes, 2.30pm. I'll wait in the lobby. Just pull into the forecourt and I'll join you.'

'Good.'

The penny dropped. Of course she'd been pushy. She was closing a business deal. She had persuaded him to employ her as his personal tour guide. How had he been so stupid? There was going to be a bill at the end of the excursion. 'I'm sorry. I should have asked about your rates,' he said. 'What does it cost?'

She dismissed this with a wave of her hand. 'Fee! No fee. It will be my pleasure to show Mr Mick Kellie-Smith around his ancestral home. It will be my pleasure.'

Nearly two hours later, Mick waited in the lobby watching the entrance anxiously. She was late. Only ten minutes, but it was enough to make him think that perhaps she had second thoughts. She had said 2.30, he was sure of it.

Her *Proton Mira* swept into the forecourt and stopped by the valet parking station. Immediately, one of the attendants stepped forward. Nancy waved him away as she emerged and slid a pair of large-paned sunglasses up over her forehead. The way they tagged in her dark hair and her model's pose – a vision in black leggings and a white stiff-collared blouse – reminded Mick of Audrey Hepburn in *Breakfast at Tiffany's*. He remembered his argument with Tifanu. He chuckled; his life *had* taken an unnatural turn.

He hurried out to meet her, hitting the overpowering wall of hot air. She held the car door open for him and he slid inside. When she had settled into the driver's seat, he said, 'Good afternoon. This is very kind of you.'

'It is my pleasure,' she said, slipping the sun shades back down over her eyes with one hand while the other went to her neck which had started to flush red.

The car's interior was cool and he should have been able to relax, but he found that sitting so close to Nancy was unsettling. He was overwhelmed by a fog of tension, anticipation and expectation and that, along with the scent of a perfume he didn't recognise, threatened to smother them both. Yes, it was something to do with their proximity in the jarring mundanity of the car's plastic-enclosed space but there was more. It reminded him of when he was much younger, on his first date with his wife. He wondered if Nancy felt anything.

As if to answer, she pushed the gear shift into first and let the clutch in too quickly. The car bounded forward and stalled. She stifled a giggle and turned the ignition again. A crimson tide spread up from the neck of her blouse. This time the car leapt forward and was immediately going too fast in the confined space of the hotel pull-in. She grasped the wheel and swerved to avoid the kerb as the forecourt narrowed. The front tyre clipped the edge and the impact bounced the car to the middle, where it stopped only inches from the give-way line marking the entrance to the main road. A passing Mercedes blared out a long warning.

Nancy took a deep breath and wiped her hands on her ski-pants. She turned the rear-view mirror towards her and checked her make-up, running her tongue across the front of her teeth.

'Are you okay? Mick asked.

She turned to face him. 'Sorry, I am not used to this car.'

'We're not in any hurry.'

'I know.' She pulled her blouse down so that it pleated over the waistband of her trousers. Now in control, she drove with fluid movements. She focused on the traffic around them and Mick, remembering how he had felt driving in the city, knew not to distract her. It gave him the opportunity to study her profile. It was her lips that commanded his attention. They were parted slightly in concentration. Her back was straight, her head held imperiously. Her torso had a slightness that intrigued him. There was something intoxicating in the contrast between the immodesty of women's clothing at home and Nancy's understated elegance.

They left the city limits and she turned briefly. 'It won't be long. Are you excited?'

He thought about it. He had come half way round the world to see this. He *should* be excited. But any anticipation of visiting his supposed ancestral home had been overtaken by another more urgent, animal excitement. He tried to rekindle his enthusiasm for the quest but the embers had cooled. Should he confide in her? Should he tell her he that *she* was the object of his interest now? That he wanted to spend time with her. That their destination was an irrelevance. 'Yes,' he said, disappointing himself as the word emerged. 'Excited!'

The land around them was flat and rows of palm trees marched off in every direction as far as he could see. The sun was still high and, in the cool of the car, he had to remind himself how hot it would be when they stepped out.

They turned off the main road following a sign for Batu Raja. This was now a single carriageway and the jungle lined it menacingly. He recalled his night at the restaurant when the animals closed in as soon as the humans departed. It would only take a few months of neglect for this road to be obliterated by creeping vines, advancing stands of bamboo and the accompanying fauna.

'That's it.' She pointed to the right.

Ahead of them, the top of a square turret peaked out over the trees in the same way as it did in the photograph folded into his wallet. He could make out the tops of window openings that bore carved stone lintels. The car followed a bend round to the right and there it was. The house stood in a clearing. The earth had been banked up to create a platform for its footings. On the front of the embankment the words 'Kellie's Castle' had been picked out in white stones.

The red sandstone absorbed the sun's rays rather than reflected them and this gave the frontage a baleful look not leavened by the two rows of unglazed windows that stared back blankly. He shivered. Had Nancy turned up the *Proton*'s air-conditioning?

She steered the car into an opening in the fence and pulled to a halt by a signboard. In front of them, a small bridge traversed a shallow fast-flowing stream that twinkled in the sunlight. There were no other cars. They were alone.

11

Mick's realisation that the visit to the house was now of secondary importance was confirmed as he stood waiting for Nancy to prepare for her guiding duties. She opened the rear door, reached in and picked up a hat and shoes. She leaned on the car to change her shoes, stretched, as if aware that he was watching her, and put on the bamboo Chinese sunhat that tied beneath her chin with a black ribbon. Large Ray-Ban sunglasses hid her eyes so he couldn't tell whether she was watching him watch her, but he didn't care; he couldn't drag his eyes away.

She smiled broadly, dragging his attention back to her eminently kissable mouth. 'Shall we?'

He nodded.

She led the way along a gravel path. He was mesmerised by the swing of her slim hips as she climbed the steps up to the base of the wall that radiated heat from the day's sun. She turned to face him. 'This is actually the back of the house. If you look behind you, all you can see is the Kellas Estate plantation. This is the best view. Let's go this way.'

He followed her to the left beneath the square tower and in through a narrow entrance. It became clear that this wing was only one room deep and all the rooms enjoyed the plantation view. An open-sided passage extended ahead of them.

'After William Kellie-Smith died the old house and the construction site were looted for materials and only the shells of the rooms remain. In the war, during the Japanese occupation, stonework from the original house was taken and used to build blockhouses and such-like.'

He looked around. 'Which original house?'

She pointed out of the first opening to their left. 'There, across what was going to be a courtyard. The intention was to link the two houses with a single storey building. After the war, the new owners made what was left of the old house safe and preserved as much of the new house as was left. All the rooms were probably wood-panelled. There was a magnificent staircase in the reception hall behind us. All gone.'

Mick nodded. He was reminded again of the greedy jungle devouring anything in its path. 'Who are the owners? Who maintains what's left?'

'One of the local plantation companies – it owns all this...' she waved her arms expansively '... the Kellas Estate.'

'Kellas – the village in Scotland where my grandfather was born.'

'Exactly. Also the name of the first house – Kellas House.'

Mick followed Nancy along the corridors on both floors, dutifully peering into the empty rooms as she described their proposed functions. At the far end on the first floor they came to the stairway that took them through a doorway onto the roof. Mick followed her to the edge where the view looked over the car park with her solitary car, the stream and the ranks of trees stretching beyond towards the distant hills and the afternoon sun.

She put out a warning hand. 'Don't go too close to the edge.'

'It's strange there are no barriers.'

'Many people come here but there's only ever been one accident.' Her voice wavered. 'A man slipped and fell from here five years ago.'

'Was he okay?'

Nancy's face was shielded by the wide brim of her hat. Behind her sunshades, she seemed to be seeking something on the horizon as though her thoughts were elsewhere. Her face was a beautiful, oriental mask; serene and unattainable. 'No. He died.' She bowed her head for a moment, sighed and turned away.

Mick followed her to look out over what would have been the courtyard. It was a scrubland of impacted soil, with, to the left, the ruins of the Kellas House. The outer faces of its pale, stone blocks had been polished to a matt sheen that glowed orange. There was a fence bearing a sign in English warning visitors not to trespass because of the danger of falling 'masonary'.

Nancy moved closer and her left shoulder touched his arm. 'It was a much prettier house, the first one.'

'But it didn't make the same statement as this. It wasn't a work of love.'

'I like to think this castle was meant to be a declaration of love for the country as well,' Nancy said. 'It was a promise to his wife: we're going to be here permanently. This is where our children will grow up. I will be able take my son to the top of the tower and tell him that one day all this will be his. These people will be your family.'

He should have been moved by his great-uncle's folly, but her eloquence affected him more. 'I hadn't thought about that aspect. How he must have fallen in love with your country. It makes it all the more poignant. All those hopes dashed when he died in Portugal.'

She stepped away. 'Would you like to see the basement?' Without waiting for an answer, she retraced their steps to the staircase and at the ground floor she took him along the cloister to the round tower where an open doorway led to stone steps going down.

The room was illuminated only by small openings set into window wells outside and they had to wait until their eyes adjusted to the comparative dark. The basement extended a short way under the length of the house. The back wall comprised a series of vaulted alcoves, presumably for wine and other provisions that needed to be kept cool. The floor here was loose sand. Their arms touched and Mick was profoundly aware that they were alone.

How could he take advantage of the situation? There was a cultural chasm between them. How would she react if he tried to... to profess his attraction towards her? Could he act as if they were in a film and take her in his arms and kiss her? Even with the supposed magic that accompanied his trip, he had no licence to act precipitously. Given their different cultures, probably less.

He cursed himself for his inaction as he feigned interest in a part of the wall that was roughly bricked over. 'What's there?' he asked.

'It was the start of a tunnel that led alongside the stream all the way to the temple. Nobody knows how long it's been bricked up. Whoever owned it after the war must have done it because of safety. There is a rumour that Kellie-Smith's Rolls Royce is still down there.'

'Has nobody asked to excavate it – to dig out the tunnel?'

'Not that we know. The locals – native Malaysians – want to forget about the colonial past. They'd probably pull this place down if it was up to them.'

'Why is it still standing then?'

'The company that owns it is Chinese.' She turned away and hurried back to the stairway. 'We must go back to Ipoh.'

'What about the temple?'

She climbed a few steps and, as soon as there was sufficient light, looked at her watch. 'We have time before it gets dark but we should hurry.'

They strode side-by-side to the pedestrian bridge over the stream and, without crossing, turned right and followed another path that took them into a copse of native trees fringed with colourful blossom: icing sugar white, lilac and blood red. The trees formed hardly more than an arched gateway to another clearing alongside the main road. Behind a pale cement-rendered wall rising to Mick's shoulder height, stood a tower faced with multi-coloured tiles.

'The temple,' she said.

'Amazing!'

'Do you know the story?' she asked.

'That he built it to appease the migrant workers' Gods when so many of them had been killed by the flu after the First World War.'

'Yes.'

Mick followed the wall to the entrance but there was a heavy chain across the iron gates. He turned to check that she had followed. 'Can we go in?'

'I do not think it's used. Come back round to the side. I want to show you something.' She pointed to a single file of plaster figurines. Each was about a half-metre high, posed, some seated some standing, on a pediment wall that extended along the length of the façade at roof height. There must have been twenty or thirty of them. Mick scanned along the row.

A pink-faced man in a brown military jacket stood to attention between a kneeling fakir playing a wind instrument as if to charm a snake from its basket and a holy man sitting Buddha-like. The western-garbed man wore a black belt across his chest and held a rifle by his side. His head was covered by a pith helmet.

'He is your grandfather,' she said.

'His brother – my great uncle,' Mick said. He felt a tug in his chest. Perhaps it *had* been important to come here. He needed a photograph of this not only for him but for Steve, the funny little statue's grandson, and he cursed himself for leaving his camera at the hotel. The prospect of having Nancy as his guide had made it slip his mind.

He stepped onto the gravel path that ran around the wall. As with the house, some agency was keeping the jungle at bay. He stood on tiptoe to get a closer look over the wall. Nancy was right, it looked as if the building had been abandoned. He turned to her. She stood at the margin of the trees scanning the ground at her feet.

'What are you looking for?' he said.

'A block of wood or a stone. Something to stand on.'

'What for?'

'So that I can see.' She pointed. 'Over the wall.'

'I can give you a boost.' Even in the fading light he could see the colour rise from her throat to her cheeks.

She shook her head and took a pace backwards 'I don't think so.'

He imagined grasping her by the waist and lifting her almost weightless form so that her shoulders were level with the top of the wall. 'Look!' He stooped and interlaced his fingers to form a stirrup. 'You only have to step into this and I can lift you.'

She smiled and came back to the wall. He leant his shoulder against it and offered his hands. She stepped in and up. He had been right, she seemed to have no heft at all. He looked up. She had grasped the top and was using it to take some of her weight.

'Yes. I thought so. Nothing,' she said.

When she had stepped down, she dusted off her hips and thighs. 'It's getting late,' she said. 'We should return you to your hotel.'

He only half heard her. He had unconsciously moved his hands and they now held hers. 'I can't tell you how grateful I am for your help today. I have learned so much more than if I had come here alone,' he said. He was trying to think how he could legitimately extend the time with her. What would be acceptable in her culture? Would it offend her if he invited her to dinner?

'It is not a problem. Has what you have seen given you satisfaction?' She smiled as if she was amused by something he wasn't party to.

'Yes. I had to come and see it for myself. And now I have.' The words sounded final. This was the opposite of the impression he wanted to achieve.

'So now you can go home?' Her eyes were downcast as if she couldn't bear to look at him. Was this a sign?

'I hadn't thought about it but, yes, I suppose my business here is finished.'

'Will you move on to the next stage of your trip – to Langkawi?'

'Yes, to Langkawi.' He didn't remember telling her of his plans.

They reached the car and he held the door open for her. As she passed him her hand touched his sleeve almost imperceptibly but the contact gave him a jolt as if from a cattle prod. Once he was settled in his seat, there was silence. She was watching him anxiously, her hand on the ignition key with the engine not yet started.

The claustrophobic, sun-baked interior encouraged a sudden swamping of sweat in Mick's underarms and around his thighs. He glanced at Nancy who appeared unruffled.

'Are you all right, Mr Mick?' she said.

She seemed genuinely concerned and he wondered if he could dare imagine that she might have feelings for him. 'It's so hot in here.' He fanned his face with a hand.

She started the car and, before the cooling effect of the air-conditioning could kick in, drove over the bridge and out of the castle compound. He looked back wondering whether this would be his only visit. Had he seen everything he should have? He had come away with nothing tangible, not even a photograph. That was it. 'Nancy...'

'It is permitted to call me by my first name when we are alone but back in Ipoh if we are in public you should call me by my family name – Miss Lee.'

'I'm sorry, I didn't know that.' She had mentioned the possibility of being in public together. Perhaps what he had in mind would not be so out of place. 'I was going to ask... I forgot to bring my camera today. Would you bring me back tomorrow? I would like some photographs.'

Her knuckles paled as her grip tightened on the wheel. 'If you need to come back, of course I will be your guide once again.'

'Good. Shall we meet in the lobby of my hotel?'

She bowed towards the windscreen. 'Of course.'

'Shall we say 10am tomorrow?'

'Yes.' The tip of her tongue fluttered where her lips were at their fullest.

12

When Mick returned to his hotel he went down to the basement business centre and sent an e-mail to Steve to let him know that he'd seen the castle and intended to return the next day to take pictures. He also mentioned that he'd spent the afternoon in the company of a charming guide called Nancy Lee and that he was thinking of asking her out for an evening meal the next day.

Afterwards, he contemplated where he might like to eat that evening. He cursed himself for not asking Nancy to continue her role as guide and help him find a restaurant. It was perfectly reasonable to ask for her recommendations and as natural as the sea meets the shore for him to casually ask her along.

Although KL's bars and clubs gave the impression of a hedonistic society, he assumed that the permissiveness of the capital did not necessarily extend to the country's north. Even in KL, Islam affected day-to-day discourse. The women mostly wore headscarves with two-piece outfits comprising a smock over loose fitting trousers. He had noticed that many of the Malaysians at the roadside cafés ate only with the fingers of their right hands. People from the Chinese diaspora, like Nancy, were a minority. If they felt beleaguered, they had every reason to retain conservative ideas about a woman's behaviour and mixing with westerners.

He had made her uncomfortable by calling her 'Nancy'. What if she had divined that he imagined them enjoying each other's company as a couple? No. This was going too far, too fast. She would be shocked at the idea. It was bad enough that he was having these notions when he was ten or more years older than her; his being a westerner made it preposterous.

What about her time in England? Even if she had lived with relatives she would have been exposed to student life to some extent. She'd have been in the company of young men – boys – her own age. If they were anything like he was in his late teens a beautiful woman such as Nancy would have learned how to fend off unwelcome advances without being offended and, perhaps, to have accepted a few welcome approaches. Here he was thinking of her as an innocent. What's to say she hadn't had her share of affaires d'amour?

As he went to bed that night, Mick resolved that by lunchtime tomorrow he would have made a simple statement and asked a straightforward question: He would like to get to know her better. Would she care to join him for dinner?

If it was so simple, though, why couldn't he put the scenario out of his mind and go to sleep? Why was it replaying over and over with each possible response making him shiver with apprehension?

Perhaps it was residual jet lag, perhaps it was anticipation of the day's events, either way, Mick woke early and couldn't prevent his mind instantly engaging gear. There was no way he would find sleep again. Sighing, he pointed the zapper at the television screen and watched *Fox News in Asia*. The lead story was about the possible sighting in Germany of Nick Leeson, the Brit who, when he lived in Singapore, had worked as a trader for Barings Bank. The bank had collapsed due to the enormity of his trading losses. He had successfully eluded the police since leaving Singapore in February, but, the report concluded, the dragnet was closing in on him. Mick speculated about the possibility of bumping into his fellow countryman in the hotel lobby. Would he turn him in? It sounded as if the bank had been extraordinarily lax in its controls. Should he treat Leeson as a victim rather than a fraudster?

In the absence of any up-to-date film of Leeson, the segment ran a montage of what appeared to be family snaps: on the beach, in a bar, at a party. In all of them, Mick discerned something about the face of the bespectacled trader, something in his eyes that suggested vulnerability. The fragility there reminded Mick of other boys who had been bullied at school. He remembered how he had tried so hard to inject steel into his own gaze, to learn indifference, to not show fear. Mick could understand how such a man would overstep the line to get ahead, to show 'them' that he could thrive in the hothouse atmosphere of the trading floor.

Which brought Mick to today. In the years that he represented the family company on the road, he had learned how to mask his victim's diffidence. Outwardly he was confident but inside he suffered an inordinate fear of rejection. His objective during the morning's tour with Nancy would be to charm her. He hoped that she already had some feelings for him and, if he could build on these, not in a forced way but naturally, he would maybe reach the point where it would be natural for him to invite her to dinner and for her to accept.

Nancy was waiting in the lobby, when he emerged from the lift and her expression of mild concern turned into a broad smile of welcome. 'Mr Mick, how are you this bright Sunday morning?'

'I'm well, thank you, Miss Lee, and looking forward to our expedition.' He registered what she had said. He had asked her to work on Sunday! He hurried after her. 'I'm so sorry. I lost track of the days. I didn't realise it was Sunday. It must be your day off.'

She stopped before they reached the revolving doors and drew him to one side. 'It is my pleasure to be of service, Mr Mick. It is not an inconvenience to me.' She looked him over. 'But where is your camera?'

He lifted the hem of his sweater so she could see the leather case.

'It's very small,' she said.

'It's the latest compact camera. Automatic. Point and shoot. It has the Advanced Photo System; the film's in a cartridge. Today's date will be recorded on each picture automatically...'

'I'm sure it's a jolly excellent camera, Mr Mick.'

'I'm sorry.' He shrugged. 'But I had to jump to the defence of my little camera.'

'You could have just said, size isn't everything.' She didn't wait for an answer and, with her hand over her mouth stifling a laugh, she swept through the revolving doors.

He caught up with her in the heat and they waited side by side for the car to arrive. She was dressed almost identically to the day before. Her crisp, cotton blouse was in a style that he would always associate with her – a narrow stand-up collar with a 'V' cut demurely into the front. She carried the same coolie-style hat in her hand. He tried to discern if there were any signals for him in the minute changes to her wardrobe and was disappointed when he decided there were none. But the 'size isn't everything' comment; if a woman back home had said this in similar circumstances he would have interpreted it as flirtation.

As she drove them out of the city in silence, Mick became aware of Nancy's perfume. It was flowery with a lasting note of grass-like astringency and he felt the need to breathe deeply through his nose as if this was her essence, the scent of her body. Once they were on the Batu Gaja road, Nancy's knuckles resumed a healthy colour and Mick said, 'Did you have a nice evening yesterday?'

She glanced at him and turned back to the road. 'I just stayed in. Washed my hair.'

Was it a joke? 'It looks lovely.'

She frowned. 'What?'

'Your hair. It looks lovely. After you washed it.'

A blush rose around the collar of her blouse. 'Thank you.'

He cast around for a topic that would take the conversation in a more fruitful direction. 'Do you have anything else planned for today? Other than me, I mean.'

'No.' She shifted the car into top gear long after they had been on the open road. 'No. I will visit with my family.'

'Here in Ipoh?'

'Yes, my father has a business here.'

'What does he do?'

She slowed down behind a heavy lorry belching smoke and, leaning to her right, peered ahead, waiting for a straight stretch of road. When it came, she pulled out and changed gears to accelerate past. Almost immediately, a car appeared from around a bend a few hundred yards ahead. Mick's stomach muscles contracted and he involuntarily pressed his right foot to the floor.

Nancy pursed her lips, changed gear down again and pressed her foot to the accelerator. The Proton's engine screamed but its response was immediate enough to press the seat into Mick's back. They could see the dark face of the driver in the oncoming car. He flashed its lights. Mick watched Nancy's face, silently imploring her to brake and resume position behind the lorry that showed no sign of slowing. Her features betrayed nothing.

The lorry driver was now blaring his horn and so was the driver of the car that was closing fast. Mick shut his eyes and stiffened for the impact. Nothing happened and he looked out to the offside in time to see the other car lurch onto the verge between them and the trees. It slewed from side to side. Mick turned and watched as it resumed the road with a final shake of its rear. Seconds later, Nancy pulled across in front of the lorry. She drove on as if nothing had happened.

'That was close,' Mick said.

'I saw he was a Bumi,' she said. 'He was always going to give way.'

He wasn't sure that he liked what this revealed. But he didn't live in Malaysia. What did he know of the inter-ethnic relations? Best to stay clear of the subject. 'You were going to tell me about your father's business,' he said.

'It's import and export. I work for the company most of the time. Being a tourist guide is only part-time, more like a hobby.'

'That's interesting. I also worked for a family company.'

'What does your company do?'

He smiled and decided to avoid that particular minefield. 'We sold it a few years ago. I have an interest in a small cinema in Richmond now but I'm basically a man of leisure.'

She turned away from the windscreen to look at him briefly. 'But you are too young to be retired. Will you be looking for another job?'

He smiled, revelling in the notion that she at least didn't see him as decrepit. 'I suppose I'm waiting for something to turn up. What does your company import and export?'

There was a hint of embarrassment in the way she breathed heavily through her nostrils. 'Palm oil, obviously, locally produced furniture; it sells very well in Europe. They are probably our biggest lines. But, basically, we export anything that we think will turn a profit.'

'What do *you* do?'

'I manage the shipping – logistics.'

'I imagine you're very good at the organisational side.'

She cast her eyes downward for a split-second. It was a gesture to indicate modesty even where, as in this case as far as he could tell, no modesty existed. 'I think it's mostly because of my English.' She nodded towards the windscreen. 'Look, here we are.'

They retraced their steps over the river and Mick stopped to take the first picture of the castle's facade. He asked Nancy to be in the foreground and, standing at a slight angle to him, she adopted a pose, holding the fingers of one hand to the brim of her hat. She crossed one leg in front of the other, knee flexed and toe brushing the gravel.

They progressed through the rooms and stairways with Mick taking photographs of the scenes through the empty door and window-openings or from the flat roof. He took a few steps down to the balustrade that ran along the courtyard side of the building, the part that overlooked the original Kellas House.

Mick leaned on the brickwork looking out. 'This job you have – import-export – is it interesting?'

She appeared to be scanning the horizon, her eyes obscured by sunglasses. 'It means I have to go to KL sometimes to sort out a local difficulty and I find travel interesting. I like the contact with our agents in other countries. But I would like to travel more. To go to Europe again.'

'Did you enjoy your time in England?'

Was there a slight fluster in her response – a blush and a hesitancy. 'Oh, yes! I loved being a student in Kingston. Even though I was under the eye of an uncle and aunt, I had more freedom in England than I have ever felt here.'

'How long did you live there?'

'While I was doing my degree. Three years.'

'And you had fun?'

'Pardon?'

'Did you make the most of the experience? Did you have fun?'

She twitched her nose. Her expression was hidden by her Ray-Bans. 'I don't think you could say that I was a typical student. I went to Kingston because that is where my uncle owns a hotel. I stayed with the family rent-free but in return I had to work. I did shifts on reception in the evening and served breakfasts before I went to classes. There wasn't much time for socialising.'

'Didn't you have boyfriends?' He was closing in.

She took a step back. 'Shall we go to the temple now? You need a picture of your ancestor's little statue.'

His heart sank. It was a clear rebuff. 'Of course.'

When they were on the path, Nancy asked Mick what business his company had been in. 'Nothing exciting. Sanitation products. That's all behind us. It's just the *Film Factory* – the cinema – now.'

'Do you have a wife in England? A family?'

He shook his head. The heat was making its way through the crown of his hat and his back was damp with sweat. 'No. I was married but we divorced fifteen years ago. Since then I have never had time to make those sorts of commitments.' He stopped and turned towards her. He needed to see her reaction. 'Not like now. I'm free but I've been thinking about settling down again.' He cursed that he couldn't see her eyes.

'So you have a girlfriend?'

Hadn't she understood? Or was she being deliberately obtuse? 'No. No girlfriends.' He sensed that it was now or never. 'Look, Miss Lee – Nancy. You must know that I think you're a very attractive woman—' He stuttered to a halt and there was a sudden rush of sweat down his sides. Oh God! It sounded as if he was going to propose!

She looked down and brought a hand up to cover the lower half of her face. It was now completely hidden.

He slowed the pace of his words, parcelling out each one precisely so there could be no misunderstanding. 'I would really like to get to know you better. I would like us to have a date—' he thought he heard her whimper almost imperceptibly '—I'd like to take you to dinner... tonight, if you're free. Would you like that?'

When she took her hand away from her mouth, she was biting her lower lip. 'Yes, Mr Mick—'

'Please call me Mick, just Mick.'

'Yes, Mick, just Mick, I would like that very much.' She smiled and Mick had to pin his feet to the ground to stop himself taking her in his arms.

13

The hotel room was too cold. It was difficult to adjust the air-conditioning to its Goldilocks setting. The problem was exacerbated because Mick was wearing only boxers while he surveyed the meagre contents of his wardrobe. He hadn't envisaged dressing to impress while he was away and nothing on the hangers inspired him.

His one linen jacket was crumpled and, while there was an iron in the room, he knew that, if they spent any time outside, the jacket would have to come off and he wanted to be wearing something better than a t-shirt underneath. Nancy had already seen the two pairs of chinos he had brought with him and both the sweaters that he had worn indoors. He looked at his watch. There was just enough time. He sniffed the armpits of the t-shirts, selected one and threw it on, followed by a sweater and his cut-off jeans. He grabbed his wallet and the room key and hurried towards the lift. The parade of shops attached to the hotel lobby was horrendously expensive but this was the last of his concerns.

Forty-five minutes and £800 later, Mick sat in one of the lobby's club chairs reading the *Straits Times*. Most of the money had been spent on the Paul Smith ash-grey blazer that he wore over a navy polo shirt. His linen trousers were also new as were the *Sperry Topsiders* that he wore without socks. He purposely kept his eyes on the newspaper, despite the urge to focus on the revolving door where Nancy would enter. He was looking at the print but not reading it. He couldn't concentrate. There was too much depending on this evening.

He heard her cough. He lowered the paper as if to check it was her, stood up and straightened his jacket. She was wearing a high collared, ivy-green cheongsam with gold detail. Her brown eyes shone with as much lustre as the cream orchid in her hair. 'You look lovely,' he said. He held out his arms and leant towards her to kiss her cheeks in the European way but she jumped back like a startled fawn. A young man stood behind her wearing a dark blue, cotton suit over a v-neck t-shirt. He wore trainers. Some sort of chaperone, Mick thought, his heart sinking.

'This is my boyfriend Lang-ren,' Nancy said.

I imagine Mick greeting this news with a stunned nod of his head. He stood motionless, trying to catch up with what had happened. Hadn't they cleared the decks? There were no attachments on either side and yet here was a 'boyfriend'.

Was she seriously asking him to accept that she was in a relationship with this scruffy, Chinese whippersnapper? He felt the ground slip beneath his expensive deck-shoes but stepped forward and held out his hand. 'Glad to meet you, Langdon.' He turned back to Nancy and raised his eyebrows.

'Lang-ren. His name Lang-ren.'

Mick held up a hand. 'Lang-ren. Sorry!' He repeated the quizzical glance at Nancy.

'Shall we have drink here?' she said and sat down on the couch opposite. Lang-ren sat alongside her but a few inches apart. Nancy crossed her legs and Mick was insulted by a tantalising glimpse of her thigh showing through the split in her dress's side-seam.

'Yes. What would you like?' Mick said, his voice flat. After ordering, he asked how Nancy had spent the rest of her day.

'I met with my father,' she said. 'We talked about his plans for business when he retires.'

She was looking at him intently as if she was trying to communicate a coded message. Mick glanced at Lang-ren to see how much interest he was taking in what she was saying. He slouched back alongside her sipping a *Tsingtao* beer. Mick turned back to Nancy and his diaphragm tightened. He realised that they were playing some sort of game and its intricate rules would always be inexplicable to him. 'Yes, the import-export business.'

'My family – my father and my uncles – we own businesses in lots of interests. We own hotels as well as the import-export business – plantations too.' Her eyes were willing him to understand.

'I see,' Mick said. But he didn't see at all. Her strained speech suggested that there was something more for him to know. If she was trying to send him a message, the ploy was failing.

Mick took a gulp of his gin and tonic and said, 'And you, Lang-ren, are you in business?'

Nancy leant forward putting herself between Mick and the young man. 'Lang-ren understands English well but is not a good talker. He works for my father also.'

'How did you meet – you and Lang-ren?'

'We are old school friends. His family, my family we go way back.' She studied her flat-heeled shoes.

Mick drained the rest of his glass and stood up. 'Shall we go for dinner? Where would you like to go?'

After a discussion between Nancy and Lang-ren in Mandarin, she suggested an open-air food market nearby. 'It is very good,' she said.

They sauntered in silence in the evening heat, three abreast, none touching and when the path narrowed it was Lang-ren who fell back and ambled a pace or so behind Mick and Nancy. The five-minute stroll took them to a square where tables were scattered around a central hub of stalls, all offering different styles of food: Chinese, Malay, Indian and 'fusion'. It dawned on Mick that this was a 'Durians welcome' zone because the air had a fetid undertone and it was difficult for him to breathe without betraying that there was something nasty about the atmosphere. Both Lang-ren and Nancy appeared to be immune.

Mick and Nancy queued for food. 'Is everything okay?' he asked quietly watching Lang-ren waiting at the drinks stall with the money Nancy had given him.

She studied the ground at her feet. 'I'm sorry for not being straight for you,' she said. She lifted her eyes and brushed away a tear. 'My father... my family...' She shook her head and pointed at the cartons of food that had appeared on the counter top. 'I will pay.'

They returned to the table with three plastic plates and an array of dishes: fish-head curry; pork and noodles that could have come from an English Chinese take-away; rice, pak choi and mixed vegetables; and another meat and sauce dish chosen by Nancy. Lang-ren handed out plastic spoons and Mick slumped into his plastic seat pondering the contrast between his expectations for the evening and the reality.

He had anticipated asking Nancy whether, if he stayed on in Ipoh, they could spend more time together. He had even dared think that after a few days they might go to Langkawi as a couple. There was something offensive about the way they had brought him to this food market when he was dressed for the best that Ipoh could offer. She and this... boy... had crushed his hopes with all the detachment of a steamroller flattening a hedgehog.

Lang-ren threw himself into the feast as if it was to be his last meal. He took something from every plate. Nancy ate miniscule portions of the rice and the vegetables with only one spoonful from the meat and sauce dish that she had chosen. She passed the foil container to Mick. 'You must try this. It is a Malaysian speciality.'

Dutifully, Mick took a spoonful and immediately recoiled. His disgust was so visceral that he couldn't hide it. He swallowed quickly and immediately took a swig of beer. He felt as if he had consumed a mouthful of the smell fouling their every breath.

Lang-ren laughed openly. Mick wanted to hit him.

Nancy chuckled. 'Sorry. I should have warned you. Westerners never like this dish.'

'What's in it for goodness sake?'

'The meat is beef. But the sauce is made from dried shrimps. They dry very slowly in the sun and this what gives them the special flavour.'

'Rotten shellfish basically!'

'If you put it like that. But I remember the first time I ate cheese I was almost sick. Chinese feel the same about cheese as you feel about what you have just eaten.'

He wondered if she had bought the dish solely with the intention of setting him up. Neither she nor Lang-ren were keen to finish it. It seemed unnecessarily cruel. Whatever the reason, the exchange had further dampened his mood. 'Am I safer with this?' he said, pointing to the fish-head curry.

'Yes. Let me serve you.' She spooned some curry sauce onto his plate and then set about peeling pieces of flesh from the fish's head. It was firm and white; after a tentative spoonful, Mick pronounced it good. He took more.

Mick ate sullenly. Nancy gave all her attention to the meagre rations on her plate, while Lang-ren chomped and slurped enthusiastically.

Mick was desperate to inject some energy into the stultifying atmosphere and decided to share with Nancy a half-baked plan that had occurred to him while he was getting dressed. 'Do you know who owns Kellie's Castle?'

She coloured and fanned her face as if she had bitten a chilli. 'I told you. One of the plantation companies.'

'Do you think they may consider selling?'

She placed the end of the spoon to her pursed lips and ejected a small bone with the tip of her tongue. 'Why do you ask?'

He shifted his bottom and his shirt peeled away allowing the sweat on his back to cool. 'Maybe it's a silly idea but the story is so romantic. The castle has huge potential as a tourist site. Surely, Ipoh, Perak State or whoever, could make more of it. As it stands, anybody can go there for free. If the authorities took it over, they could charge admission and earn revenue for the people.'

'I think politicians too corrupt to make it work. The state and the city have no money.'

He sat back. 'I have money. What if I bought it and gifted it to Perak? What if I stayed here to make sure it was done properly?' Inadvertently, he realised, he was asking her to reconsider this charade.

She shook her head. 'You are a westerner. Non-Malays are not allowed to own property. Every company must have Malays on the board. You could never make it work.'

'Even if I stayed to oversee it?' He wanted her to have no doubt about what he was implying.

She shifted plates around as if she was looking for a dish she hadn't yet tried. 'There nothing for you here, Mr Mick. You no understand our ways. Malays *and* Chinese. So complicated. You best to just go home.'

What had happened to her command of English? Why was she suddenly talking like a cartoon? Mick sighed and covered his face with his hands as if the sweat from his forehead was stinging his eyes. He nodded. Any words he could conjure up would stick in his constricted throat.

Lang-ren said something to Nancy in Mandarin and signalled to Mick's plate. 'Lang-ren says you should have the cheek. It is most tasteful part.' She delved into the side of the fish's face beneath its eye. Her spoon emerged with the shining prize on its tip and she fed it directly into Mick's mouth. It only served to emphasise the lost intimacy of the evening.

There was another conversation between Lang-ren and Nancy and this time she shook her head. He leaned across in front of her and plunged his spoon into the fish's eye socket, dug out the eyeball and sucked it into his mouth greedily. He turned the head over and repeated the operation, laughing at the look on Mick's face.

Nancy retrieved the cheek on this side and Mick signalled that she should have it. Her eyes sparkled in the electric lights as she placed it, like a pill, on the tip of her tongue and took it into her mouth. The sensuousness of it was a kick in the pit of Mick's stomach. He'd had enough. He stood up and tossed back the rest of his beer. 'Well, thank you for a lovely evening. I think I'll stroll back to the hotel now. I have an early start.'

Malaysia was over for him. He couldn't bear to spend any more time there. The thought of being alone at the Langkawi beach resort, a notion that had been appealing when he had planned it, now promised only solitary confinement. Next morning, he would return to KL and bring forward his flight home. 'Well, it's been lovely,' he said.

Nancy stood and offered her hand. 'Enjoy rest of your stay.' They shook hands and Lang-ren stood, lowering his head like a bullock preparing for a time when it had horns. He proffered his hand and grunted.

Mick turned back to Nancy and searched her eyes for any

sign that he was making a mistake but they were blank. The idea that she was drugged flashed into his head but he dismissed it. No, he was sure he hadn't been mistaken, behind the cold exterior, there was sympathy, perhaps even attraction. For a second, he was out of the shit-smell of the food court and alone in a scented cocoon with Nancy, if only he had the nerve to pull her to him and...

Lang-ren hawked in his throat and brought Mick back to the present. He turned on his heel and walked away, tears of frustration welling in his eyes.

14

The Malaysia Airlines plane was late and I'd been waiting for nearly two hours by the time Mick emerged. I'd heard very little from him while he was away and was desperate to learn more about the land and the castle.

'Good of you to come,' he said. We shook hands. 'How's it all been?'

'It's only been a week. We've managed – somehow.' I checked my watch. 'Come on, we'll save some money if I pay for the parking in the next five minutes.'

We hurried through the concourse, dodging suited men and women as they trundled across our path towing executive suitcases. Once we were in the car and on the A4, he turned to face me. 'I found the exact spot where that picture was taken.'

'Picture?' I was focused on whether to use the inside lane to overtake a taxi that was rattling along, belching black smoke, at a few miles an hour below the speed limit.

'You know, "the land".' I sensed he was making speech marks with his fingers. 'The castle is there behind it like in the article you showed me. But it's abandoned.'

'Who owns it?'

'It's a plantation company. It's sad that they're not making more of it. It would make a great tourist attraction—'

'But you can just go there and look around?'

'It's not fenced off and there's a car park. There's even

a notice board with the story about your grandfather. But they're not making anything of it.'

'But it's clear that it was built by my... our family?'

'As far as anything is. Why?'

His disinterest irked me, but he'd only known of the castle's existence for weeks. I'd had five years of living with the knowledge that my family had built it – far, far away. In all those years, I was the one who could – should – have gone there were it not for my timidity. I changed the subject. 'You cut short your visit. Why didn't you go on to Langkawi? It looks fabulous in the pictures.' I glanced across.

He was looking out of the window at the residential properties that lined the road approaching Kingston. 'I lost interest.'

'That's very enigmatic. What happened?'

He sighed. 'To be honest, Steve, I'm knackered. Can we discuss it another time? Over a pint perhaps.'

A couple of days later in *The Duke's Head*, I broached the subject of his early departure. The bar staff were fussing round us hanging skeletons, blood-smeared zombies and witches on broomsticks from the ceiling in preparation for a Hallowe'en party night.

'I didn't want to stay there on my own.'

'Why not?'

'I met this woman.' He leant forward as if we were conspirators. 'I made a bit of a fool of myself over her.' His lip trembled and for a moment his face crumpled like paper. He was looking out across the bar as if he could see all the way to Malaysia.

I reached out and touched his arm. 'How?'

'We bumped into each other, literally. In the hotel lobby. She was a stunner. Tall, slim, dark hair...' He examined something at the bottom of his pint glass.

'What's her name?'

'Nancy. She's Chinese. Her name's Nancy Lee.' He drifted away again watching the ghoulish preparations.

One of the helpers brushed past me with an armful of fake cobweb. Some of it attached itself to my shoulder and I brushed it away. Finally, I asked what happened.

'She works for her father's company but does part-time work as a tourist guide. She took me to the house – the castle. She knew the whole history. She seemed to be really interested in me and the Kellie-Smith thing. We started getting along. I thought we had a spark. I really did. I fell for her, Steve. Really fell for her...'

It was time for me to study my pint, holding it up to the light to check for cloudiness. 'Did she give you any inkling she felt the same way?'

He shook his head and when he looked up his eyes swam with tears. 'Nothing obvious. But I felt she liked me.' He wiped a palm across the table top. 'I felt – you know in a sort of body-language way – that she fancied me. That there was chemistry. But I worried about the difference – our ages and her being Chinese and me a Brit.'

'How old is she?'

'Dunno. Maybe early-thirties.' He took his wallet out of his pocket and removed a photograph. 'Look. This is her in front of the castle.'

Nancy Lee was everything he had described. It was easy to see why he had fallen for her. 'Hmm. What are you, forty? That's no difference. Maybe the cultural thing, I can see why you may have held back. Did you make a move?'

He snorted as he took the picture from me and studied it. 'You can hardly call it – what do the Americans say? – "coming on to her". I just asked her to join me for dinner one night.'

'Nothing wrong with that. Did she turn you down?'

'No, worse.' He had such a sad smile. 'She brought her boyfriend along.'

'Oops!'

'It got worse: he was obviously so not her boyfriend. Not romantically anyway. He was such a lightweight. Okay, they may have known each other – she said since school – but even I could tell there was nothing romantic. He just sat there talking Mandarin, or whatever it is they speak; he was there to keep me at bay. His name was Lang-ren. What sort of bloody name is Lang-ren?'

'She wanted you to know that she wasn't up for... romance.'

'That's pretty much the size of it.'

'What did she say next day?'

'I didn't wait to find out. I checked out, drove to KL and got the first available flight.'

'You haven't spoken to her?'

'I couldn't face it. I'd really fallen for her. There was something about the trip that set me up for meeting her. After a couple of days, I was ready to ask whether I should stay in Malaysia. Whether she might think about coming to the UK. I wanted to talk about the future... our future... and she brought that stupid Lang-ren.' He stood up abruptly. 'I need a pee. I'll get another round in on the way back.' He rubbed his face as he dodged between the swinging dummies of the undead on his way to the toilets.

Life returned to the routine. I oversaw the operation of the cinema and Mick and I held our regular meetings. He seemed to be on the mend. He never mentioned Nancy. Nor did he address the elephant in the room – the fact that we were cousins – each other's nearest relative.

When he came back from Malaysia and told me about Nancy, I admit it didn't take me long to realise that she, or someone like her, represented, not a threat exactly, but a different take on our relationship. The cinema was fine; we had a partnership agreement. I was comfortable with us being business partners first, friends second and our being cousins hardly mattered at all. I was ten years older than him so I had no reason to consider that Mick's money might play a part in my future. But if he married and I was no longer his next of kin, what did it mean for me?

This conundrum whirled in my head for weeks and when the envelope from Malaysia arrived – its origin obvious from the row of garish stamps along its top edge – addressed in a shaky hand to *Mick Kellie* at the *Film Factory Picture House, Richmond, Surrey*, naturally I steamed it open.

That same evening, after reading the contents, I glued back the flap, added a strip of *Sellotape* to cover any signs of it being tampered with and put it in Mick's postbox.

15

Dear Mr Mick

I have been crying most of time since you left. You went without saying goodbye. I did not have chance to explain. This is what I do now.

You were such a gentleman with me but not knowing how I felt about you right from when I bumped into you in the hotel lobby. Of course, this was not a mistake. I meant it that we meet this way and when I explain why, I hope you be kind to me and forgive me.

When we were on the roof of the castle you went to the edge and I told you be careful. I told you that a man had fallen there five years ago. But I didn't say I knew this man. His name Luis Escobar. Like you did, he said he was relative of Mr William Kellie-Smith. When he came to Ipoh my father tell me to act as his guide. Why he do this? Because my father S Y Lee. His company own the Kellas Plantation and the Kellas House land. I'm sorry I could not tell you this.

Mr Luis was finding out that maybe the transfer of land to Leeyate Holdings was not safe and he could say that Kellas Land still belonged to Kellie family. But before he could try he have accident at night and fall from roof. He the man who died.

That time I worked in bank and came to Ipoh special to see Mr Luis. Now I work in Ipoh for my father and he call me in and say another relative to Mr William Kellie-Smith is fishing around. This time man called Mr Mick Kellie.

When you came out of restaurant I made sure to bump into you and drop my leaflets. You were gentleman. Helped me to get up and collected my dropped. You held my hand and I felt like in electric storm when neck tingles. Your blues eyes made me feel things like I had not felt since being teenager. I am blushing to remember such feelings and now feeling same again I am shaking almost!

I think you must knew how I feel when I nearly drive car into wall! And you all time, you so cool Mr Westerner not flustered like me. When you look at me I go to jelly almost but you not feeling the same way I think.

You thinking, but Lee Lai Ping (yes you can call me by Chinese name if you like) was student in England. She must have gone out with English boys. This is a little true but no feelings from those days was like the first hours with you.

Did you have same thunderbolt – same feelings for Lai Ping? I see now that you think Chinese girls be treated properly like lady. But all time I did not want it so much.

At end of first day I could tell you like me just a little bit. You like me being thin with good figure. I am taller than most Chinese girls. And more you gave me feelings that maybe you like me the more trouble I took to look good for you.

You made me feel in small ways that you like me too. When I laughed when you made joke you made joke again because you liked me be happy.

But all time with you I behave like good daughter and, even though trembling with emotion because with you, I show you round Kellas House and explain the story of family and building and what happen.

When you said we would have dinner I knew it was you like me. I also know that you (even though I did not feel this) could be westerner who takes advantage. You ask me to dinner and then to have coffee in your room. I know if this happen I not able to resist my body wants. I could not let this happen. My father – my place in business – all make it so wrong. So I bring Lang-ren along as my boyfriend. It make me sad now I remember your face when you see me with Lang-ren in lobby of your hotel. It was cruel trick.

In dinner you ask why S Y Lee's company not make house a tourist attraction. You also felt romance in house. You said about buying it from my father's company and donating it to people of Perak. This make you so noble and I felt even more bad about how we trick on you.

But I also see that if my father decide to sell to you, what if you find house didn't belong to him? How much money he loose? And if he decided not to sell it make me afraid to keep you safe not like Mr Luis.

It is real thing you not be safe. I engaged to Tommy Lee, but I not love him so will break with him if you care something for me. Then his family loose face and make trouble.

I had to let you think nothing here for you in Malaysia and you go away. I was wrong. There is something here for you if you still want. It is me. You should not come back here in case it not safe. Also me coming to you not safe because is Tommy's side of family own Number 8 Hotel not far away in Kingston. This side of family not good for us so your stay away from them.

But I can escape my father if you help me. If you want it we plan something so we live together somewhere where S Y Lee can't find us. Not until after we find if feelings between us are good and true.

Will you send for me? I will go anywhere in your arms.

Your Nancy Lee (Lai Ping)

16

Of course, Mick wanted to discuss the letter with me. Who else did he have? He took it out of his pocket as we sat in *The Duke's Head*. Halloween had been and gone. The hanged dummies of the undead had come down and only we regulars remained to scare the occasional drifter-in away.

'What's that?' I asked, my eyes wide.

'The letter that was sent to *The Factory*. The one you dropped by.'

'From Malaysia,' I said.

'That's right?' His frown and the rise in his tone questioned how I knew.

'The stamps,' I said. I had to be on my toes here, pretending to be unaware of its contents. Before the letter arrived, I had only known that Luis had died in a fall from the castle roof. I hadn't known for certain that he had been suspicious about who owned the castle, nor that Nancy had been Luis's guide and she suspected his death may not have been an accident. 'Who's it from?' My brain was racing at top speed but I had to keep my voice in a low gear.

'Nancy.' He shuffled the pages. 'It turns out she *did* feel the same about me. But there were complications...' He shook his head as if he was looking for something on the pages that wasn't there.

'Complications?'

'Her family – our family.' He shook his head and swore

under his breath. 'Families! Who'd bloody have 'em?' He sighed. 'It's a long story. It turns out that I had a relative – a second cousin I think he'd be. He went over to look at the castle about five years ago.'

Should I have said that I had met Luis Escobar – that he was *my* cousin? No. This was Mick's story. It was more important now to focus on where this thing with Nancy Lee was going. But I still needed to react properly. 'A cousin. We have another relative. There's not just the two of us?'

'There was another but he died.' He riffled the papers as if seeking confirmation.

'Blimey!' I said.

'Nancy – my Nancy – showed him round too. Only *he* was interested in finding out whether the Kellie Smith family had any claims on the plantation and the house. She implied his death may not have been an accident.'

I paused as if I was putting two and two together and acted confused. 'But why would one thing lead to another? This cousin finding out something and then dying. How would she know?'

Mick tutted as if I was missing a point. 'Because her family owns the damn castle. They think anybody connected to the Kellie Smiths is a problem for them. Or at least for her father, this S Y Lee character.'

'So when you went along saying, "I'm a Kellie Smith" they weren't so pleased to see you.'

'Exactly. When I was there asking about why the owners weren't doing more with the house she was worried for me.'

'You can understand it. If she really believed that this other cousin had been killed because he was too nosy, knowing you were going to... try it on with her—' I rolled my hands around each other in what I hoped was a moving-things-along gesture '—she anticipated that the longer you stayed, the more questions about the castle you'd have. She took her boyfriend to the date to stop you in your tracks. She was only looking out for you.'

'Yes! But now she's had second thoughts and wants to meet up – more than that, she suggested we go away together—' it all started coming in a rush '—more than that even. She wants to run away from her family. But not here. They'd know she'd be here and her father has family in Kingston. They'd find her and take her back. She wants me to tell her where and she'll come to me. It's not much of a plan. The upshot is that she wants us to try out how we feel about each other. That makes sense, doesn't it?' He gulped back some beer.

'I don't know. Where could you go? What about *The Factory?*'

He gave me an exasperated look. 'Where's your sense of romance, Steve? She wants me and I want her. We'll go somewhere and see if it works. If it does we'll confront the... mundane things like her family and what to do with *The Factory* then.'

I held myself back when he called our connection mundane. 'That's how it looks to you. But what about her family? What if they come after you?'

'But I'm not a threat to the land – I couldn't care less about the bloody castle. It's the daughter I want.'

I sucked air between my teeth. I recalled how, in her letter, Nancy had told Mick that Tommy Lee's side of the family would lose face and could react badly if he and Nancy went ahead with her plan. 'It depends on the family, I suppose, and how modern they are. To them it could be worse that you want the daughter.'

He waved this aside with a flick of his wrist. 'We can worry about that when the time comes. Look, she's in her thirties, for God's sake. They've got no hold over her. They let her live over here for three years when she was a student.'

The germ of plan was sprouting at the back of my mind. I wasn't totally sure what had prompted it, but I knew that I should maintain some influence over where this was going. 'All right then. Let's say you're going to meet up and spend time together. It's got to be somewhere nobody expects you to go. Somewhere with modern communication so I can keep you up to date with what's going on here... but obscure.'

'A European capital would be good. With connections.'

I had only been to one European capital and it was the obvious choice. I had to make it appear to be his idea. 'Let's look at the options: Paris is too near, Berlin may be too far east. Needs to be western Europe... Spain might be good or Por—'

'Portugal! Lisbon, of course! It's the romantic choice.'

'Why?'

'Don't you remember? It's where William Kellie-Smith went while he was building the castle.'

'But he died there.'

'That's what makes it romantic.'

'It's certainly not obvious. There's no reason her family would look for you there.'

'Lisbon! We'll meet there!'

'How can you organise it without her family knowing?'

'We'll both set up one of those new AOL personal e-mail things. They're safe.'

'That's settled then,' I said. 'Let's drink to Lisbon.'

For the next two weeks Mick was off my radar with only occasional contact to check in on the cinema. At those brief meetings, I'd ask how it was going with Nancy or he'd tag on notes to his e-mails: *She's coming to Lisbon! We're sorting out flights.* That sort of thing.

My routine managing *The Film Factory* allowed me time to think. After Luis died, in the years before I chanced upon The Vineyard and the empty Kellie factory, I had given up on the idea of finding a family. I had come to terms with being alone. Mick's branch of the Kellie family fell into my lap and I became his friend doing something that I really loved. The prospect of his marriage to Nancy was unsettling; it put a barrier between me and my newly-found family. This was how I felt when he called and asked for us to meet on the Monday morning in the foyer of *The Factory*.

We stood next to the new push-button machine while it chuntered and whirred out two cappuccinos. I glanced guiltily through the window at the coffee shop on the corner that we no longer needed to frequent. We took our cups and sat on one of the Chesterfield sofas that were positioned either side of a low table.

Mick looked out through the smoked-glass frontage as if he too had been thinking about the coffee shop.

'You okay?' I asked.

He shook his head as if to spin his thoughts away. 'Yeah. I was just thinking. Twenty... no thirty... years ago, when this was the only Kellie factory, I used to work here in the school holidays and on Saturdays.'

I contemplated my cup. 'Long time.'

'I used to fetch sandwiches and drinks for the shop-floor workers from that place over there.' He pointed to the coffee shop. 'It was a Colonial Stores—'

A sharp pang of recollection tightened my chest. For a split-second I was back wearing a Colonial Stores apron as I pedalled along the Waterloo Road on my delivery bike.

'—You know, a place where they sliced and weighed out ham and other cold meat to make up sandwiches and rolls. They sold cakes – iced Chelsea buns. The machine operators here all loved the iced Chelsea buns from over the road. They're not the same these days.' He sighed, took a pensive sip of his coffee and smiled. 'But I didn't ask you to come over to talk about Chelsea buns.'

'Why *did* you want to see me?'

'Just to let you know, I'm off on Friday. I've cabled money to Nancy and she's driving to Singapore on Wednesday. She's flying from there to Paris, getting a train to Schiphol and from there flying to Lisbon. We'll meet there on Saturday.'

'Blimey! She certainly doesn't want to be followed.'

'That's not the end of it. Depending on how things go, we'll move on.'

'Back to here?'

'No. We're thinking maybe America. A road-trip.'

'A Las Vegas wedding, perhaps?'

He blushed. 'Maybe. Who knows.'

'What's the plan? Keep your heads down until you get married and then come out into the open. Fait accompli'

'If it works out. If that's what we both decide. Can you look after this place for a couple of months?'

'Absolutely no problem. You gotta do what a man's gotta do.'

'We should increase your salary—'

I shrugged. 'To be honest, living like I do I don't spend what I get now. No, let's leave it a couple of months – until the end of the year – see what the profits look like. Perhaps there'll be enough for a bonus. No hurry.'

He shuffled to the edge of the sofa. 'Look. I want you to know I appreciate what you've done here. This place has given me a new lease of life—'

I held up a hand. 'Trust me, Mick, whatever you've got out of this place, I've got so much more. It's been a lifeline for me.' As I was saying it I thought to myself how true it sounded... how true it was.

'You're not horrified at the prospect of me being away?'

'Not at all. It sounds like a good plan. We can keep in

touch by e-mail. I assume you'll be staying at hotels where the rooms have modems.'

'I'll make sure they do.'

'Good. You know where you'll be in Lisbon?'

'Yes. *The International*.'

'Inside a week and you'll be over there. With Nancy.'

'Yes. I feel like a bloody schoolboy.'

I chuckled. 'Love'll do that to you.' As if I knew.

I saw Mick briefly on the Friday morning when he called in to *The Film Factory* on his way to Heathrow. Soon after he left, I called British Airways to confirm my own flight to Lisbon.

17

On the Tuesday before Mick left for Lisbon I had been sitting behind the computer dealing with work e-mails, when I started thinking about Nancy's letter and, specifically, the warning that she had given Mick about what her family was capable of if it was crossed.

I had always harboured suspicions about Luis's accident. If Nancy was right and Luis had died because of what he knew, Mick was clearly exposing himself to danger by whisking S Y Lee's daughter away. Mick was the only family I had left. I could not stand aside and lose him.

Another thought nagged at me. If he and Nancy settled down together, abroad perhaps or even here in Richmond, where in their future lives was the space for me?

I flicked through Yellow Pages to the 'Hotels and Inns' section and picked up the telephone.

The *Number 8 Hotel* in Kingston was an unprepossessing building comprising a row of linked houses on a main road nearer to Surbiton than its bigger neighbour. The signage and decoration implied that it was probably used more by salespeople on the road than by tourists or families.

Mr Sammy Lee came to meet me in the cramped reception area dressed as if he were a character in a drawing-room comedy who was just 'orf' to a rowing regatta. The garish stripe of his blazer clashed vividly with the paisley cravat at his neck. When he welcomed me, it was with the smooth assurance of an Old Etonian. Given his urbane manner, I didn't expect his office to be little more than a broom cupboard nor that it would reek of cigarettes.

After I had declined his offer of tea or coffee, I said, 'You don't know me, Mr Lee. There's no reason why you should. I'm here because I am in the cinema business with my partner Mick Kellie—'

'I don't know—'

'Let me finish please, Mr Lee. All will become clear.'

Sammy Lee sat back in his chair and a cynical smile tainted his otherwise blank expression. He must have thought I was intending to sell him something and he was giving me some leeway before shooting me down.

'My partner Mick Kellie recently visited Ipoh. While he was there, he met a relative of yours –' I paused for effect '– your niece, I think, Nancy Lee.'

Sammy Lee's smile faded. 'You have my interest. Go on.'

'My business partner and Nancy Lee have strong feelings for each other, so strong, in fact, that she is prepared to break off her engagement to your nephew Tommy Lee.'

'You seem to be remarkably well informed about my family.'

'I have seen a letter from Nancy to my cousin. She appears to be very much in love with him.'

Sammy Lee maintained his neutral expression but his body had tensed as if he was steeling himself to jump across the desk.

'My business partner also happens to be my cousin. He is the only family I have. I would not like to see him come to any harm.'

There was no movement, no answer from the other side of the desk.

'Perhaps I need to give you more background.'

At last a response: he nodded slowly. 'Please do.'

I took a deep breath. This was the delicate part. 'About five years ago another cousin of mine visited Ipoh. We have a family interest in Kellie's Castle. My grandfather built it. Do you know it?'

'Of course. It is part of the Kellas land owned by our family.'

'Exactly.'

'And?'

'While he was there he discovered something that might have been unwelcome to your family, your brother S Y Lee in particular. It would have affected your family's right to own the castle. Before my cousin could prove anything, he had an unfortunate accident and died.'

Sammy Lee frowned. 'That is most unfortunate. I'm sorry for your loss. But I still don't see what this has got to do with me – or my step brother.'

'My cousin, Mick Kellie, has arranged for your niece to meet with him and effectively elope. Your nephew Tommy will no longer be part of her life.'

'I don't see how this can happen. My step-brother will prevent it.'

'I'm afraid the plans are already in place.'

'I still don't understand why you are telling me all this.'

'Let me put it like this. I wouldn't want Mick to have a nasty accident like my cousin. I would rather he didn't put himself in harm's way.'

Sammy Lee stood up. His eyes narrowed and his voice had lost the all trace of its previous miserly warmth. 'I am not sure I fully understand what you are saying but it seems to me that you have an out-of-date view of how families in the Chinese community behave. We are not some sort of Mafia. You have been watching too many Triad films, I think.'

I clasped my hands together. 'Please, I'm sorry if I have

offended you. Perhaps I've got the wrong end of the stick.' The idiom didn't appear to confuse him so I ploughed on. 'I have written down certain details on the back of this business card. I will leave it with you and you can decide whether to pass them on to your step-brother.' I placed the card on his desk.

'Why are you doing this? I don't understand. Surely you don't believe we would harm your cousin?'

I spread my palms. 'Let's just say I'm leaving nothing to chance.' He was right. I was trading Mick's future happiness against the vague possibility that, if he and Nancy went ahead with their madcap plan, he might be harmed, die even.

If Nancy and I were wrong, and Luis's death had been an accident, Mick was in no danger; I was making a dreadful mistake. The image of Mick and Nancy playing happy families passed momentarily across my mind's eye. No, this was the right thing to do. I pointed at the card that he had left untouched. 'You have the information. You decide what to do with it.' I stood up. I had done what I had come to do.

Sammy Lee reached out for the business card and, theatrically, when his fingers were only millimetres away, withdrew his hand and stood up. 'You need not have come, Mr Cross. Your cousin has nothing to fear from us.' He pressed an intercom button on his telephone. 'My assistant will show you out.'

The door opened and a youth sidled in with a toothpick twitching at the corner of his mouth. He slouched by the door, his feet anchored to the floor by bright, golden trainers that looked three sizes too big.

'Stand up straight, idiot boy!' Sammy Lee's order made the youth stiffen to attention. Turning to me, Sammy Lee said, 'You just can't get the staff.' He smiled as we shook hands. My assumption, that this Henley-blazered caricature was any kind of violent Triad boss, was, in that moment, ridiculous.

18

Once I had negotiated the arrivals procedures in Lisbon Airport, I went straight to my hotel, dumped my case and returned to the ground floor. The cold drizzle swept across the doorway and I threw my raincoat over my shoulders for the few steps to the waiting taxi. We stopped off at a flower shop on the way and, when we reached the *International Hotel*, I asked the taxi driver to wait, gripped the lilies, blooms downwards, in my right fist and ran into the lobby. It was bland and bright, dotted with dark-suited businessmen. Tourists were rare in November. I could have been anywhere in the world. The receptionist smiled a welcome.

'I'd like to see one of your guests – Mr Mick Kellie – that's Kellie spelt with an "i" and an "e" at the end.'

'Of course.' She checked her computer and pointed to a bank of telephones behind me. 'If you take the first one on the left I'll connect you to his room.'

As I picked up the telephone, one of the businessmen came alongside and lifted the receiver next door.

'Hello?' Mick's voice sounded tentative; the response of a fugitive.

'It's me... Steve.'

'Is anything wrong?'

'Absolutely nothing. But I'm here in Lisbon, in your hotel. Downstairs.'

'What!'

'Downstairs. I thought I'd surprise you.'

'Yes. Well, you've certainly done that.'

'Is Nancy here? Have you met?'

'Yes. The poor girl's tired out after being on the road since Wednesday, but she's here. She's safe.'

'Good. Look do you want to go out? There's something I want you to see.'

'I can't. Nancy's asleep.'

'I thought she might be. This needs only you. Only an hour. Let her sleep. Leave a note.'

'An hour?' His voice dropped to a whisper. Perhaps Nancy had stirred. 'What's it about?'

'Come down to reception and I'll tell you. Or should I come up? Which room are you?'

'Room 808. Don't come up. Like I said, Nancy's sleeping...'

'Room 808, did you say?' I glanced at the businessman on the phone next door. He hadn't yet spoken.

'Yes, but don't come up. Can't this wait?'

This was more difficult than I had hoped. 'I've come all this way.'

'I didn't ask you to.' He was waiting for me to give up on it.

I held my breath. The man next door put down his phone and sauntered over to the lobby's far corner to confer with a similarly suited colleague.

'You still there, Steve?'

'Yes.'

'Okay.' I could hear his exasperation. 'Give me a minute. I'll come down.'

I put down the phone, sat on one of the armchairs facing the lifts and tried to slow down my breathing. The lilies lay across my lap.

Mick exited the lift a few minutes later. He was dressed to go out in a zipped waterproof top and carried an Indiana Jones style hat. I stood up and we shook hands like strangers.

'Everything okay upstairs?' I said. I proffered the flowers. 'These are for Nancy.'

'Thanks,' Mick said. He looked disorientated with the lilies suddenly thrust into his care. 'I'll just leave these...' He went across to reception and passed them over with a few words of explanation. When he returned, he said, 'What are you doing here? What's all this about?'

'I'll explain in the taxi.'

'What taxi?'

'I said. I want to show you something.'

'But Nancy—'

'You said she was asleep. It won't take long.'

He shook his head. 'I don't understand.' But he followed me out through the revolving doors.

As we crossed the pull-in road, where the taxi was parked, I was relieved to see that the rain had stopped. I looked up. The clouds had gathered on the horizon giving the weak sun an unfettered view of the city.

Once we were settled in the back of the cab and I'd given the destination: the British Cemetery, I turned to Mick. 'I've got a confession. I haven't been entirely straight with you. I've been to Lisbon before. I met our other cousin, the one who Nancy mentioned in her letter. It'll be easier to explain when we arrive at the cemetery but for the moment I just want you to know that as far as the cinema is concerned I've been totally honest. From the second I first saw the old factory and had the vision of the picture house and wrote to you, right up to today, everything between us has been above board.'

'I don't understand.' He shook his head, frowning. 'What do you mean you haven't been straight? How else—?'

I could see we were already on the far side of the square from the cemetery gates. 'Look. We're nearly there. You'll understand soon enough.'

Mick pressed his forehead to the window. In a small voice he said, 'Is it about Nancy? If you're going to tell me something bad about her. I couldn't bear it...'

The taxi pulled up outside the gates and I handed over the Escudos with a good tip. I led the way down the wide central path, turned off to the right and stopped at the Celtic cross.

Mick read the inscription aloud. 'William Kellie-Smith.'

'Yes. This is your grandfather's twin brother. Your grandfather Kenneth started the factory in Richmond. His brother, William –' I pointed to the name on the stone '– started the Malaysian plantation and built Kellie's Castle. This is *my* grandfather's grave.'

'And what's this got to do with—'

I took his elbow and steered him to the next grave along. 'This is his daughter.' I pointed to the name on the headstone *Helen Escobar*. 'She was Kellie-Smith before she married.'

'Escobar! That's the name of the man in Nancy's letter.'

While he was talking, I noticed a small plaque had been planted at the base of the headstone. On it was picked out: *Also the final resting place of her son Luis Escobar who died in Ipoh, Malaysia on 21st November, 1990 aged 40.* I hadn't expected the plaque to be there but it helped me make my point. 'In 1990, I discovered I had a cousin, Luis, and came to see him in Lisbon. He told me about the castle but only decided to go there after meeting me. I sparked his interest. I was the reason he went there.'

'Where he died.'

'Yes. In an accident that I always had doubts about and which Nancy mentioned when she warned you about her family in her letter.'

Mick shook his head as if he was trying to shake something loose from his hair. 'I don't get it. This is all too much. Why are you in Lisbon? Why are we here?'

I pointed to a shelter with a bench. 'Let's sit down and I'll try to explain.'

It was cold and I regretted not bringing a winter coat. Neither of us could stand a drawn-out explanation but I needed to take my time if I was to keep him safe; I leant forward with my elbows on my knees studying the ground. I dared not look at his face. 'You never asked me for the whole story about how we're related and I think I'd better start there. I told you how I never knew my father, Anthony Kellie-Smith. He was William's son. He was born in Malaysia but was in the UK when World War Two started. It sounds like he was a high-up in the RAF in London when he was killed in a flying-bomb attack in June 1944. I was born in January the following year – 1945. He never married my mother but they were engaged. Perhaps he didn't even know she was pregnant. She died five years ago.'

Mick mumbled a commiseration. He studied his shoes and rubbed his palms together to warm them.

'Your grandfather, Kenneth, died in the same air raid as my father. My father met your grandfather in the London Blitz and a bastard Doodlebug landed on them. When my mum died – she'd been ill a long time – I felt desperately alone and started to search for my family – some remnants from my father's side—'

'And you found me.'

'No. Not until much later. This was five years ago, remember.' I straightened up. 'I found Luis Escobar first and he told me about the land in Malaysia and the Castle.' The story was garbled. I feared he wouldn't be able to grasp it all.

He pulled me round to face him. 'You knew all that stuff about the land five years ago. But you—'

'I know. I could have told you about it before but there was no reason to. Not until you showed me the picture of the family land. That's when I gave you the magazine to put you on the right track.'

'You had the article all along.'

'I'm sorry. Yes, I'd had it for years. Perhaps subconsciously, I thought that if I told you and you went to find the castle you might have an accident like Luis. But you did go and you came back safe. Except—'

'Except I'd found Nancy.'

I watched the sparrows flitting from bush to bush in the thin sunlight. Their twittering filled the silence while I contemplated how to lead into the part of the story that I had rehearsed over and over.

'None of this explains why you're here now. Why *are* you here?'

'I thought if you saw where Luis ended up it might impress on you the huge risk you're taking. It's not too late. I think Nancy was right. I think her family was probably behind Luis's death. They are capable of murder. If you do this. If you take Nancy from them...'

I turned and faced him. 'After Escobar died I had a sort of breakdown. My new family had been snatched away. I went off the rails for a bit, drinking and not looking after myself. I was getting my life back on track when I saw the old Kellie factory and had my vision for the cinema. I knew about this stuff and it didn't matter that you didn't know. But because of Nancy... suddenly it seems important that you should know what they will do if you cross them. That's why I came here. I had to make it as clear as possible what they're capable of.'

He rose from the seat and started for the gate. 'I'm going to have to think about this. It's weird. *You're* weird. You must know nothing's going to stop me and Nancy. Not now.'

I tugged at his sweater. 'Of course, I know it. But I have to do this... for me. Family's important and anything that jeopardises it... well, I've just tried to keep you close. It wasn't important that *you* cared whether we were related but it matters to me.'

He looked at his watch and shivered. 'I'm cold. Come on. I ought to be getting back.' He led the way to the gates and flagged down a passing cab.

I checked my watch. We'd been gone long enough.

19

'Would you like to meet Nancy?' he asked as the taxi approached the *International*. 'Either that or you keep the cab.' It was as if the conversation in the cemetery had never happened.

'Can I come in? I'd like to meet her if she's up.'

We crossed the lobby towards the reception desk together. The clock told us it was nearly five. Mick took the key and the lilies and we waited silently as the lift took us to the eighth floor. My stomach was churning and I regretted not having eaten since I left London.

Mick knocked on the door and said, 'Nancy, it's me,' before opening it and stepping inside. He turned back. 'Wait here.'

I held the door ajar and peered in.

Then came the startled shout. 'Nancy!'

I followed Mick, half-expecting to see Nancy's body on the bed. It was empty, its duvet half-strewn on the floor.

'She's gone!' He barged through the open bathroom door, came back wide-eyed, looked around frantically and tossed the flowers on the bed.

I stood, not knowing what to say or do.

'Come on!' He rushed out to the corridor and I ran after him as he sped to the lift. He pressed the call button as if he was sending an urgent message in Morse code. His lips were drawn back against his teeth. His face was pale as if dusted with chalk powder. 'Come on!'

He shoved through the still opening doors and stabbed the ground-floor button and another to close the doors. 'Come on!'

The receptionist was cool and calm. 'Yes, we saw Ms Lee leaving about thirty minutes ago. She looked distressed.'

'Why didn't you stop her?'

'We had no reason to. She was in the company of two businessmen – men in dark suits.' She leaned across the desk and whispered. 'They were of Eastern appearance like her. Perhaps they were relatives. I wondered whether they had brought her bad news.'

'Did they say where they were going?'

'No, sir. They walked straight out and went off in a limousine.'

'What do you mean *limousine?*'

'Not an ordinary car. Not a taxi. A black limousine. I could see it waiting.' She indicated the glass frontage with revolving doors.

A man whose lapel badge identified him as the duty manager approached. 'May I assist you?' he asked, as he signalled to the receptionist to move along the counter and deal with another guest.

Mick turned to him. 'My... fiancée... Ms Lee. She's staying here with me. I think she's been kidnapped.'

The manager gestured that we should follow him to the quieter end of the reception desk. 'I'll call the police,' he whispered.

'No!' Mick held up a hand. 'Not yet. We have to find out what's happening first.'

The tall, grey-haired concierge signalled from his post by the doorway. The manager excused himself and went to join him.

Mick pulled me towards the lobby entrance. 'It's probably her family,' he whispered. 'That's why I don't want to involve the police. They must have tracked her down. How could they have done it so quickly?'

I shrugged. 'Maybe they traced her tickets. She hasn't used a credit card since she arrived, has she?'

He looked at me as if I'd had a lobotomy. 'Don't be stupid.'

Out of the corner of my eye, I could see the duty manager returning. He cleared his throat. 'I've been talking to the concierge—' he gestured to where he had been standing '—about your fiancée's leaving, sir. He suggests that you might go to an area of Lisbon where the Chinese trading companies have businesses. They are in the few streets north of the square called Martim Moniz. If she's been taken by Chinese people perhaps she will be there. That's all I can suggest short of calling the police.'

'Where did you say?' Mick said.

'The streets north of Martim Moniz Square.'

A taxi was disgorging passengers on the forecourt. 'Quick, we can take that cab,' Mick ordered.

I dived into the taxi after him and he called out the name of the square. 'North side!' he shouted. He jittered and fidgeted while the driver waited for the traffic to clear so he could pull out. 'We're in a hurry!'

'Try and calm down,' I said.

'Calm down! They've taken Nancy. She'll be on a plane back to Kuala Lumpur before we can blink. We've got to stop them.'

'How do you know it's them?'

'Who bloody else would it bloody be? But if it is, when they see how much I care... Can it be that bad marrying a gweilo? I've got money for Christ's sake. It's not as though I'm some sort of bum.'

'Just be careful.'

When the taxi stopped by the narrow streets at the top of the square, it was obvious why the concierge had suggested this area. The names of various companies were spelled out in Chinese lettering with English translations using the words 'trading,' 'import' and 'wholesale'. Mick led the way along the widest street looking for signs of a black limousine. The entrances on both sides had closed double doors. The car could have been parked beyond any of them.

'This is hopeless,' I said. 'We're not going to find it.'

The street lights were beginning to come on. I shivered. We turned into a street called Rua Calçado Mouraria. There, a hundred metres along, was a red sign with yellow Chinese lettering and the translation: *Leeyate Trading*.

Mick dragged me by my sleeve. 'Leeyate! That's the name of their hotels. Come on!'

He ran up to the sign. The frontage was uncannily like the entrance to the factory yard of the old Kellie's premises in Richmond. The wooden, triple-garage-width sliding gate boasted a Judas door. Mick banged on it with his fist. Nothing happened. He bashed it again, rattling the hinges. There was a sound from beyond and a spy panel opened at chest height. Mick stooped to see who it was. 'I've come for Nancy. I know you've got her. If you don't open up I'll call the police.'

The spy hole slammed shut. Nothing happened on the other side for perhaps thirty seconds while Mick paced in a circle wringing his hands and banging on the door every time he passed it. 'Okay. I'm calling the police now. This is kidnap!' he shouted.

Again, there was no movement. Mick was about to turn away when we heard bolts being drawn back. The Judas door opened to reveal a cobbled yard with a black Mercedes parked in the middle. Mick ducked in under the lintel and I followed.

A Chinese man was stationed at each corner of the car, two in business suits and two dressed like peasants in a paddy field. All four nonchalantly dangled pick-axe handles from their right hands. My heart raced. My throat felt blocked as if I'd half-swallowed my tongue.

A small man in his sixties stood in front of the car's radiator grille. He bowed his head but there was no politesse here. Despite his age and the fact that he held no weapon, he looked ready for violence. 'You must be Mr Kellie,' he said, his voice reedy. 'Well, Mr Kellie, my daughter has decided to return Malaysia of her own free will. She not kidnapped.'

'I don't believe you. I want to see her – to hear it from her,' Mick said. He unzipped his jacket and allowed his hat to slip from his hand. It fell to the cobbles between us. Was he seriously contemplating taking them on?

The man, I assumed him to be S Y Lee, ignored him and turned to me. 'And who you?'

'I'm a friend. Just a friend.'

'Then I suggest, Mr Just-a-friend, you step back. Leave. This not your quarrel. You both no understands Miss Lee. She is very loving daughter. She wants to be with family. She has responsibilities in family business. She knows these duties and she wants go back home.'

'She's old enough to make up her own mind,' Mick said.

S Y Lee nodded as if conceding the point. 'She *is* old enough and she chooses go home.'

'Let me see her,' Mick's voice wavered. He was beginning to understand the hopelessness of his case.

My mind, sharpened by adrenaline, was honed like a razor. I considered the options. I had no wish to be beaten up alongside my cousin. But I couldn't allow him to doubt me. I stood firm. The different paths the immediate future might take were clear. Neither of them saw Mick and me leave that yard with Nancy. We could either leave in an ambulance or with our faces and limbs intact. The latter was preferable; it was up to me.

I had to extricate my cousin from danger. I looked around. My line of sight took in the bottom of a flight of wooden steps and followed them up to a half-paned door. A tall Chinese woman stood watching. She raised a hand and pressed her palm against the window-pane.

Back by the limousine, none of the four young men had lost their menace. S Y Lee shifted his hand from his pocket to behind his back and I heard the click of what I assumed was a switchblade.

This was what it had come to. This was a fated moment. All the possible futures detonated after Mum's death had collapsed into this one pinhole of now. There were only five words of the English language that I could utter that would be appropriate to this place, to this time.

I picked up Mick's hat and dusted it off, feigning nonchalance. I gripped his elbow and shoulder, twisted him away and steered him towards the street. Never have I said five words with such feeling.

'Forget it, Mick,' I said. 'It's Chinatown.'

PART THREE –
1995–1996

1

Back in Martim Moniz Square, Mick turned to face me, his features twisted with contempt. 'What the bloody hell did you have to say that for?'

I could only shake my head and shrug. It had seemed like a moment of destiny. How often are you able to quote the immortal last line of a classic film in exactly the situation for which it was written? It was foolish. But it had worked. He had allowed me to lead him through the Judas door and away.

He pressed his fingers against his temples and drew his hands downwards. For a second it looked as if he would drag his eyes out of their sockets. 'If only you hadn't come here. That ridiculous charade with the grave; what was all that about?'

I knew better than to answer.

'If you hadn't taken me away—'

I couldn't let him get away with it. 'They would still have come for her. You'd have been beaten up at the hotel.'

'What am I going to do?'

I touched his arm. 'Why don't you go back to the *International* and rest? I'm sorry about the cemetery thing. It was stupid. But how could I know what was going to happen? I needed to let you know what you're dealing with...'

His cheeks were wet and he wiped the end of his nose with a sleeve. 'You go back to *The Film Factory*. You shouldn't have left it. I'll try to work out if I can do anything here.'

I put my other hand on his shoulder. 'Is there anything—?'

He shrugged me away. 'Yes! You can fuck off back to England!'

A week later, Mick called me to arrange a cinema meeting. I unlocked the glass door of the foyer and pushed the buttons for two cappuccinos so that the drinks were on the table between the sofas for when he arrived.

While I was waiting for the coffees, I looked around. The white and silver Christmas decorations conveyed the subdued but classy effect I had been aiming for. When I saw Mick's face, it was obvious he wasn't in the mood to notice the tinsel. He was pale, his cheeks sunken and his eye sockets were dark hollows.

'You okay, mate?' I said.

'Course I'm not bloody okay. I've lost her.'

We weren't going to be talking much about the cinema. 'You don't know that.'

He stabbed a finger at me across the table. '*You* don't know anything. She's told me. She has no choice. She does what her father says. She wants to get away from the whole family thing but it's too powerful.'

'She won't run away again, then.'

He shot daggers with his eyes. I took it as a no.

'You're still in touch with her, though?'

He nodded. 'By e-mail. She says her dad isn't monitoring it. But it's his company's computer. Who knows?'

'It's a good sign that she does—'

'But it's not going anywhere...'

We moved on to discussing the film programme and the cash flow but his interest was perfunctory. I shuffled together the spreadsheets.

'Look, before we go,' he said, 'we ought to talk about what you told me in Lisbon – before they kidnapped Nancy.'

Blood rushed to my cheeks. 'It's okay...'

'No. Obviously, it would have been better if you'd been straight about it all from the start. But, the family stuff over there in Malaysia, it means nothing to me. For me, Malaysia means Nancy, nothing else. Now I've got to find a way...'

'I understand. But, if I'd told you about Luis and his visit, maybe you wouldn't have gone and you wouldn't have—'

He put up a hand to stop me. 'Don't try and make it better. It won't get better. And as far as us being cousins is concerned, well, I understand it's important to you because you never had a family but for me our partnership in the cinema is what counts. Sometime maybe, you can run the family tree by me again... if we're cousins, we're cousins. What difference does it make?'

I nodded. Okay, for him it didn't mean much; to me it was... I was part of a family again. What do families do at Christmas? 'Have you got anything planned for Christmas Day?' I asked.

He shook his head. 'I've been going to a pub for Christmas Dinner since my dad died. Why?'

'I was wondering if you'd like to come to mine. We could have couple of pints in *The King's Head* while the turkey cooks and I'll do the traditional thing: roast potatoes, sprouts, stuffing. The full hit.'

He sighed and agreed cheerlessly.

As soon as Mick left, I started planning the lunch. I'd make sure that his Christmas dinner would be better than anything he'd have had in a pub. Perhaps it would help him come to terms with the fact that the cinema and I, we were his future, not Nancy.

2

The Film Factory showed *It's a Wonderful Life* on Christmas Eve. We only had the main screen open and it was a full-house. As George Bailey's family and friends jostled around him, handing over their money and singing *For He's a Jolly Good Fellow*, I found it hard, as always, to hold back the tears.

Mick had stood with me in the foyer to wish the audience members Happy Christmas as they left and we closed down the building together. I set the alarm and we stood outside listening for the warning beeps to stop. We turned in unison to face the street and he twisted up the collar of his overcoat. Blobs of watery snow fell around us like May blossom. My blouson jacket wasn't warm or waterproof enough for this weather, but I only had to walk a few yards to the house next door.

'See you tomorrow, then, Steve,' Mick said, 'Happy Christmas' and hands in pockets, he sauntered off towards Vineyard Passage and the town. His shoulders were hunched against the cold and he carried a heavy sack of grief on his back.

It must have been the scream of the racing car engine and the squeal of brakes that woke me because I'm sure I was already out of bed when I heard the crash and felt the house shiver. I jumped to the window as the alarm started screeching.

With my cheek against the glass, looking down I could see

the tail end of a hatchback sticking out from the front of the cinema. A spiral of dust and smoke rose around the car's rear end. I ran downstairs and out onto the street in time to see two men scarper around the corner into Onslow Road. A second car flashed across the junction. By the time I had passed the wrecked cinema doorway and reached the corner, the two men and the second car had gone.

I retraced my steps and edged past the hatchback's rear end, shattered glass crunching underfoot. The bonnet was doubled back against the open windscreen. The engine compartment breathed electric-smelling smoke. I grabbed the foyer extinguisher and dusted the engine block. I went back to the house, called the police first and then Mick.

The blue lights scanning the house fronts reminded me of the night Mum died. A few gawkers had gathered on the opposite pavement and watched while a tow-truck tugged the hatchback, screeching and tearing, back into the street. Sharp-edged stones of glass and twisted lengths of aluminium fell around it. Officers from a police patrol car had visited us briefly. They put the crash down to joy-riders, saying they'd investigate the ownership of the car, already assuming it had been stolen. They said we would hear from the station in the morning. I called the insurance company's 24-hour helpline and was given the name of a glaziers who would come out straight away and secure the premises. They were not due for another hour or so. It was after 2am. Mick and I both had pyjamas on under our overcoats.

'Did you see what happened?' Mick asked.

'I heard the crash and looked out of the window.' I signalled in the general direction of my bedroom with my thumb. 'I saw two guys running away. A car picked them up around the corner.'

'What about the CCTV?'

We both glanced up at the camera set on the wall of the house that pointed at the cinema doorway.

'We should take a look. Hand it over to the police,' Mick said.

'I told them it wasn't working; that it wouldn't be any help.'

He raised his eyebrows. 'Why did you do that?'

'Dunno. Just a feeling. Something about the two guys, their height, the way they ran. I don't know what made me think it but maybe they were Chinese.'

'What!'

'I know it's a big leap. But when we look at the film, maybe you'll feel the same way. Do you think it could be Nancy's dad sending you a warning?'

We stepped through the open frontage, our shoes scrunching the glittering jewels of glass. Ignoring the smell of spilt petrol, we entered the back office and I rewound the tape, watching as two men ran backwards to the car and Fosbury flopped into their seats. The building frontage rose back into place when the car reversed out and sped backwards up the hill towards Richmond Park. When it was out of the frame I pressed play.

The car, a black VW Golf, sped into view and immediately swerved right, then left, straightened up and speared into the building. Nothing about it was accidental. The car's doors opened and, simultaneously, two men, both short and in baseball caps, ran to the corner and waited for two or three seconds. One of them was wearing hi-top gold trainers that, reflecting the light from the street lamps, flashed like the lens of an Aldis lamp as he hopped from foot to foot. It confirmed what I thought I had seen.

'What are they doing?' Mick said.

The answer became clear immediately. The second car drove up from the south side of the junction and the men ran off in the same direction. I appeared on the corner a second or two later but by then they must have been out of sight over the top of the hill.

I pressed the 'stop' button. 'See what I mean. Something about them...'

Mick was thin-lipped, pale. 'They could have been joy-riding kids.'

'But the other car came for them. It was all deliberate – planned. Didn't you think, the way they ran... they had sort of bandy legs—'

'Oh! And Chinese men have bandy legs.'

'I'm not saying that. What I am saying, though, is that someone did it deliberately and maybe it was a warning from Nancy's father. Maybe he knows you and she are still in touch. He's telling you to keep away.'

'Let's sleep on it. But it's probably best to put another tape in the machine and we'll tell the police we forgot to turn the system on or something.'

It rained on Christmas Day. I woke late after the disturbed night and looked out of my window. The pale boards covering the gap in the glass were streaked where the water had dripped down from the broken guttering.

When Mick arrived we were of the same mind, agreed without words, that the best reaction to the previous day's events would be to find drunken oblivion as soon as possible. By the end of Christmas dinner we'd had three pints in *The Duke's Head*, Champagne while I cooked the veg and a bottle of Rioja with the meal. We sat side-by-side in front of the television that was showing the opera *La Bohème*. The sound was turned down so that we could continue chatting about the *The Film Factory* and our plans for building the business in 1996. We were both slumped down in the sofa cradling half-full tumblers of Glenlivet on our chests. Mick had said as he poured them, 'I'll make them big ones so we don't have to keep getting up.'

The subject of the cinema ran its course and in the silence that followed, I felt my eyes closing. I couldn't remember feeling this settled. It must have been before Mum had been ill. Could that be nearly twenty years ago, when I was in my late twenties? Meeting Mick and building the business together had come to my rescue. I took a swig of the whisky and wiped my eyes with a tissue.

'Tell me about your family,' Mick said.

With the rain battering against the window and the television now merely flashing images in the background, I slurred my way through the story: my mother on the Barnardo's doorstep, my parents in the war, my father's death, my upbringing by a mixed-race, single mother and how I cared for her until she died.

'And how are you connected to my family? Run that by me again.'

My rambling account culminated with how our grandparents shared the same paternal DNA because their fathers were twins and how this made us direct cousins.

'You're the only family I have, then,' he said.

'And you're the only family I have.'

He raised his glass. 'Cheers!'

'Cheers, cousin!' I said

The television took centre stage again and we watched Mimi singing the tear-jerking aria *Donde lieta uscì* in which she tells Rodolfo that she is leaving him but still wants to be friends. Mick was deploying a discreet tissue. 'Something about meeting Nancy made me think it was meant to be, you know it was our fate to be together,' he said.

'What do you mean?'

He recounted the uncanny events leading up to his arrival in Ipoh. 'When I got there, I was primed for something momentous. It made me feel out of kilter. I was listing – like a boat about to capsize. I met Nancy and she straightened me up...' pause '... yeah, you could say that she straightened me up...' pause '... figuratively and literally.'

We both exploded into our whiskies, snorting and giggling like two old topers in *The Duke's Head*.

Mick's voice wavered as he described their time together exploring our ancestral home and his subsequent disappointment when Lang-ren turned up at their 'date'. 'And I'd spruced myself up like a Christmas tree. Even put talcum powder down my underpants.'

We spluttered again.

'You *were* optimistic,' I said.

'If you'd been in my shoes, you'd have done the same.'

I couldn't even remember the name of the last woman I'd slept with. In that moment, it didn't seem as important as having a friendship that meant you could sit alongside someone, watch something on television that neither of you understood, and guffaw at each other's feeble innuendos.

Later, when I stood at the door watching Mick stagger down *The Vineyard*, the boarded frontage of our cinema triggered an image of Sammy Lee running his hotel in the borough next-door and a shiver of fear for Mick's safety tickled my back. I reassured myself that not even a heathen would attack a man on the evening of Christmas Day and closed the front door reassured.

Washing up in the warmth of the kitchen, drinking the last of the champagne, I considered my friendship with my business partner and cousin and realised that if something happened to him, or even if Nancy came back into his life, it was *my* mental cargo that would be in danger of shifting. I wasn't sure I could face that prospect again.

The police were right about one thing. The VW was stolen. Without the benefit of the film showing the second-car pick-up, they concluded that the crash was the work of teenage joyriders. They based this on my comment to the attending officer on the night that I had seen 'small men' run away. I doubt whether they bothered checking the car wreckage for evidence, forensic or otherwise. It was another case best filed away and forgotten.

Next time we met in the pub, Mick told me that he had mentioned the crashed car to Nancy in one of his secret e-mails. She had said that, if it was a message from her father, it would have been delivered by the Lee family in Kingston, the same people she had stayed with when she studied at the polytechnic.

'I'm going to see them. Find out for myself,' he said. 'I'm not going to give her up.'

I didn't know what to say.

He sighed. 'Look, if you really are my cousin don't you think you should be on my side here?'

What was he implying? It felt like I was in the dock and that anything I said would have sounded incriminating.

'There has to be something I can do to make her father accept me. I'm not a bloody waster. I can look after her as well as any member of her bloody family. I have to persuade him somehow.'

3

There's no doubt about it, Mick's heart would have been thudding and his underarms pumping as he pulled onto the frontage of the *Number 8 Hotel*. It was on the main road that linked Kingston with its neighbour, Surbiton. It was so unprepossessing that he had driven along this road many times during his selling days and never noticed it.

He had telephoned in advance and made an appointment to see the General Manager, whose name, unsurprisingly, was Lee. Mick didn't know how senior this Mr Lee was, but was hoping to find out.

Mick wore a suit and, as he approached the front door, he imagined himself as a James Bond character entering the evil mastermind's den. In the books, this direct approach to the enemy was usually the only way for Bond to bring resolution, save the world and, incidentally, the girl. But it was never without danger and Bond usually had to survive torture and other trials at the hands of Dr No or his equivalent before winning through.

The reception door opened automatically and the bell press on the unattended counter sounded an innocent ping. A Chinese youth with a toothpick between his lips slouched in. So far so good.

Sammy Lee wore a blazer over light-grey trousers. With cut-glass accented, public school assurance as he asked Mick to be seated and whether he would like tea or coffee. The office was a small room cluttered with box files. The acridity of stale cigarette smoke was knitted into the room's fabric.

After he had used a grubby, white intercom machine to ask for two coffees, Sammy Lee asked Mick why he had come.

It had been a long time since Mick he had been on the road representing *Kellie's Janitorial Products*. He had failed to prepare an opening and felt vulnerable relying solely on his wits. 'I'm not sure that you can help me. But if I explain how I became connected to your family, perhaps it's a start.'

Sammy Lee made space on his desk for the coffee cups that appeared from behind Mick, carried on a tray by a sullen youth. Mick wondered whether this had been part of Nancy's role – how many years before? He drew a deep breath. 'Mr Lee, I went to Malaysia recently and I met and fell in love with a relative of yours. Her name is Nancy Lee and she lives in Ipoh. Her father is S Y Lee. He too runs a hotel – *The Leeyate Plaza*.'

'Of course. Nancy Lee is my niece.'

Mick was disarmed by the man's honesty. 'You don't seem surprised.'

'My step-brother S Y Lee has told me about you. He was most disturbed when Nancy ran away from home.'

'She hardly ran away. Nancy is not a child.'

Sammy Lee bowed as if accepting the point. 'We remember Nancy from her time here. She was an exemplary student and a good worker in the hotel. How did you know about my connection to her – to her father?' His eyes had narrowed and he placed his hands flat on the table as if he was preparing to react in some way to what Mick said next.

'Nancy told me about her time at the polytechnic and how she had lived with her extended family at the *Number 8 Hotel* in Kingston. It wasn't difficult.'

Sammy Lee's shoulders relaxed. Apparently, Mick had passed a test he hadn't recognised. 'So how can I help you?'

'I would like Nancy and I to be together. Perhaps even to get married. We are, neither of us, young. We feel that, left to ourselves, we can decide whether it is a realistic prospect. Unfortunately, though, Mr Lee – S Y Lee – has set himself against the idea of us being together. So much so that he kidnapped... detained his daughter in Lisbon, where we planned to spend some time together, and now forbids her any contact with me.'

'This is most unfortunate for you. I can see the problem. Mr S Y Lee is very – what you and I would call – "old-school". He is set in his ways.'

'I have no way of letting him know that my intentions towards his daughter are entirely honourable. He is so set against me that I believe he warned me to stay away from Nancy by sending men to crash a car into my premises.'

The eyebrows on Sammy Lee's mobile face almost disappeared beneath the dyed-ebony of his hairline. 'When did this happen?'

'Christmas Eve.'

'Are you sure it was him?'

'I'm sure it was something he could have arranged.' Mick felt as if the air had been sucked out of the room. The temperature dipped and the only sound came from under the table as Sammy Lee tapped out the seconds with his toe. It was as if the taint of old cigarettes had consumed the room's oxygen.

Finally, Sammy Lee nodded. 'Perhaps it was.' He smiled showing small, pointed teeth. A shark's smile. 'But I still don't know why you have come to see me.'

'Because, I have no way of communicating with S Y Lee. He refuses to accept anything from me. Nancy can't speak to him on my behalf. I was hoping that you could pass on a message.'

'What message?'

'That I am no threat. In fact, quite the opposite. I am genuinely in love with his daughter. I am a man of means. She and I could live independently. I'm prepared to live in Malaysia with her, if that's what it takes.' He leaned forward, realising that this would be his only opportunity to press his case. 'The only thing wrong with me as far as being a suitor to his daughter is concerned is that I'm not Chinese. I'm a good man. I'm a relatively rich man. If I came to Ipoh to live permanently I would sell up here and be able invest in business there. But this can only happen if he lets Nancy and I work things out. We feel strongly for each other, but who knows? We need S Y Lee to give us time and space.' He leant back, suddenly aware of the sweat trickling down beneath his shirt.

Sammy Lee smiled his orcan smile. 'You are a very persuasive man, Mr Kellie. I can see why my niece admires you.'

'Does this mean you'll do something?'

For the first time, Sammy Lee engaged Mick eye to eye, his dark irises and rictus smile pinned an invisible text behind his words. 'Of course. I will tell S Y Lee about our meeting. I can tell him what you have said. I'm not sure that it will make any difference. *I* can see that you could be the right man for my niece. But S Y Lee – who knows?'

There was no more to be said. Mick leant across the desk and offered his hand. 'Thank you so much, Mr Lee.'

'I hope we can resolve things to your satisfaction, Mr Kellie. Who knows, we may meet again as family.'

Mick was smiling as he returned to his car. His smile faded when he remembered Nancy's warning in her letter that Sammy Lee was from the same branch of her family as her fiancé Tommy. He shook his head to spin the thought away. His visit couldn't have made things worse than they already were.

4

Mick was buoyant when he told me about the meeting, convinced that Sammy Lee would contact his step-brother to put Mick's case. I was more circumspect, by no means certain that Sammy Lee was the urbane 'Englishman' he would have us believe. The golden trainers were irrefutable proof as far as I was concerned. Not for the first time, Mick had been seduced by the inscrutability of the East.

As I anticipated, nothing happened to give Mick hope over the next few weeks. It seemed that, even if Mick's case had been put to S Y Lee, it had bounced against a Chinese wall.

The insurance company paid up and we repaired the cinema's frontage in time to cope with the big freeze that swept in from the east towards the end of January. Despite the sub-zero temperatures and snowstorms that made Vineyard Passage impassable on three evenings, our audiences were big enough to maintain The Factory's profitability. Mick and I had our management meetings and he would bring me up to date with his clandestine e-mail correspondence with Nancy. S Y Lee was still resolute in his opposition to their spending any time together. Then came the breakthrough.

We met that cold February morning in the lobby at The Factory. A 25-metre stroll for me but a stiff-kneed skid along the compacted-snow alleyway for Mick. He shook melting snow petals from his coat. 'Bloody brass monkeys out there.'

'I'll get the coffee,' I said, hurrying to the refreshment counter. When I returned to the table by the window, Mick was looking up into the pregnant sky. 'Looks like more on the way.' When he turned back, his face was animated by a wide smile.

'Wow! You won the lottery?' I asked.

'I've had some great news. Nancy has persuaded her Dad to see me! He's had a change of heart.'

'That *is* good,' I said. 'Sammy Lee came through for you, then.'

'Nothing to do with him apparently. But, when I emailed Nancy about my conversation with Sammy Lee, I mentioned how I was prepared to sell up in the UK and find something to invest in over there.' He grinned. 'Apparently, she had no idea how much money I have. She'd always thought every penny was in the cinema.'

This was news to me. What did he mean 'sell up in the UK'? What did it mean for *The Factory*, for me? I let him go on.

'She didn't tell me everything but it seems that she's worked this up into an idea that might get her dad onside.'

'What idea?'

'She said it was to do with the castle; something I said to her in Ipoh about how it should be a tourist attraction.'

'And she's definitely persuaded him to see you?'

'So she says.'

'You'd better get out there before he changes his mind then.'

'I know. I'm going to book the flights this afternoon. But I wanted to talk to you first. To make sure it's okay with you.'

'You should go. Go get the girl.'

Mick booked a flight leaving two days later. I didn't want to spook him by reminding him about what had happened to Luis, but I thought he should have his affairs in order, as they say. If S Y Lee had been responsible for Luis's fall, might Mick meet the same fate? His share of *The Factory* partnership would probably come to me, but what about the rest? There was his flat in Richmond, his car and the money from the sale of the company. I'd looked up the rules and if he died without having made a will, without any known relatives, his money would revert to the state. He wouldn't have wanted that to happen.

In the end, I decided on what I hoped would be a sufficiently robust solution that wouldn't spook him. I found a local calligrapher through an advertisement in the *Surrey Comet* and commissioned him to do an urgent job for me.

The tube containing the document arrived by courier only hours before Mick was due to leave and I hurried over to his flat.

'Everything ready?' I asked.

He sucked in a long breath, puffing up his chest. 'I'm hellishly nervous.'

'You'll be fine. He's agreed to see you. It's a good sign.'

'I really think my future happiness depends on this.'

'You're in love.'

'What did you want?'

'Well mainly to wish you *bon voyage* and all the best but I also wanted to show you this.' I held up the cardboard tube. 'I ordered it after Christmas but... just let's say this seems the right time.'

'What is it?'

'It's a bit cheesy but I had a calligrapher draw up a sort of family tree. Your side and mine. Look I'll show you.'

I unrolled the faux parchment and ran my finger down a hand-scripted family tree from the twin grandparents at the top through the next generation to where Mick and I were the only two people in our row. We were linked through a box containing the word 'Cousins'. Below our names there were spaces for Mick and me to sign.

'I know this doesn't mean much to you,' I said, 'but remember I never had a family. This makes it all seem real. It's not a big tree, is it? Two names at the top and now only you and I left at the bottom – but I'd treasure it.

He looked from the document to me and back again. 'No, I understand. It's important. For both of us.' His gentle, blue eyes were shining. I could have hugged him.

'It would mean a lot if you'd sign it, recognise that we're family. I know it's silly but I'm going to get it framed.' I proffered my best fountain pen. The one they had given me when I left Scotia.

'Of course,' he said. Leaning over, he signed in his space and handed the pen back to me. 'If it all goes well in the next few days we'll be adding to this. First Nancy's name and, who knows, a next generation.'

I signed in my space and waited for the ink to dry. 'Let's hope that it does. This thing looks a bit narrow. It could do with broadening out a bit. It's about time somebody in this family did some proper breeding!'

Mick laughed. 'Well, I'm keen to start work on it!'

I clapped him on the back. 'I'd better go and leave you to your packing. Good luck, cousin.' I rolled up the family tree and slid it into the cardboard tube.

'You too, mate,' he said as he ushered me to the door. We shook hands and I skipped down the steps to the ground floor exit. Everything was in place for Mick's trip.

5

I can only imagine how Mick's heart would have lifted when he saw Nancy waiting at the barrier as he trundled his case through the arrivals gate. She rushed to him and their hug turned into a long, passionate kiss. She pulled away, breathing sharply, looking around and smoothing down the front of her cheongsam. She blushed.

Hand in hand they hurried to the exit where a wall of hot, humid air took Mick's breath away and triggered a rush of sweat under his shirt. They joined a queue for the taxi rank at the head of which a uniformed lackey motioned them towards the next cab in line. Once settled inside, Nancy held Mick's arm tight against her chest. 'It's so good to see you again, my love. I was afraid we would only ever have Lisbon.'

After sneaking a look to see if the driver's eyes were on the road or the rear-view mirror, Mick turned and kissed her on the mouth. 'I see you've ditched Lang-ren,' he whispered, nodding towards the driver's seat.

Nancy giggled, hiding her mouth behind her hand, and patted his arm. 'It's just you and me tonight. We have a room in the Istana Hotel. It's very swanky.'

'What have you told your father?'

'A friend is covering for me. As far as my father is concerned I'm spending tonight with her and we will pick you up at the Istana in the morning.'

He placed his hand on her knee, his little finger twitching

towards her thigh. 'I like the idea of just me and you in the *swanky* hotel.' He stifled a yawn and looked at his watch. It was late afternoon. 'This jet-lag! I fear that I'll have to have a lie down as soon as we arrive.'

She nodded and frowned as if she was considering a question. Finally, putting her hand over his and inching it imperceptibly higher, she said, 'This sounds like a most sensible plan.'

The next morning, they were on the rear seat of a Mercedes taking them north towards Ipoh. They sat inches apart, holding hands. Nancy had warned that, although Lang-ren wasn't driving, the chauffeur was still one of her father's men so they would have to be circumspect from now on. Sitting upright with only their hands touching, they watched the increasingly rugged landscape swish by.

Part of Mick's brain was formulating his side of the discussion with S Y Lee. Nancy had briefed him over their room-service supper the previous evening. He knew now that SY Lee had a dream for the castle but was having difficulty financing it. Would Mick's ability to put up the money overcome S Y's prejudice about westerners? Last night, he and Nancy had pledged, rashly he now knew, to spend the rest of their lives together. This would be much easier with S Y's blessing, if only he could be convinced. The arguments that he rehearsed silently, focused on how he saw himself as merely the money man. The grand, new, spa hotel would be run by the Lee family – principally Nancy – as part of the *Leeyate Group*. Mick's involvement would be only as Nancy's partner and, he hoped, husband.

When they arrived at the hotel, Nancy clasped his hand tightly, let it drop and hurried off to her room. She called him later to confirm that S Y Lee would see him first thing in the morning and she indicated that it would be best for them to stay apart until after the meeting. 'His spies are everywhere,

Mick. We can wait until tomorrow. Fingers crossed. Sleep tight.'

After a solitary breakfast, Mick announced himself at the reception desk and was escorted to the private lift for the penthouse floor. He wore the same expensive jacket and trousers that he had bought on his previous visit to Ipoh.

The lift doors opened directly into S Y Lee's office. The small, balding man, whom Mick remembered from the Lisbon Chinatown courtyard, sat straight-faced behind the desk. It was only as Mick stepped forward that he realised that the desk was on a dais. The blinding sunlight through the wall of glass behind S Y Lee was another feature of the room designed to disarm the visitor.

Determined not to be intimidated, Mick ignored S Y Lee's signal to take a seat and stepped onto the dais, his hand extended. S Y Lee shook hands without rising.

'It's good of you to see me,' Mick said. He smiled, still standing in front of the desk. 'It is much more pleasant here than in Lisbon.'

S Y Lee evidently failed to see anything to smile about. He indicated the chair again. 'Please, sit down.'

The raised platform extended across the window side of the room and Mick moved past the front of the desk to one of the windows and looked out. 'You have a terrific view.' He pointed. 'Is that the railway station?' He knew the answer.

S Y Lee swivelled in his chair. If he was irritated by Mick's refusal to step down and take a seat, he didn't show it. 'You be more comfortable sitting down, Mr Kellie.'

'I'm fine here.' He perched his backside on the window ledge. He hoped that S Y Lee would be impressed by his refusal to be intimidated.

'I am most disappointed that you ignored warning and stayed in touch with my daughter, Mr Kellie.'

Mick shrugged. The car through the cinema window *had* been to reinforce S Y Lee's message.

'You know that she engaged to be married.'

'Call me Mick, please. What I know is that Nancy and I are in love and I would like your blessing to marry her. Clearly, this would require her to break off her engagement.'

'This make many peoples in my family very unhappy. But Lai Ping has asked me listen to what you say, Mr Kellie. I her father. I would like her be happy but I need her to hold obligations to family.'

Mick stood up, half-facing the window and half-addressing the man behind the desk. He paused, waited and, at the precise moment that S Y Lee appeared to lose patience, said, 'When I was here in Ipoh, Nancy could tell how I felt about her. I think she already had feelings for me. She sent me away because of her daughterly obligation to you and to your family.

'One of the last things I said to her was that it was a pity that the building I know as Kellie's Castle wasn't marketed as a tourist attraction.' He spread his hands. 'I didn't know then that you owned the house and, because of my family association with it, I suggested rather romantically that I could buy it and give it to the state of Perak. I think this is the first inkling that your daughter had that I am quite a rich man.' He paused to let the fact sink in. 'When we were planning Nancy's trip to Lisbon...'

S Y Lee leaned back in his chair and crossed his arms.

'... Something that I now realise was a mistake and for which I apologise; while we were planning Lisbon, Nancy came to appreciate that my resources meant that my suggestion to buy the house was not a romantic delusion but a financial reality.'

S Y Lee held up a hand. 'Sorry I stop you in middle but I very rude and not offered tea or coffee. Would you like?'

Mick imagined the coffee cup being placed on the table alongside the only chair on the room's lower level. 'No, thank you.'

'I sorry. Go on.'

'I was saying that Nancy came to realise that I have considerable resources and that I am looking for investment opportunities. She may have told you that my first business venture as an entrepreneur is a small cinema in South London—'

'Near Kingston.'

'Just so. Near Kingston. Anyway, when Nancy understood the situation, she told me about your plans for Kellie's Castle.'

S Y Lee's noisy intake of breath stopped him in midflow. The older man grimaced. 'This was breach of confidence. I'm not sure I can forgive.'

'Nevertheless, the idea of a luxury spa hotel in the north of Malaysia strikes me as a sound business proposition. It is something I would like to see happen to the old building that I have come to regard with affection. In short, you and I share the same dream for Kellie's Castle.'

Mick had anticipated that S Y Lee would respond at this point and when no reaction came, he pressed on. 'I understand that you don't have the resources yourself and you are suspicious of outside investors. My proposal to you is that, if Nancy and I were together, she would receive sufficient funds from me to rebuild Kellie's Castle as the hotel. She would run it. Naturally, this would mean that she would have to stay in Ipoh. If I was lucky enough to be her husband, I would be honoured to be part of your family living in Ipoh and perhaps having a role in one of the Leeyate businesses—'

S Y Lee shook his head.

'—or not. I only play a sleeper role in my business in the

UK. Perhaps I will have to be content to do the same here. These are details. The main question is: are you interested in my proposition?'

S Y Lee shook his head again. 'Lai Ping prepared you well. She knows how much I have this dream for the, how do you say, flaghead hotel.'

Mick thought it best not to correct him.

'But there is so much more about this.' He started counting on his fingers. 'My family's objection to end of engagement to my nephew. Even if we get over this, are you a fit person for my daughter—'

Mick stood up. 'She thinks so—'

'But *I* make this decision—'

Mick spread his arms. 'She's an adult, she can—'

'I her father. That end to it,' S Y Lee snapped.

'I apologise.' Mick perched back on the ledge.

S Y Lee's voice softened. 'You have to understand. It is the way of me, our culture. Even though Lai Ping is different generation, deep down she need my blessing.'

'Of course.'

'This is all to be thought about even before the... not sure of right word... practicality.' He stood up. 'Do you have any more say?'

Mick clasped his hands together and shook his head.

'Lai Ping ask me give serious thought to what you propose this morning. This I will do. I talk to her this afternoon and let you know decision. If it possible we can discuss in more detail.'

'I hope you decide to make me a happy man.' Mick allowed S Y Lee to usher him to the lift and press the call button. The doors opened soundlessly and he stepped inside. When he turned back to face the room, as the lift door closed, Nancy's father was already in his place behind the desk.

Nancy had been waiting in the lobby watching the floor

indicator above the penthouse lift door. She rushed to Mick but stopped short and looked around. 'How did it go?' she asked. Her voice trembled in a higher register than normal.

'Well, he didn't shoot me!'

She slapped his arm and checked herself. She took his elbow and led him into the furnace outside. 'That's not as funny as you think. Seriously, what did he say?'

Mick took off his jacket for the short walk to the mall and put it on again in response to the blast of cold from the air conditioning.

Nancy punched his arm playfully. 'Tell me! What happened?'

He peered over the balustrade to check out the English-style coffee shop. 'Come on.'

Once they had ordered coffees and were ensconced in one of the booths at the back of the room, he turned to her and nuzzled against her neck. Her perfume was exciting. The mere touch of his lips against her skin was enough to make his blood race. 'I love you,' he whispered.

She moved away from him. 'I told you. Not in Ipoh. Not until... look, for goodness sake, tell me what happened.'

'Like I said, he was okay. At least he heard me out. He's worried that the family won't accept you breaking off your engagement.'

'That's going to happen anyway.'

'He doesn't know that.'

'What about the hotel?'

'I think the trump card is that it will be you – your money not mine that makes it happen. Although, I think he doubts whether I have enough.'

'Do you have enough?'

He shrugged. 'Labour is cheaper here. Even if it takes everything I have...'

'You're so sweet.' She checked around the room. 'I love you too!' She whispered.

'He's going to see you this afternoon to give you the verdict. If he's still open to the idea when you see him, you'll have to persuade him that you'll only be happy with me. Maybe you don't have to go so far as to tell him that you'll break off the engagement whatever he says. But once he gets the message loud and clear I think the whole thing is going to be about business. If he thinks you and I have enough money to bankroll the project, I think he'll give us his blessing.'

She locked her eyes on his and, hidden from others in the café by the table, placed a hand on his thigh. 'I can't wait,' she said.

Their roles were reversed later that afternoon. It was Mick who sat in the lobby watching the unchanging floor indicator above the private lift entrance. Nancy had been with her father for over an hour. Even with his jacket on, Mick was cold. He had shifted his seat twice to try and find a space that was not immediately under a freezing airjet.

He had tried to read the paper but couldn't focus on the print. A revolving screen above the reception desk publicised Ipoh's tourist attractions, tellingly omitting any mention of Kellie's Castle, but he had become bored after watching the same reel three times. He had studied the comings and goings of the passing guests, making a game of guessing their nationalities. He had observed the concierge, who waited patiently at his station until a guest presented with a query, whereupon he would make a phone call or shout for a bellhop boy so that between them they could send the guest away happy. He had wondered, if he and Nancy were successful, what role might be his in the maelstrom of tourism and commerce that swirled around him. He looked at his watch for the umpteenth time and checked the floor indicator stuck on '8'.

It moved to '7' and counted through the numbers to '0'. He hurried to greet her. The doors opened.

He could tell from the wide smile on her face and the tears in her eyes. She stepped out of the lift and into his arms. There was no need to hide.

Over the remainder of that week, the three of them met every day to work up S Y Lee's plans into a real project. The architect who had drafted them provided a ball-park estimate for the construction to a finished five-star, spa hotel. The figure was big enough to use up nearly all of Mick's capital but he had no qualms. It would secure his future with Nancy.

Together, they had visited S Y Lee's Chinese lawyer and set up a new separate company solely for the new hotel within the tourism branch of the *Leeyate Holdings Group*. S Y Lee, Nancy and Mick held equal shareholdings. Much to S Y Lee's ill-camouflaged disgust, one of the lawyer's Malay partners was drafted in to take the minimum stake required by legislation. Mick set up a bank transfer for his first injection of capital.

It was agreed by the end of the week that Mick should return to the UK to tidy up his affairs. While he was there, S Y Lee would deal with the issue of Nancy's engagement to Tommy Lee and the building project would progress to an initial stage. Once the project plan was agreeable to all parties, S Y Lee would arrange a Buddhist blessing in Ipoh for their civil marriage, which, he suggested, should take place outside Malaysia.

Throughout the negotiations, S Y Lee called Mick 'Mr Kellie' and Mick called him 'Mr Lee'.

6

For the whole of the journey along the Great West Road from Heathrow towards Richmond, Mick burbled like a boiling kettle on a low heat. How clever Nancy had been to spot that their marriage was the key to S Y Lee achieving his dream. How she had primed her father so that all Mick had to do was convince him he had the funds to make the hotel real. How he and Nancy would be able to build a life together in Malaysia with her running the hotel and him... well, he would find a role somewhere.

It was only when I turned towards the River Thames at Isleworth that he paused long enough for me to contribute: 'Everything's been fine here. Good houses. All very smooth.'

'Sorry, I should have asked.'

'No problem. I totally understand that *The Factory* is way down your priorities now.' I coughed to try and eliminate the whining tone that had appeared in my voice. 'I get it.'

'Hell, Steve. You're wrong. I've been thinking about us too. Of course, *The Factory*, will be yours. Call it a parting gift. You'll be the sole owner.'

'Seriously?' This bald statement of his generosity was like a punch to the solar plexus. In that instant all sense of driving the car fell into a void. I had to consciously settle my backside into the car seat and grip the steering wheel tighter to regain my equilibrium. 'Are you sure?'

'Of course. Makes sense. My life will be in Malaysia. Why have the hassle? I don't want any loose ends.'

'It's very generous.' I didn't know what else to say. It was all coming at me so fast. I hoped he couldn't see the tears obscuring my view of the road. My dream, the one I had when standing opposite the abandoned factory had become far more real than I had ever hoped. Not only that but the asset value of the property added to my Scotia pension meant that I'd have enough to live on and more for the rest of my life. Why then did I feel so empty?

I dropped Mick off at his flat and took the car back to the Vineyard. It was dawning on me that when I came to *The Factory* and joined Mick in this partnership, even living in this house, I had somehow taken over his life. I had attached myself to him like a limpet to a rock. What happens to a limpet when a tsunami dislodges it?

Mick was my family, all I had. He had used his power to fulfil my hopes but at the same time he was abandoning me. He intended to invest his money and his future in Nancy. I would lose him. The house felt cold and empty. It echoed to the sounds of ghosts from the time when my cousin played among the carboys. Germs of worry wormed into my brain that evening and multiplied over the following days.

Next time we met, after the usual business agenda, I raised my concerns. 'Has it occurred to you that Nancy and her father might have cooked up a scam between them? They get your money but you don't get the girl?'

He smiled. 'I know you're looking out for me, Steve. But you really don't get it. We're in love. She desperately wants to marry me. She didn't know about me having money when we fell for each other.'

'But you never thought of going into the hotel business, did you?'

'I never thought of going into the cinema business!' He

chuckled. 'I don't care what I do for a job. I have no idea what I'll do once the hotel is built and Nancy's running it. Perhaps I'll bring up our children. Be a househusband. All I know is, I'll be happy with her and will do anything to make it happen.'

The feeling in the pit of my stomach nagged at me, pressing the notion that Nancy and the notorious S Y Lee were conniving to get what they wanted and that they would leave Mick pitiful and impecunious. It would not go away.

As the weeks went by, all Mick's conversation focused on the project in Ipoh and how it was taking shape. He told me how the plans had been submitted with the necessary inducements to ensure a positive result and that the work was being costed in detail. The spa hotel and country club truly would be the *Leeyate Hotel Group*'s jewel in the crown, rivalling anything in Kuala Lumpur. His eyes would light up and sometimes I wondered whether this, rather than his marriage to Nancy, had become the driving force behind his intended move.

Then those same blue eyes would fill with tears as he turned his laptop towards me to show me the latest picture she had sent him.

One day, Mick explained that as part of his desire to tidy up his affairs before he left the UK, possibly for good, he would like to formalise the transfer to me of his share in *The Factory* on the day he married Nancy. This would require a lawyer and, on the appointed day, we drove to Twickenham in his Alfa Romeo with the top down making the most of some unseasonably warm, spring sunshine.

The radio was on and focused on breaking news from a town in Scotland called Dunblane. A man had gone into a primary school and, in cold blood, shot dead at least one teacher and as many as ten pupils. There were possibly more fatalities and other injured children in hospital. According to some eye-witnesses, the gunman had killed himself. It was as if the clear sky clouded over as the mood in the car darkened. We could only catch each other's eyes and shake our heads.

In the continuing silence, Mick swung the car into an asphalted enclosure alongside a Georgian house that had been converted to the offices of Blewett Trewithian, solicitors.

We were shown into Kenver Trewithian's office at the back of the building on the first floor. He wasn't there and we both automatically went over to the Georgian-paned sash window. Below us, a garden led down to the Thames riverbank. I dared not imagine what Mick was paying for an hour of Kenver's time.

When he swept into the room, the lawyer, who was short, with the muscular stockiness of a rugby hooker, greeted Mick with a hug and shook my hand before commanding us to sit.

Without preamble, Kenver explained to Mick (using his first name) that he had drawn up the contract as requested and that, on his marriage to Nancy Lee, I would be *The Factory*'s sole proprietor. It was to be conditional on him marrying Nancy and would be irrevocable. 'There's no going back on this, Mick.'

Mick nodded. 'I want to make a clean break. Once Nancy and I are married I'll be committed to Malaysia.'

Kenver twirled his wedding ring on his finger and looked up at the ceiling. 'This is what the contract—' he pointed to a folder on his desk '—specifies. It's very straightforward. However, have you thought about what happens if, for some reason, the marriage doesn't go ahead?'

'But it will. What's to stop it?'

Kenver shrugged. 'We don't need to go into specifics but am I right that, in the event of the marriage not taking place, everything will go on as before? You will want to retain your partnership?'

Mick nodded.

'And you?' Kenver said, turning to me.

'Of course.'

'That's straightforward then. This contract does the job.' Kenver's brow furrowed. 'But there's another possibility. I don't like to mention it but, with the news today from Scotland, it's something it would be prudent to consider—'

'But what?' Mick looked at his watch.

'Let's just say things can't go on as before if you die before the marriage takes place.'

Mick sighed. 'I won't care, will I? I'll be dead.'

I leaned forward.

'But you have a will,' Kenver said.

I stayed silent.

Mick stuck out his lower lip and shook his head, 'Never really thought about it.'

'Who would be your beneficiary if you died intestate?'

'Eh?'

I bit my lip. Sometimes Mick could be very obtuse.

'Your relatives. Who are they?'

'I don't have any—'

I raised a hand from my knee.

'Well, Steve here is my cousin.' He nodded for me to explain.

'Mick's father and my father were cousins. Our grandfathers were brothers,' I said.

'You have no nearer relative than Steve, Mick?'

Mick shook his head again. 'Not that I know of.'

'It seems to me, Mick, that you ought to make a will as soon as possible.' Kenver said.

This may have been good advice but I suspected that Kenver also knew how to squeeze the last drop of fee income out of any situation.

'Obviously, Mick, this moves into realms that are only for

you to decide,' Kenver said, glancing at me. 'If you put a will in place now it would ensure that your wishes for your share in the cinema business and your other assets were not subject to dispute should you die before the marriage. I really think it would be prudent to do it. Any will you make now will only be temporary. It will be nullified by your marriage. After that, when by virtue of the contract here,' he pointed to the folder, 'Steve gets the cinema, Nancy automatically becomes your next of kin and is in place to inherit everything else. Although I'd still suggest you make a new will then.'

'I'll think about it. Is our business about the transfer of the cinema done?'

The solicitor nodded. 'Yes. I just need you both to sign this.' He took the pages, bound with a blue ribbon, from the folder and pointed to where we each should sign. I used my fountain pen and Mick scratched his name with a ballpoint from the desk. He pushed the contract back to Kenver, who signed as witness. In the hiatus while Kenver added his details, Mick turned to me. 'Look, we're done here. Do you mind leaving us and I'll sort out the other thing? Obviously, I want you to have the cinema if anything happens to me.'

Kenver stood up. 'You'll have to make it clear. It won't necessarily happen as things stand.'

'I'll leave you to it,' I said shaking hands with Kenver. I could as easily have hugged him and kissed his neck. 'I'll be downstairs.'

Mick came into the ground floor waiting room twenty minutes later. As we stepped out onto the pavement, he said, 'I don't think there's any point keeping it to myself, except for a bit to charity, I've left the whole bloody lot to you. It's so much easier and quicker than faffing about. It's only until I'm married to Nancy. Then everything will be sorted properly.'

'Okay,' I said, not knowing how to greet the news. Him dying before his wedding was an eventuality so remote that it didn't seem appropriate to thank him. There was no reason for me to either be pleased or proud that he was legally acknowledging me as his relative. It puzzled me that he wasn't leaving his money to his fiancée. 'What about Nancy? Don't you want her to be able to build the hotel if you're not around?'

He snorted. 'Kenver suggested it. I did think about it. But I'd only want her to have it if I'm there to make sure that her father doesn't take it all.'

I could see the sense in this but I can honestly say that I would have been happy with only the cinema.

Back in the car on the journey to Richmond we learned that 16 children and one adult had been killed in what was already being called the Dunblane massacre. So many families torn apart.

7

Three weeks after he had signed his will, the first he had ever made and a month before he was due to leave for the first of the extended stays in Malaysia that would lead to his marriage to Nancy, Mick slipped in his shower, banged his head as he fell and suffered a brain haemorrhage.

I discovered his body that morning. He had fallen half out of the shower cubicle and eventually the water splashing on him that had escaped the shower tray had found its way into the apartment below. The occupants knew that I held a spare key. They called me and I rushed down, entered Mick's apartment and, hearing water running, ran straight for the bathroom. Mick was naked and slumped across the threshold of the shower cubicle. His blue eyes were open, blank. His cheek had settled against the floor tiles like the hull of a stranded boat. His jaw was agape. The white crust of dried spittle lined his lips. There was no pulse in his cold neck.

While I turned off the tap and wrestled Mick's lower body out of the cubicle so I could cover him with a towel, the neighbour who had followed me in called the emergency services. Mick's legs were warm. The electric shower had been sluicing them with hot water for... how long?

Sitting on the puddled bathroom floor, I tried to make sense of it. What was it about me? First Luis, now Mick. Thank goodness there were no more cousins to find, cousins to curse.

Naturally, the police's suspicion fell on me when it was discovered that I had recently been made sole beneficiary of Mick's will. Two police officers in plain clothes appeared on the step of my house and escorted me to Richmond police station, a typically solid, red-brick municipal building from the inter-war years. I was shown into a cell-like interview room, the walls glubbed with lime paint.

The female officer, D.C. Quinn, pressed a button on a tape recording machine and, looking at her watch, announced the time. After giving her name and that of the other officer sitting behind her, a darkly unshaven man called D.C. Key, she asked me to identify myself. She read out the police caution from a card that had been taped to the desktop. 'Do you have anything to say?' she asked.

'I don't understand why I am here,' I said.

'We're investigating the death of your business partner—' she looked down at her notebook '—Michael Kellie.'

'Mick. He called himself Mick.'

'Mick Kellie, then. What do you have to tell us about his death?'

'Nothing other than I found him.'

'You had a key to his apartment.'

'Yes.'

'Why?'

The implication of the questions that followed were that either Mick and I were more than business partners – more than cousins – and, on the night before he was found, we'd had a lover's tiff that ended in violence, or that I had gone to his apartment with the intention of harming him so that I could benefit from his will in the short window before he married Nancy. D.C. Quinn was keen for me to admit that either scenario, or a combination of both, was the backdrop to Mick's death.

I told Detective Quinn the truth and nothing but the truth

as I would have done in court had it come to it. Eventually, she seemed to accept that my presence in *The Factory* on the night before Mick's body was discovered would have been witnessed by enough trustworthy people for it to be a genuine alibi. I also suggested that the only time I could have appeared on the security cameras in the streets leading to Mick's apartment building was the morning I arrived in response to the summons from Mick's flooded neighbours.

The questions and answers went around in circles before Detective Quinn shuffled her papers together, looked at her watch, announced the time and declared the interview was at an end. She and D.C. Key showed me out. She warned me not to leave the country, that they might want to question me again.

After a week of hearing nothing, I called Detective Quinn to discover that I was no longer a person of interest; it would be up to the coroner to determine what happened next.

The coroner's court in Fulham was sparsely attended. The neighbour who summoned me to the apartment that morning was there and I was surprised to see Kenver Trewithian take a seat. The coroner, from her raised bench, explained why she had asked the solicitor to attend. 'It is quite unusual for people of the deceased's age to die within a short time of making a will and your evidence will help me to determine whether I should give any significance to the timing of these events. Could you tell us, Mr Trewithian, how Mr Kellie came to make his will?'

Kenver, standing in the witness box alongside the coroner, took her through the main points of his meeting with Mick and me. He described how, after I had left, he had persuaded Mick that he ought to have a will to take effect in the period before his impending marriage. 'I assumed that Mick... Mr Kellie would want to make sure his estate would go to his fiancée. When it came to it, however, he was adamant that his cousin, Mr Cross, should be the beneficiary.'

All the eyes in the room turned towards me.

'Did he say why?' The coroner asked.

Kenver twisted his wedding ring on his finger. 'He did, but I think it would betray my client's confidence if I were to say.'

The coroner leaned forward. 'I understand. But did you perceive the reasons Mr Kellie gave for the wishes as he expressed them in his will to be reasonable.'

Kenver smiled. 'Yes. Very reasonable... and sound. Very sound reasoning.'

When it was the turn of the doctor who performed the autopsy to give evidence, we learned that Mick's stomach contained a recently swallowed, full-dose aspirin. A cache of identical pills was found in his bathroom cabinet. The doctor went on to say that Mick's medical records revealed that he had attended his General Practitioner's surgery expressing a morbid fear of suffering a stroke like his father. 'He had asked to be prescribed blood-thinners on many occasions. He had been advised that it would do no harm to take a daily, low-dose of 75mg of aspirin. If Mr Kellie had been taking more than this for a prolonged period, and it seems that he took at least 200mg on the day of his death, it would have significantly increased the chance of a blow to the head causing a brain haemorrhage.'

The coroner made a note ostentatiously before looking up over the top of her reading glasses. 'Are you able to help us with the deceased's time of death, Doctor?'

The doctor shook her head. 'Sadly, not. In the interval between Mr Kellie's fall and his body being removed from the shower cubicle, it was subjected to a constant stream of hot water. Once he had been moved and the shower was turned off, it made it impossible to accurately recreate the circumstances: the water temperature in the shower, the pattern of splash coverage, how much water was escaping, how long it took to seep into the flat below. These were all unknown. Specifically, the extent of the splashing of Mr Kellie's lower body and the shower water temperature made it impossible to estimate time of death using the usual factors such as residual temperature, rigor mortis and lividity.'

Based on what she had heard, the coroner determined that, whenever it had happened, Mick's fall had been an accident, the force of his head hitting the floor being sufficient to cause the brain haemorrhage that killed him.

The architect of Mortlake Crematorium had created a façade that was imposing, palatial even, while retaining a human scale. Its single story was composed of red brick and the chimney tower rose in the background. The colours, the tower and the scaled-down grandeur reminded me of the pictures I had seen of Kellie's Castle.

Inside the church-like interior, where Mick's coffin rested on a curtained bier, the rows of pews were dotted with Mick's neighbours in the apartment building, some of our young staff from The Factory and the landlord from The Duke's Head. Neither Nancy nor S Y Lee had come from Malaysia but the family was represented by Sammy Lee from the Number 8 Hotel in Kingston who offered me a discreet nod of the head.

It fell to me to give a eulogy and I spoke of how I had been inspired by Mick's enthusiasm and energy when we started The Film Factory together. 'We weren't merely business partners, we were also cousins and I know that the family connection between us was as valuable to him as it was to me.' After talking about the cinema and The Duke's Head and recalling some funny moments, I moved on to the most recent past. 'I was very pleased to be present in his life when he discovered love with Nancy Lee in Malaysia, who sadly can't join us today. Not only had he fallen head over heels for Nancy but he had also found a new project. We had discovered an ancestral home in Malaysia called Kellie's Castle, a dream house built by my grandfather for the love of his life. Nancy and Mick shared a new dream for the house that sadly won't now come to fruition. Mick's death leaves a gap in our hearts here in England but also, as in a previous generation of our Kellie family, leaves a dream abandoned many thousands of miles away.'

Sammy Lee nodded to me again as we left the crematorium but did not join us for a drink at *The Duke's Head*.

8

I may have told Detective Constables Quinn and Key the truth and nothing but the truth about Mick's death but I had omitted to tell the whole truth. I hadn't disclosed that, before Mick's accident, I had met Sammy Lee at *The Factory*. He had been waiting at the entrance when I arrived to open up one morning a few days after Mick and I had met Kenver Trewithian when Mick made his will.

He bowed. 'Good morning. Do you remember me, Mr Stephen Cross?'

'I do,' I said. 'From the hotel in Kingston.' I could hardly forget his trademark paisley cravat and blazer.

'Yes, Sammy Lee, step-brother to Mr S Y Lee in Malaysia, uncle to Miss Nancy Lee. I have a favour to ask you concerning your partner Mr Kellie.' He spoke carefully like a barrister addressing a judge.

I was surprised at this out of the blue visit but since, as far as I was aware, Sammy Lee hadn't sought to obstruct Mick's plans once they were agreed by Nancy's father, I had no reason to suspect his motives. 'Come in.' I shouldered the glass door aside and led him into the lobby. 'Take a seat. Tea? Coffee?'

He viewed the windows sceptically. 'Is there somewhere more private, perhaps?'

'Of course. Look I'm getting a coffee. You sure you won't have one?'

He shook his head.

I went behind the counter and pressed the buttons for a double espresso. He hopped from foot to foot, eye-checking first the doors then the windows, then back again. 'I won't be a second.' I said. 'Are you expecting someone?'

He shook his head.

With my coffee in my hand, I led him through to the smaller screen room and sat down in the first seat in the back row. This left space for him on a couch on the other side of the aisle. I placed my drink in the armrest cup-holder and swivelled to face him. The subdued light emphasised the deep, pock-mark scars on his cheeks.

'How can I help you,' I said.

His smile seemed genuine. 'Forgive me for coming unannounced. I am here on my niece's behalf – Miss Nancy Lee in Ipoh. She has asked me to make a surprise errand for her. When I say, surprise, I mean it is a surprise for her husband-to-be Mr Kellie.'

'It sounds intriguing. What could it be?' I took a pull at the espresso and felt an immediate boost at the familiar, bitter taste.

'It is very simple, actually. Miss Nancy wants to surprise her husband with a wedding gift. Probably a piece of Chinese sculpture. Something with age. An artefact.'

'If you're hoping I can help you to choose...' I shook my head.

He held up a hand. 'No! Not in choosing such a thing. Miss Nancy will do that. No, she would like somebody in her family over here—' he pointed at his chest, '—me, to take photographs of the inside of Mr Kellie's home. We need to get inside but we can't ask Mr Kellie himself; it would spoil the surprise.'

'Why?'

He steepled his fingers in front of his chest and studied his fingernails. 'Do you remember coming to see me, Mr Cross?'

'Of course, Mr Lee. I provided you with information—'

He nodded slowly – almost a bow. 'Information that I didn't use – didn't even look at.'

I returned the bow. 'Of course. I didn't expect you to.'

Now that he was satisfied that we understood each other, Sammy Lee narrowed his eyes pensively. 'It is not so much. We merely need to find a way to access Mr Kellie's apartment—'

'You said, but I still don't see—'

'If you'll permit me to finish... Miss Nancy is keen that the wedding gift she buys for her husband is to his taste. If we can access Mr Kellie's apartment we can take photographs and send them to Ipoh. She will be able to see his furnishings and possessions and, knowing his taste, choose a suitable artefact.'

'But they won't be living here. He's moving to join her in Malaysia.'

'Yes, she told us this. The photographs are to get his style... his taste. She will be able to see the sort of things he likes.' He flashed his teeth. 'I was hoping you may be able to get a key—'

'I already have a key, in case of emergencies—' I immediately regretted blurting it out.

'So much the better. All I ask of you then is that you lend me your key when you know Mr Kellie will be out – perhaps when you have a meeting with him. I will arrange for the photographs to be taken and return the key on the same afternoon.'

Within a week, the job was done. Sammy Lee only had the key for a few hours and came to my front door to return it with a wink. Mick never said anything so I assumed that

Sammy and his henchmen had taken the photographs without disturbing the furniture.

It was only after Mick's death that I realised the full implication of my giving the key to Sammy Lee: the man probably behind the VW crashing into the front of the cinema; the UK representative of that part of Nancy's family most closely related to her jilted fiancé Tommy Lee. This Tommy being the man who styled himself after a psychopathic Mafioso who shot people for fun. What if Sammy Lee had simply made a copy of the key giving him access to Mick's flat at any time of his choosing?

Perhaps the instruction from Tommy Lee in KL had been for Sammy Lee's enforcers to kill the man who had brought him such unhappiness and made him lose face. After delivering one fatal blow to the side of Mick's head, his murderers had arranged his body to look like he had fallen in the shower.

Perhaps Tommy had told Sammy and the boys to merely rough up Mick and demonstrate what it meant to have an intractable enemy in Malaysia. What if one of them had crept up on Mick in the shower, hit him and the blow caused the fatal haemorrhage?

Perhaps they burst into the bathroom and, in his shock and surprise, even before one of them had touched him, Mick slipped, fell and banged his head.

Perhaps Mick had fallen in the shower prior to the planned raid and it had never happened.

Perhaps, there was no planned raid and, while Mick was in the meeting with me, as he had promised, Sammy Lee and an associate had entered the apartment, taken a few photographs and left things exactly as they had been before.

There's no doubt about it, I was not responsible for my cousin's death. I didn't wish for it. I didn't engineer it. There's equally no doubt about the fact that I benefited hugely because he died before he married Nancy. Nevertheless, he was my family, I didn't want him to die. Even though, within a month, he was going to be lost to me.

These certainties should have meant that I could face my solitary, but financially blessed, future with equanimity. However, I could never forget that, thanks to me, for a few hours, Sammy Lee had the key to Mick's apartment. In the darkness of its shadow I think about Mick's death and my part in it and I'm forced to conclude that there's *every* doubt about it.

9

I cut my hair, bought a tropical weight suit and flew to Malaysia with Mick's ashes. I had considered scattering them from Richmond Bridge onto the waters of the Thames so that they could be swept out to the North Sea and beyond. However, Mick had shown little enthusiasm for the river, other than that its oblique view enhanced the value of his apartment, and so I decided to take him to Kellie's Castle. I made the arrangements through a travel agent who booked me into the *Leeyate Plaza Hotel* in Ipoh.

It was the first time I had been in contact with Nancy since I had called her with the dreadful news. She responded to thank me for thinking of her and to say that she had persuaded her father to agree to the urn being buried in the grounds of Kellie's Castle. She added that she would like to accompany me.

When I arrived at the *Leeyate Plaza*, the receptionist told me that I was the guest of its owner and that my suite on the seventh floor and anything else I needed were complimentary. An invitation to join S Y Lee that evening was waiting on a table alongside a lavish display of tropical blooms. I turned my cuff to check the time on Mick's Patek Philippe wristwatch.

Mick had told me what to expect when I stepped out of the lift and I wasn't surprised to find the hotel owner sitting behind his desk in front of the array of windows. I hadn't anticipated the breath-taking, panoramic view of the city's rooftops with white and red vehicle lights criss-crossing behind him like silent fireworks.

He stood and we shook hands. 'These sad times, Mr Cross,' he said. 'I see you have booked with us two nights. A short stay after long journey.'

Thank you for your very kind hospitality, Mr Lee, but I need to be back in the UK by the end of week.'

'A flying visit then. Can I get you drink? Please sit.' He pointed to the low armchair.

After we had agreed that we would have white wine, he picked up the telephone and barked an order into it.

'My daughter will join you tomorrow. What time you want go to house?'

'At eleven?'

'Excellent. I will organise cars. Chauffeur-driven, of course.'

I thanked him and paused while a uniformed waitress served us both with chilled white wine.

'Cheers!' S Y Lee said, still seated.

'Cheers! You have a wonderful view from this room,' I said, lifting the glass.

'Yes.' He didn't bother looking behind him. Instead, he leaned forward. 'Do you suspect why I asked see you?'

I shook my head. I had assumed it was merely a courtesy but didn't think I should say so.

'I wonder whether you know plans your business partner had for the house, so-called Kellie's Castle?'

'Yes. He told me about the project to turn it into a hotel.'

'Not just hotel, magnificent spa hotel. I still want this happen. Sadly, not possible without Mr Kellie's funds.'

'No. I understand that.'

'Do you know if Mr Kellie made arrangements my project go ahead even if something happen to him?'

I shook my head. 'As far as I know he did not.'

'Where his money?'

'I'll be straight with you, Mr Lee. I'm not sure that there was as much money as Mr Kellie may have given the impression there was. Perhaps he allowed his love for your daughter to make him promise more than he should have. To be honest, I don't really know the situation. The only person who knows is his solicitor and executor.'

S Y Lee's expression didn't change. 'This most disappointing. Perhaps we have claim against Mr Kellie estate.'

Before I left England, I had called Kenver to check this possibility and I knew that, although the seed money was lost, there was no further liability. 'If you put your lawyers in touch with the executors I'm sure that the estate will meet all the terms of any contract you have.'

S Y Lee stood up. Neither of us had tasted more than the first sip of wine. 'Well you have been most helpful, Mr Cross. Thank you coming to see me.' I stepped up on the dais and we shook hands. 'I hope you have successful day tomorrow,' he said.

Next morning, I waited in the lobby at 11am holding Mick's ashes. Nancy emerged from a lift and I was struck by her frailty. Her cheeks were hollow and her wrists and ankles were thin as twigs. Her shift dress was black and she carried a wide-brimmed black hat. She walked as if her slipper-style shoes were on broken glass, her gaze fixed on the floor in front of her. When she lifted her eyes, she saw what I was carrying and stopped, stepped back and half-turned away as if she had changed her mind about coming.

After a few seconds, she straightened her back and started towards me again.

'Thank you for bringing him back,' she said, shaking my

hand. Hers was cold and limp. Her eyes were pools of sadness.

'I am so sorry about what happened,' I said.

She took a handkerchief from the sleeve of her cardigan and dabbed the points of her dark eyes. She looked at the urn, clamped her eyes shut as if to banish the idea that Mick was in there, and half-stumbled past me. I caught her elbow and she allowed me to walk beside her through the doors and outside into the heat. There were two limousines waiting, the lead one for her, the trailing one for me. There was no question of travelling together.

After the cars had parked up, Nancy and I walked side by side along the path towards the building. It was my first sight of the ancestral home and I was struck by how its elevation and the loftiness of the walls and towers created the impression of a fortification, a barrier to outsiders. I had expected it to be welcoming, embracing and instead was troubled by its antagonism. My grandfather had evidently recognised the natural enmity between natives and their colonial masters.

A bonfire crackled and spat nearby and its acrid smoke hung around us as we climbed to the elevated lawn. Somebody, presumably the gardener who stood leaning on his spade at the end of the building, had dug a hole in advance and Nancy and I stood by it in the hot sun. She removed her cardigan revealing gaunt arms and nodded to me. Reverentially, I laid the urn in its place. The hole was too big and the container looked forlorn, stranded, as if it would fit better somewhere else.

I stood up straight and watched Nancy mouth a silent prayer. She signalled to the gardener to finish his task and took my arm as we negotiated the slope, neither of us turning back when we heard the gardener's spade, first cleaving into the earth pile and then swishing soil into the hole.

Standing by the door to her car, Nancy took my hand as if to shake it but held on in a desperate grip. 'Thank you again for bringing Mick back, Mr Cross. He will have wanted to be here.' She took off her Ray-Bans and looked me in the eye for what seemed the first time since we had met and her hand tightened around mine. 'I never really believed Mick and I would marry. Not even after my father agreed because of the damned hotel. It was better for Mick not to be part of the Lee family, I think. My marriage to him would have been hard for others to accept.'

Guilt about my arrangement with Sammy Lee rose in my throat like bile. I considered asking her whether she had involved her uncle in a plan to photograph Mick's apartment, but the idea was so ludicrous that I already knew the answer.

Instead, I squinted up at the sandstone edifice radiating the sun's heat, thickening and stirring the air above it like broth. Crows circled above the curling smoke making their plangent call. 'What about this place?' I asked. 'Do you think it will ever be rebuilt?'

'Not by my father.'

'And you?'

'I will never come here again. Not even for...' She scanned the walls before her gaze settled on the gardener still swinging his spade. In that instant, taking in her wide-brimmed hat and crisp cotton dress, seeing the likeness to Audrey Hepburn that Mick had mentioned, I recognised the woman that he had fallen in love with; the cool, elegant woman who had reminded him of a drift of bamboo swaying under the influence of a warm breeze.

We watched the gardener finish and walk away leaving a mound of turned tilth. 'Will you mark the place?' I asked.

She sighed so deeply that it sounded from the depths of her before morphing into a choked sob. Whispering, so that I had to lean in close enough to smell the dead-leaf musk of her perfume she said, 'Mick will be more peaceful if nobody knows he is here. He is our secret. You. Me. My father.'

Still she stood facing the castle, half-turned away as if she couldn't force herself to leave. Malaysia's unrelenting sun toasted our backs while, from behind the screen of trees, the bonfire, that had been the soundtrack to our visit, cracked out a volley of pistol shots.

Abruptly, without warning, Nancy spun on the soles of her fragile shoes and the chauffeur guided her into the limousine. Its engine had been running to keep the interior cool and without further delay the car exited the castle grounds and turned towards Ipoh.

I thought about my cousin Luis who had fallen to his death not far from this spot and my cousin-partner who too had died daring to dream a future for the building that loomed before me, shimmering in the smoke like a mirage. My generation of the family destroyed because of this building. Me, the only surviving Kellie, too timid to take it on.

Curious about the bonfire, I followed the path that ran parallel to the stream and broke through an archway of blossom into a clearing. On the far side, the ornately tiled walls of the temple rose above the shrubbery. A pair of gates were open and the bonfire bristled and flared on the asphalt. Two men carried planks and scraps of broken furniture out of the building and threw them onto the flames, sending embers spiralling upwards, sparkling like tinsel.

I walked over and waited for one of the men to return. 'What's going on?' I asked, immediately regretting my haughty colonial tone.

'The temple is opening again,' he said, 'for worship.' He cast his armful of lumber onto the fire and, from the bubbling paint, orange flames knitted new spirals of black smoke that twisted towards the house.

I nodded, and in turning to retrace my steps, spotted the

row of painted figurines on top of the temple wall. Halfway along, the cartoonish plaster representation of a pink-faced colonial officer stood sentry, as he had done for over seventy years. My grandfather peered through the smoke, over the top of the blossomed copse, towards the remnants of his dream house, waiting, always waiting.

KUALA LUMPUR TO LONDON

10th May, 1996

The dull throb of the Jumbo's engines weaves a brain-fog from which emerges the spectral outline of Detective Quinn. While others had accepted the coincidence of water twice smudging the certainties of death-scene science, she harbours suspicions that this is my *modus operandi*. I had both motive and opportunity; I must be implicated. And, as I spin the tuning knob in my head, searching the frequency for sleep, my eyes gritty and squeezed shut, her phantom presence forces me to confess one truth, that I have withheld even from myself.

Perhaps, even while I have been in Malaysia, D C Quinn has been scrutinising my telephone records and has discovered that I made a call to Sammy Lee. I imagine she will have read much into the fact that it is dated after Mick had been persuaded to make his will in my favour. She will drive a wedge in the gap between fact and this undeclared truth. The call was merely to check that Mick would be safe when he went to Ipoh again, but her certainty will plant doubt in my mind.

In the face of her circumstantial evidence, after relentless questioning and near-tortuous levels of sleep deprivation,

I will admit that, in the meeting that followed the call, I connived with the mob side of the Lee family to kill my only cousin, my only friend. From there she will cast doubt on how my mother died. New truths will emerge. Guilt piles on guilt.

Like Robert De Niro's character, Noodles, in the final scene of the film *Once Upon a Time in America*, I need strong dope if sleep is to come and wipe away the strife, the mistakes that have sentenced me to suffer the innocent's dread of unwarranted discovery. No ordinary daydream scenario can lead me step by step down into the soft-cushioned cellar room of sleep.

I sketch out a new storyboard: I will sell the cinema to a property developer. The funds from it, the sale of Mick's flat and his micturition money will be more than enough to start a new venture.

Take one: As I once vowed I would, I have returned to Lisbon and made a home there. I have immersed myself in its lifestyle and its music. After spending the evening at a *Fado* bar, I stand on my night-time terrace, nightcap sherry in hand, and scan over the roofs searching out the mercury band of the river. Warm, dusty eddies of laughter and bantering conversation waft up from the streets below. They share the clamour of revellers; I am alone.

The scene fades. 'Alone' doesn't work anymore. Anyway, Lisbon was only temporarily the natural sequel to what went before. If this dream-catcher is to work, it must be about family and this means the castle. My father bequeathed me its romantic story and it is the key to my future.

Screwing up my eyes, I dive into the deepest reaches of my imagination. I surface with a new storyboard.

Take two: I am sitting on the first-floor veranda of a modern property, ice clinking in a cut-glass tumbler containing gin, tonic and a twist of lemon. The distinctive, juniper and quinine fizzes in my nostrils. I look out towards a tropical sunset. To my right are the earthworks that signify that an eighteen-hole championship golf course is in development. To my left *Kellie's Castle Spa Hotel and Country Club* is bustling with activity. The hardened sun-worshippers catching the last of the rays are still by the pool. Most of the guests are in their rooms preparing for dinner. My money has made this happen.

But still I fail to slip away. It needs more. I screw my face down into the pillow. If the next one doesn't work I might as well give up and watch a movie.

My destiny is in my hands. I am ready to step into Mick's shoes. Not in a *Talented Mr Ripley* way, but by commandeering the future that was to be his. How easy it would be for Nancy Lee and me to become close during the time we spend together planning and building the hotel.

Take three: I am sitting on the first-floor veranda with a view across the hotel complex towards the golf course. Nancy, my wife, is beside me. We are waiting to be summoned to the dining table where we will be attended by the house staff. Our children, Michael and Louise, are in the nursery. The nanny is in the room next to theirs.

I am marvelling at how fate has brought us together. 'Do ever think about Mick, Nancy?'

She chinks her glass against mine and takes a sip before responding. 'I loved Mick. I do think of him. But everything I felt for him I feel for you and more.' She stands up, takes my hand and leads me to the railing. 'Look at all this. You should be very proud. It would not have happened without you.'

Nuzzling my lips against her bare neck, I say, 'It means nothing to me without you and the children – my family.'

She spins round slowly, still enfolded in my embrace. We kiss.

This scene is working. I am teetering on the precipice of

oblivion. A member of the cabin staff passing now would look down at me and see that my face is split wide by a dopey-grin gash as if I'm floating in the arms of Morpheus like a junkie in a Chinatown opium den; the pipe's harsh, kind smoke thick in my lungs.

In my last residue of wakefulness, in the nanosecond that is the present, I happen upon a significant conclusion. Yes, the past is over. It *is* recorded on ticker tape – immutable, reviewable, open only to interpretation. The future, on the other hand, is elastic. It can stretch to anything, even a Hollywood ending.

Author's note

The author visited Kellie's Castle near Batu Gajah in the Malaysian state of Perak, at about the same time as Luis Escobar's fictional visit in this novel. The romantic story of the castle's builder, William Kellie-Smith, was written in English on a weathered notice board in the car park. There was nothing to say who owned it.

Internet research infers that a private company has acquired Kellie's Castle. It has made the fabric of the building safe and opened it to the public. Visitors can read about the house's history and see various exhibits that show how it might have looked had it been completed.

It is a popular tourist attraction with thousands of visitors every year. The tunnels were excavated but appear to have been dead ends. There never was a Rolls Royce.

There are reports that the castle is haunted by William Kellie-Smith who is desperate for it to be completed so that it can be lived in by any of his descendants that may yet be found.

Acknowledgements

Novel writing is mostly a thankless business, especially as I spend my writing life unnoticed by the literary establishment. So I would like to take this opportunity to thank the friends, family and strangers who continue to motivate me with their encouragement and positive responses to my work. My family, bless them, are uncritical and unwavering in their acceptance that this is the way I choose to spend my time and their money.

Among my friends, I have to mention specifically fellow scribe Bruce Johns who, despite operating in a higher orbit of our 'craft', is ceaselessly enthusiastic about my workaday efforts. As is customary, Valerie was first reader for this manuscript with Linda Gallagher and Chris Smith both seeing early drafts. It has benefited from their insightful comments.

In terms of professional editing, I must first mention Hadyn Middleton of Writers' Workshop whose devastating critique of an earlier version of Steve Cross's story ensured that it morphed into this work which reads better than it did and should be error-free thanks to direction and suggestions from Anna Johnson.

During my research, I visited Lisbon and was fortunate enough to stay in Tiago's apartment where one passes through a Hobbit doorway onto a unique rooftop terrace with its view over the city's rooftops. Tiago introduced us to the *Restaurante Devagar Devagarinho* where our Fado experience was the template for the fictional one that Luis and Steve enjoyed. My main purpose of going to Lisbon was to visit the British Cemetery and thanks are due to Andrew Swinnerton there for helping me find the grave of William Kellie Smith.

Patricia Borlenghi, the driving force behind Patrician Press, has been a generous friend and meticulous publisher. None of this would have happened without her. Thanks to David Janes for the cover design, based on original artwork for the *Chinatown* film poster by Richard Amsel. The illustration of Kellie's Castle is by Charles Johnson.

I'm sure that I've omitted people I should have thanked and I apologise to them. Apologies also to you, the reader, for any errors of fact or in syntax, spelling or production that have survived the publishing process; the buck stops with me.

Finally a note about inspiration. This is the second of my novels inspired by films; this one the timeless classic *Chinatown*. As well as starting with the intention of purloining its final words, I have tried to borrow from the film its spirit of beguiling duplicity. This is why the book ends with a scene that mirrors the end of another classic movie, *Once Upon a Time in America*; De Niro's manic smile undermines everything that went before. As Jack Nicholson playing Jake Gittes says, 'In Chinatown, you can't always tell what's going on.'

BV - #0032 - 270220 - CO - 216/138/19 - PB - 9781999703059